Web Of I

by

Christine Long

ISBN: 9798676198695

Copyright © 2020 Christine Long

PublishNation
www.publishnation.co.uk

Acknowledgments

First and foremost my husband Ray who has given me lots of support to finish this book.

Darren Long my son who has been there for me all the way he's been wonderful. Renate Long daughter -in - law brilliant.

Gemma Ridgley and Joyce Panunzio friends who had faith in me.

Then last but no means least another dear friend Shirley Reading who has been telling me for years to write a novel.

Thank you.

Web of Lies

Chapter 1

Slate Moors Prison

Jake Farrendon was well prepared for the events that were to take place, just a few last-minute details to discuss with Luke Stamford then they'd be off to heaven knows where? The two men had gone over the escape plan time and time again, to make sure there wouldn't be any mishaps. So today was the day Saturday 10th March. Jake had been waiting for this with bated breath but was very nervous of what might happen. The two were so pleased the weather conditions were just perfect for them, with continuous heavy snowfalls; he was apprehensive about the whole set up and realised he was putting his life on the line, also his future, if he should be caught. But he felt this had to be. 'He hated this environment.' 'He hated this prison.'

Anyway this man Luke had been let out of his cell for some exercise, to go round the pen grounds, even though it was snowbound and difficult to walk. He was usually kept in another part of the building, but no one knew what crime he had committed, however the men gathered it must be something bad to put him in a cell on his own. The guards were keeping it very hush-hush. There were jobs which needed to be done in Luke's cell, a blocked loo was one and new pipes to be fitted, so for a week he was able to mix with some of the other prisoners, but he was certainly not liked. The sooner he was put back in his cell the better, most thought.

But it was Jake he wanted for this breakout. Why? Should he go in with this dreadful person's plan? Or not? Thinking back now it all came about when Luke sidled up to him one day and got quite chatty. It was out of this situation that an idea formed

1

between the two, to escape from the prison. Jake at the time was very worried by the whole dilemma, because he didn't like the man. his thoughts were the same as the other prisoners, to keep well away because he wasn't sure he could trust him. But when he thought of the escape, it got Jake thinking it just might work. He wanted to get away from here, that was uppermost in his mind now. After hearing the man's scheme it sounded good, so he decided to take this big chance with Luke, when he heard the whole set up. The two had to be careful though and not show they were too chummy, which would never happen with Jake and this person it was purely that he wanted. Out!!!

He had to be careful though as both of them were often watched by the inmates. With one or two shaking their heads, probably wondering how Jake could get friendly with this person. So over the last few days, they had talked briefly, whilst outside in the yard, not making it too obvious. Quietly, they worked out everything, down to the last detail. As it happened Jake was a bit of a loner in the prison, not really wanting to mix with any of the other men, but Luke knew he was in with one particular guard, so that's why this escape could work. Anyway when told about it Jake was willing to take the chance.

The snowstorms had been unbelievable on the moors, with heavy drifts, which they both hoped would play a big part in this venture, if it carried on. Jake was nervous but had thought over and over again in his mind about what the two were about to do. It was certainly a big chance to take, but he couldn't stand another year or so in here. Also Luke was not a man to turn down, as you never know what he might do. It was all rather worrying but Jake couldn't change his mind, not now. He would just have to go with the flow and stick with this awful bloke, thinking at the back of his mind, he could be dangerous. Luke hadn't asked anybody else to breakout with him in the prison, because he felt Jake was the only one he could trust, knowing that he never got involved with other prisoners, because of their despicable ways. Which, when he told the vile man in front of him, a smile crossed his ugly face, probably thinking how stupid Jake was. One of the inmates, Ginger Watts, was a man who was very irritating with his remarks, which Luke didn't always take lightly, and Mack Goff was another person who revelled in picking a fight, but he never picked on Luke because he might get more than he bargained for. These two men knew something was going on, but never said.

Jake had always behaved himself inside, he was not a troublemaker or violent, did as he was told and never took drugs. But at times he was very depressed and muddled by his situation. He couldn't believe he had been accused of killing his wife, whom he'd thought he'd loved at the time, when the whole thing had been an accident, he hadn't meant for her to die. He didn't know that she would fall and bump her head on the stone fireplace. After all, he only pushed her in a fit of anger, when he found out she was having an affair with their friend Matt. He and Kate had befriended him and taken this so-called friend, under their wings when his marriage had collapsed. Letting him have a room, meals, and the run of the house, never thinking there might be anything going on between his own wife and his so-called mate. It was unbelievable! Well Jake was accused of murder and got six years. When it was after all an accident, a push, that's all it was, something you might do to one another at times in anger. So he was devastated by the Judge's decision. Manslaughter!! It was a terrible shock to him and everyone.

How he would love to live on the outside again, which had seemed a long way off, now he was thinking differently. He had to get out of here, before he took his own life, that's how low he had been feeling lately. Even though he didn't like anything about Luke, in fact he hated him, but couldn't do this break without him, as it seemed fool proof. So they both planned their getaway unbeknown to their inmates. If all went well and they got away with it, the two would separate eventually. Which Jake was more than happy to do, but of course was worried about what the consequences might be if they were caught? He probably would end up in prison for longer. But it didn't put him off, all he could think about now, was getting himself out of here and not getting caught, then starting a new life. He hated Ginger and Mack, they were always pestering him; yes he knew what they wanted! But they weren't going to get it, not from him. He'd make sure of that. (Luke wasn't an option.) So what with everything, the time seemed right. Staring at Luke over the canteen table as they ate their fry up now, he began thinking what was he about to take on with this dreadful bloke who stood so tall, big and ugly?

"Won't be long now," Luke said, as he passed Jake the tomato sauce in the breakfast hall.

"Not so loud you might be overheard," Jake whispered back.

"I think we're going out at 11 o'clock today."

"Right," Jake answered curtly. He was beginning to shake a little now and Luke noticed it.

"You okay?"

"Yes of course I am," Jake told him. "I've been skipping round my cell this morning, what do you think?"

"Alright! Alright! I only asked. So that's why your shaking eh?" He smirked.

"Just want to get started that's all. I hate this waiting around." He couldn't believe what he was about to do, or why, because he knew with good behaviour, he might have been out in two years. But he couldn't take any more in here.

"Well me too."

At two minutes to eleven the men were lined up ready to walk outside. In the past few days the prisoners had been going out in parties of ten, to remove the huge boulders which had fallen from the hillside onto the road through the bad weather, making it highly dangerous for motorist's, this is what they were told. So the men were ready, visibility was very bad they'd heard, still the inmates had to do this, for the safety of others. Not that most were worried about that.

Luke had managed to get some cutters in the tool shop, when he was working there one day, they had been sharpened and were just what they needed for today. So he had passed them over to Jake one morning when they were having their breakfast, giving him some string as well, which he'd found lying on the floor. Jake had hidden them under the jacket he was carrying and took them back to his cell. So that when the time came, which was today, he would tie them to the bottom of his inside leg. They weren't too big, but they were sharp, however he had concealed them easily, when he was alone in his cell. It had been nerveracking though, to hide them from the officers who had been walking around checking things.

4

They never bothered Jake too much, as they knew he wasn't a troublemaker, so that was good. Luke had always told him that he was the right person for the getaway, as the main guard George Trent never checked him properly because he trusted him, and Jake got on really well with him; thank goodness. The older man often told him jokes which were very funny. when they met up from time to time. He knew how to cheer the prisoner up when he could see he was low, well Jake didn't want to laugh today. It made him feel guilty what he and Luke were about to do and was going to let George down. What would he think of him? He didn't like to deceive him, but it had to be. The older man would frisk him quickly, when they made trips out and when they came back, before searching other inmates whom he didn't trust and it took longer. Anyway they were all ready now. Jake was sweating under his coat, thank goodness he didn't go down the bottom half of his leg, because he would have felt the offending implement, which was strapped tightly to the inner side of his right leg.

At two minutes to eleven the men were ready to go out onto the open road, having all been checked. Thank goodness that ordeal was over, the chain gang was ready. As Jake and Luke began battling against the heavy snowdrifts, wondering would this situation be successful or not? The shuffling of chains was apparent, and the deep snow didn't help. It was so cold Jake pulled his coat collar up. They had to pick these huge boulders up which had fallen from the bank putting them into a heap at the roadside edge. Five officers were now walking out with them, two carried rifles. It was later when Jake and Luke noticed three guards were having their break in the cabin; Dan Glover, Scott Mitchell, and George Trent. Dutch Mackay was guarding the prisoners at the front of the line and Jim Harper was at the back. The prisoners had been working for half an hour when Luke in front gave Jake the nod which he just about saw through the blizzard. He began to feel very nauseous as he waited for the right moment. This dreadful human being would tell him when to go. Only two of the men, Ginger and Mack, knew what was about to happen, as they had been informed by Luke who told them not to say anything or else! Jake wasn't happy about that when he heard. Fancy telling them! But they wouldn't let

5

anything out, because they would have to deal with Luke, who despite all their bravado they wouldn't want to face in a fight. Jake was pondering now and had thrown the boulder down onto the side of the road, when he heard.

"DUTCH YOU'RE WANTED IN THE HUT? I'LL KEEP AN EYE ON THEM!" The prisoners heard Jim the other guard yell out through the thick gusts of heavy snow.

"Right," the officer yelled back as he made his way down to the end of the line, where prisoners were working as fast as they could in the terrible weather conditions, not seeing what was about to happen at the other end.

Jake got Luke's signal when he noticed him nod. 'This is it!' He bent down to release the string as the cutters fell to the ground.

Suddenly a prisoner who was chained to Jake said, "What are you up too?"

Luke overheard and called out through the heavy snowfall:

"None of your bloody business nosey sod, get on with your work. Jake hurry up and pass those bloody cutters".

The men in their group stared in disbelief.

"And you lot, I wouldn't interfere if I were you, or you might be sorry".

Nobody would argue with Luke. All the prisoners were now aware of what was about to happen and they weren't going to cross this man that's for sure. The freezing cold was getting to most of the men.

"Quick," Luke said, noticing Dutch had battled through to where Jim was standing in the full-blown snowstorm. As it happened they weren't watching the prisoners at that particular moment, because the two men were deep in conversation, before Dutch walked off to the cabin. Jim took his mind off the men for a second as he bent his head down trying to pull his hood up further, from the heavy flurry's. When he looked up, he could hardly see anything in front of him now the men were in a full-blown snowdrift, that swept into everyone's eyes.

Jake was now cutting through the heavy chain which was difficult, nevertheless he used all his strength and it worked. Taking a quick glance at Luke he threw the cutters over to him, just missing one of the prisoner's heads as he ducked. When suddenly officer Jim at the other end, began to look their way but with difficulty. Thankfully the men carried on doing their work, trying to make everything look as normal as possible. The blizzard was horrendous, as dark clouds spread across the sky. The atmosphere being very heavy, but it was the perfect weather for the two men who were about to escape. The officer who had taken over from Dutch was on his way up. Jim pointed to the line telling him something. Mitch put his thumb up as he began to pull his fur hat down and fasten the flaps before struggling with his coat collar. Jake knew Jim had seen he was doing something from that distance, so he had to be quick if he wanted to escape, before Mitch got to him. He never really thought of the consequences; this was it, no time to waste, or wait for Luke, which he didn't want to do anyway. Jake noticed that he was having trouble cutting his chains, still that wasn't his problem. He had to look after himself now.

Turning he gave the other man the thumbs up, before running towards the bank and climbing up with difficulty, it was very slippery. The prisoners were all watching the scene behind them and the guard was almost at the place where Jake had been working. Everyone stared into the distance as Jake ran, waving his hand in the air to all the men.

Suddenly Dutch came flying out the cabin after hearing Jim shouting "BREAK!!" He could see everyone was pointing in Jakes direction and shouting at the top of their voices. Jim and Dutch were moving as fast as they could to catch him, getting closer, but with difficulty, as the snow was covering them all in seconds.

Then Scott shouted out to the two guards: "Quick he's getting away."

Everything happened so fast. the men were amazed by the whole situation, all but the ones who knew what was going to happen.

Dutch yelled from way back: "STOP OR WE'LL SHOOT!"

But Jake was moving as fast as his legs would let him when he heard the gun being fired, thank goodness into the air, but it made him duck.

Luke sighed, it was too late, the so-called cutters had let him down, they'd gone blunt, and he wasn't able to cut the chains. So he threw them into some bushes not realising there was a concealed well there and they went straight to the bottom as he heard in the quiet atmosphere; plop!! He didn't want anyone to know he was the instigator of Jakes escape. There would be another time for him. But he was thinking now, he should have gone first. After all it was his idea to breakout from the prison.

Chapter 2

Jake was moving fast across the moor as he headed towards the nearby wood. He and Luke knew this was there, as they had both seen it when they first came to the prison on the coach at different times. The snow was making it difficult to get along and his trainers were so heavy as it stuck to his soles. The adrenalin was pumping now, as he hurried as fast as he could, hearing a gun go off again. Missed!! Thank goodness. Frightened, he increased his strides as much as he could, feeling very determined. Mind you he didn't want to be shot at, but they were mainly shooting into the air to frighten him, which it did. He wasn't going to stop now not as he'd come this far, he was going to see it through. He looked back again to see if Luke was following, but the weather was so bad, he actually saw nothing. Not even the guards. Luke wasn't going to make it he was sure. Good! If he was a kidnapper, molester, murderer! Whatever!! He should never be released. But Jake at that moment began to think of his own situation, he hadn't intended to do what he did. Suddenly in-between the blizzard, he entered the nearby wood in front of him. Steadfastly he ran in and out of the huge trees, which were now heavily laden with snow, their branches bending all ways.

"Who's escaped? Who's escaped?" Mr Trent was shouting to the guards as he approached them from the Cabin, after hearing all the commotion.

"It's your friend Jake Farrendon." Scott smiled, a little cocky.

"WHAT?" The man was lost for words that Jake had betrayed his good nature and felt devastated by what he had done. Well he had to pull himself together as everyone was looking at him.

"Okay, Okay," he struggled to say. "Jake has gone for now but he wasn't my friend, just somebody I took to inside, because he hardly ever put a foot wrong and did all you asked him to do, more than some I could mention."

The officer look down, embarrassed by his outburst, when he was one of his mates, pulling himself together he thought it must be the cold getting to him. Sorry! He said quietly.

"So anyway let's get these men back to the prison George was saying it's very cold and I'm sure there's lots more snow to come down," he told his men that were left. "Line up," he yelled out to the prisoners, through the heavy snow storm. This must have been well planned, he began thinking because he had never suspected a thing. Clever! Now as he looked towards where the two guards were chasing after Jake. He thought. "They will never catch him in this snow."

Dan, Scott and George were all shouting to the inmates now, "Get in line you lot, we're going back to the prison."

How bedraggled everyone looked as they dropped the rocks they were carrying, to the side of the road. Their huge chains jangled in the blizzard, which was getting worse. The men were hardly able to see the person in front of them as they whispered and sniggered about the break, many wishing it was them who had escaped.

Ginger and Mack were now talking about Jake having made this jail break. "Who would have thought that quiet bloke Jake Farrendon would break out of this prison." Ginger shouted.

"You're right there," the other agreed. When they saw Luke staring at them both as he pulled one of his sneering looks. The two stopped talking.

Dutch and Jim were still chasing the prisoner but they couldn't get near enough to catch him. Jake had disappeared into the blizzard and the shot from the gun hadn't frightened him, because he knew that they wouldn't want to shoot him, well not on purpose, so the shot went into the air.

It was going round that Luke had been involved in this escape. And the prisoners had noticed why he hadn't gone too? Ginger and Mack knew all about it having seen the two chatting together at times, probably planning this get away from Slate Moor unbeknown to all. But it had rather backfired on Luke as he didn't get away.

"We will be apprehending your partner in crime, very soon." Officer Dan told Luke pushing him in the back. "How did Jake manage to get out of those chains? What was the tool he'd had?"

The man shrugged his shoulders, he wasn't saying anything:

"Don't ask me, I've got nothing to do with it." He smirked.

"Well Jake will soon be caught," Dan said.

George had gone very quiet now, feeling let down by Jake, the man had betrayed him. Disappointing!

"You hope, 'dick head'," gobby Ginger shouted out. "He fooled George Trent here," he laughed, which started them all off doing the same, but then they saw the two officers faces and went quiet.

George butted in, when he heard what was being said. "Okay that's enough from you," he told Ginger. Then began thinking Jake would never have done that on his own, or even planned it. However he suddenly realised that he hadn't frisked him well enough when they all went out today. It was his fault, for trusting the man, well not anymore. We'll soon get him back and he won't fool me again, he thought. That was it, he wouldn't trust another prisoner ever again. Well he wouldn't have to soon, still this would happen now.

"When we get back, questions will have to be answered," he yelled out to the men. "Now let's get going!!"

He waved to everyone, officers as well, he was in charge. George began to take in the scene as he looked round at them all. "Also don't get any ideas he told them, you won't get as far as Jake."

Going back wasn't easy as the men needed constant watching. They were getting rather rowdy as the inclement weather got worse. He'd never seen conditions like this, as he began staring across the moors, which were misty. All that could be heard were the men's chains jangling in the silent atmosphere. Looking now he could see Dutch and Jim struggling their way back. But without Jake.

Annoyed that he hadn't got away himself. Luke realised the cutters had been too small to cut both chains, as they had gone blunt after Jake had cut his. He should have had bigger ones, but they would have been difficult to conceal. Nevertheless he should have been the one to escape, after all it was his plan, but at the time Jake was the one who hardly ever got frisked. Luke began to feel so angry now about the whole situation and that he was going back to prison when he should be out.

Would he ever be able to get away from the prison? It would certainly be a lot harder because, the guards would be watching him closely. Since his own cell had had problems and having been put into a temporary cell, it was confirmed by the governor, he was to be allowed into the food hall to eat as the other cell they had wanted to put him into was over in another building and they wouldn't have had enough men to guard him. Also there would be the problem of his meals as an officer would have had to keep running across the yard with food all the time. Luke had found out it would be a few days before his cell was up and running, also he realised he was being closely watched most of the time and knew he wasn't liked, but he wasn't worried about that. Well he had never thought that Jake would agree to his plan, so he must have been pretty desperate. He had organised it all whilst over this side of the prison, but unfortunately it had all gone wrong for him, as now he was walking back through the prison gates again.

Dutch and Jim joined the other officers and looked whacked by all that hard running across the moors, the snow having got much worse now. There was disappointment on their faces at not having found their prisoner, as the wood went on for miles and the conditions were dreadful. As their boots began disappearing into heavily fallen snow. Jake Farrendon had gone...

"How did this happen?" Asked the governor, Peter Trehern, to the five men who stood before him.

"Well sir I just don't know? said Dutch. One minute the men were hard at work clearing the rocks and the next minute, Jake Farrendon was scarpering across the fields to the woods."

"I see, his boss answered. "Well there is a big hunt on now, looking for the prisoner. Also I've just contacted the police. How far were you both from him?" The governor asked.

"Couldn't get any nearer to him," Jim told Trehern, backing Dutch up. "The weather conditions were horrendous, so we were unable to go any further, as we actually couldn't see where he'd gone through the snow storm and he just disappeared."

"I understand you liked him Trent, didn't you?"

George Trent was totally embarrassed by this remark. He swayed back and forth on his legs: "Yes sir, he was a good prisoner and did everything you told him to do. I never for one-minute thought that he would escape from here. He only had probably another two years to go and he might have got out earlier, on good behaviour. Now he's blown it."

"Did you not search these men, before they went outside?" The governor asked them all.

"We did." Scott spoke up, glancing in George's direction. "But we found nothing."

"Well Jake Farrendon must have been hiding those cutters somewhere. Possibly up his arse! Would you say?" Trehern remarked with a smirk.

"I don't rightly know sir. I think that would have been a bit difficult." George answered him with a half-smile.

"Funny Trent, anyway we've got to find Jake Farrendon he can't have gone far, mind you that wood is thick, but I don't think he will be in there for long, I'm sure. I understand Luke Stamford was also going to escape, is that right?" (He saw George nod.) Also has he disclosed any information to you as to where Jake was heading?"

"No sir not a word, he's adamant. I spoke to him earlier, but he wouldn't divulge anything, saying he had nothing to do with the break. Lies! Lies! Because, we know now he also was going to escape today, as we heard a whisper? It didn't work for him but there was a tool involved, of course which we hope to find. Possibly cutters, we will look when the snow clears. Luke must be annoyed Jake got away and he didn't, because I think he would have escaped first. Jake however must have had cutters hidden somewhere probably on his leg, I did search him, but not enough, I know that now. Luke evidently knew he wouldn't be checked like the others are, because I was easy with him, so that's why he got away. My fault entirely sir, you see I trusted him, so I do apologise. Its taught me a lesson a little late though," George was saying.

13

"Knowing Jake Farrendon he couldn't have planned all this on his own. Thank you men, we will just have to wait and hope he gets caught soon. Or else there will be lots of explaining to the powers that be, in London." He walked towards the heavy window and stared out at the snow. "Once this weather clears, he will be found."

"There's no let up yet, sir, so I heard on the radio," added Dutch continuing to stare at his boss.

"As I mentioned before, we will get him eventually." Then in a more friendly tone, he suddenly dismissed the men. "Not you Trent I want a word." Closing the door Peter Trehern turned to the older man. "You've only got until this Saturday haven't you George before your retirement? How do you feel about that?"

"Rather apprehensive at the moment, by what's happened sir. I'm so disappointed in Jake that he let me down. When I put my trust in him, which I shouldn't have done. You see I did like the bloke."

"It's unfortunate that this has happened, but not to worry about it now I'm sure we'll get him soon. I can't believe you've been here twenty-five years George," he told, the worried looking man in front of him.

"No, neither can I sir and this situation has never happened to me before. I'm not usually wrong about people. I've had a long time here to weigh a person up and his character. But this one has foxed me. I put my trust in prisoner Jake, I know what he did was bad, but it was an unexpected accident. I didn't think he deserved that sentence but I really thought he'd do his time and go. It just shows sir you can't trust anybody nowadays. The only thing was I knew he was getting pressurised from somewhere in here, but he wouldn't say who was causing his many panic attacks, because whoever it was, might have beaten him up. I heard this information, in the sick bay one day. So I think that made him do what he did." George sighed.

"You're probably right, but you know the judge's decision was paramount." He stared at his main guard, noticing the deep-set lines in the man's face and how grey his hair was. This work has taken its toll on him, the governor thought. It's funny how time goes by so quickly and you never really notice it he thought.

14

Anyway don't worry old chum he'll be caught eventually. You just think about your retirement."

George Trent looked at him: "It will remain a worry for me until he's caught." And in the next breath, he said: "Do you fancy a cuppa sir? It's been a long day…"

The other man put a hand on his shoulder and they both walked out the office. George was now thinking about when two days ago all the officers congregated in the canteen, and Peter Trehern presented him with a Rolex watch, for being at the prison twenty-five years. It was a lovely speech he made, which he really didn't deserve now, after what had happened.

And George had thanked them and said he would miss them all with their little quips that had kept him going when prisoners were playing up. It had been hard at times. Well he could imagine what they were thinking now.

Chapter 3

Jake was not as far from the Prison as he would have liked to have been. The snow storm was getting worse. He could hardly lift his feet up, and his trainers were getting so heavy as he walked. He pulled his coat collar up again, as the particles fell down the back of his neck. Stealthily he moved in and out of the huge oak trees, standing as close as he could to them, just in case the officers happened to be near, but as his eyes scanned about, he saw no one. The heavy snow made the atmosphere still and quiet. Suddenly in front of him he could make out the road he knew. He began to think the people at the prison, must have worked it out by now, that he had been linked up with Luke.

He had to get out of this wood. Keeping low before making his way out to Roaden Beach, which he knew so well. The tide was out now as he climbed the wall. Sliding down the other side he walked along the wide ledge, taking it very carefully. This part of the beach was usually slimy quicksand, which he didn't want to fall on or get stuck in, although today it looked quite firm, probably because of the cold weather. Still he wasn't going to take any chances, he'd got this far, and didn't want to disappear now through carelessness. When the sound of shouting and whistles being blown suddenly came to his ears, he kept very close to the wall, where he couldn't be seen from the road. With a bit of luck he could get to the far end of the beach and disappear into another nearby wood, heading for the open moor and hopefully a new identity. He was wet through, his jean jacket was like a limp piece of cloth as was the blue prison shirt underneath, which he knew he had to dispose of, as it just might give him away at some point. Luckily he had a clean T-shirt in his bag, that would be dry but wouldn't keep him warm and he really needed warmth. Still he would sort that out later. He stopped walking hearing the sound of voices.

"Nothing over here sir."

"Morgan and you Slater," Detective Inspector Thornton called out, I think we'll call it a day and start again tomorrow,

Farrendon won't get too far, not in this weather, because it's getting worse. He'll have to appear at some point but I'm sure he's taken cover for the night, he could be anywhere. Come on let's go home," he yelled out. With that the three got into the car driving slowly away, on the slippery road.

Jake was very pleased to see them disappearing in the distance. So far so good he thought, reaching the end of the wall and climbing up onto the path. Not a soul was in sight now, probably all in their lovely warm homes. He felt the stillness of the evening, as the weather began playing a big part in his escape again. Hurriedly, he made his way back across the road in the heavy snow storm, but he began to realise he had to be very careful not to take the wrong path, which would be so easy to do in this weather, that might lead him somewhere he didn't want to go. Sliding and falling now a couple of times, he picked himself up, brushing the snow off his clothes, and made his way towards another wood. He looked up and couldn't believe how the sky looked, full of it, but the moon gave off a brightness which made the surrounds glisten in the still of the night. So he was able to see where he was going; just!! As the huge flakes covered him.

It was continuous snow falls and it must be at least two feet deep he began thinking. The police car had gone into the mist. He began pushing the snow laden branches away as he walked slowly, step by step, to where he had no idea, but boy was he cold? When he'd planned the breakout with Luke he knew it was going to be hard with these conditions, but had never experienced anything like this. Blinking his eyes he shook the snow away from his lids. Was he seeing things? No! It was a small hut he could see in the distance and not a soul about, it seemed to be in the thickest part of the wood. As he made his way towards it. A few minutes later he was trying to open the door by pulling the bolt across hard, when the wood at the bottom of the door scraped the ground, moving huge mounds of loose snow as it gradually opened, he pulled it with all his might falling unexpectedly backwards into the deep snow. Jumping up Jake began brushing himself down before he entered the hut and pulled the door to before the snow drifted in. It was small inside but a lot warmer than outside. It would be ideal to hide in, as he felt he'd walked miles from the prison. Surely nobody would be around on a night like this. In the corner he found some sacks, next to piles of wood. Taking his jean jacket off, he hung it onto a small nail to dry, and then reached into his bag for the tee shirt, not warm but better than the wet prison shirt. He had to get rid of the shirt it wouldn't be wise to keep it, not with prisoner printed on it. Looking around the shed he picked up two sacks in the corner, wrapping them around his body he covered himself completely with them, which made him feel a lot warmer, they were rough but better than nothing. Jake felt so very tired now, it had been a long day, however he began to feel very hungry, when all of a sudden he remembered he had a few squares of chocolate in his pocket, which Mr Trent had given to him two days ago, and he'd forgotten to eat it. The man was always doing things like that. Nice person, he thought. He must be very upset by me at the moment. But he's saved the day again. Reaching into his trouser pocket he pulled out the piece of chocolate and popped the squashed bit into his mouth. 'That's filled a hole for the time being.' Then without realizing, he fell into a deep sleep. Only to be woken by what sounded like a big vehicle somewhere in the wood.

He jumped up, not knowing what time it was because his watch was in the hands of the prison warders. He could see through a hole in the shed that it was light, when he noticed through the window a four by four vehicle with a trailer on the back, heading towards the hut. He must get out he thought, reaching for his coat which was still very damp as he put it on. Looking round there was a small part of the hut that was broken, he walked quickly towards it, as whoever it was, would come bursting through the door any minute. Seeing a wrench in the corner, he slipped it under the wood and pulled with all his might. It split the timber and made a bigger hole than before. They wouldn't have heard that crunch, because the trailer was making so much noise. Now he was pushing his body through the gap, which was very difficult, ripping his coat as he went, once outside he buried his shirt and pushed it right under the shed into a hole, he hid behind a tree because they might see him in the snow, as the whiteness would show him up. So he cowered nervously. When he saw a young fellow go to the shed door, whilst the man was busy cutting the engine of the vehicle and that was Jakes moment to move fast!!

"Can you open the door Sam," the man shouted.

"Yes dad the bolts unlocked," the boy pulled hard and it opened. Looking around, he suddenly noticed the hole in the side of the hut.

His father got out the car picking up bits of machinery from the trailer, hurriedly following his son as he carried them into the shed and laid them down. "Come on son get a move on, we've got to pick up wood down further to put on the trailer, all before lunch. You know how long it takes to load up...? What are you looking at?" When he saw his boy pointing.

The fifteen-year-old turned to his father. "I think someone's been here!"

"What makes you say that?" Then he suddenly saw the hole where Jake had gone through. Why yes, you're right!" He bent down and took a piece of blue cloth from the torn wood and showed it to his son, before throwing it in the corner. Then he noticed the wrench lying on the floor next to the hole. "How did anyone get through that? But whoever it was must have heard us coming, and scarpered." He watched his son pick up a small piece of a chocolate wrapper, which was screwed up on the floor.

"Well they liked chocolate, the young boy told his dad. I'll just go outside and look around, while your sorting this lot out."

"You be careful Sam you never know who's out there. On second thoughts. I'll come with you," Tom Franks told him.

"Dad, don't be silly I'm big enough to look after myself now."

"That you maybe, but I'm still coming out with you."

Outside the two looked around, their boots disappearing into the deep snow. When Sam yelled out. "There're footprints over here, leading from the hut, but whoever was here has gone, that's for sure!" He told his dad.

"Well I expect they might have wanted shelter from the snow. But why would they rip a hole in the side of the hut unless… they saw us coming and didn't want to get caught? Somebody was cowering in here from this awful weather," Mr Franks said to his son. "Come on let's go and pick that wood up, but first I must put another piece over that hole, in the hut, we don't want anyone else in here. Also I think I'd better put a lock on this door I will look in my tool box. We have some important equipment in here but that's funny nothing has been taken."

"Yes, that is peculiar Dad."

Needless to say Jake was long gone and he was now running as fast as the snow would allow, but it was very deep underfoot. Thank goodness he hadn't been found. It was sometime later and he'd been walking what seemed like hours. His jacket which had dried slightly after hanging it up in the shed, was now soaked again. How he would love to wear something that wasn't wet. He needed dry clothes, but only had three pounds left in his pocket from his prison jobs. Even if he came across a shop somewhere he couldn't go in looking as he did because he might be recognised. The day went by quick and it was now late evening and quiet everywhere, so he decided to move towards the roadway where the snow looked a little less deep. He began to walk with a heavy heart. Where would all this end he wondered?

Trudging along with his hands in his pockets he was frozen to the core, having been on the go all day, without any food, apart from last night when he had the chocolate. His feet felt like lumps of lead and his body began to ache. All in all, he was worn out. Had he done the right thing? Because he was beginning to wonder? It must be miles from the prison now, well he was hoping. When he came upon another path leading off to who knew where? But he decided to follow it. Jakes legs were getting weaker by the minute, against these terrible conditions. His jacket and trousers were sticking to him and he was shivering uncontrollably now. Never noticing the bright light approaching him, in the distance, until it was almost upon him. His head was down as he pushed the weather back. But the cars headlights were glaring as he turned round seeing in the half-light that it was getting closer. Jake wondered if it was the police. Not wanting to be caught, not now, having got this far, wishing he'd kept on the other path he had been on, where he wouldn't have been seen. Only a madman would be out on a night like this. That he wasn't! Too late to hide. He turned and looked at the car as it got nearer, it was very old which the police would definitely not have had. Better keep walking and try to act naturally. The car was in line with him now, as he put one weary foot in front of the other. When he heard a voice coming through the snow storm, someone was shouting.

"I say would you like a lift?" A woman's voice asked.

He bent his head down a little, surprised by the invitation as he walked up to the car and looked through the open window: "Thank you that I would."

She leaned across opening the door as he then fell heavily onto the front seat. Banging his overhanging feet outside before shutting it. One thing in his favour he hadn't lost his good manners which he'd always had before prison. The warmth of the car heater was wonderful, and he was steaming, embarrassingly so.

"Are you alright?" She asked.

"Yes, I'm fine, just very cold. I'm so pleased you happened to come along though."

"What are you doing out here, in this awful weather?" She asked him, as she put the car into gear and moved slowly away.

He was too tired to even work out what he could say to this woman and needed a few minutes to think: "I've been walking for ages."

How worn out he looked she thought. "Where do you want me to drop you off then? That's if we get through this snow storm."

"Wherever you're going, then I'll walk the rest of the way, thank you," He puffed the words out.

"Oh! Oh! Okay!"

He sounded peculiar and on turning slightly, she noticed he'd all of a sudden fallen asleep. The poor man looked exhausted, walking in these conditions. A feeling of apprehension came over her, as she wondered who he was? He could be dangerous!! She really shouldn't have picked up a complete stranger at this time of night and in such a lonely spot too. But the weather was so bad and he had needed a lift. Anyway she took a chance, and he never attacked her when he got into the car, so he must be okay? She'd ask him questions when he was a little more with it. Where in the world was he heading? In the heat of the moment she decided to take him back to her cottage, just for the time being, anyway no way could she just dump him on the side of the road again, he'd freeze. Also the weather was horrendous and he wouldn't be able to walk in this deep snow. She hadn't seen anything like it in years, however she must concentrate as it was getting dark and difficult to see where she was going. Still her cottage wasn't too much further she hoped, finding it rather hard to recognise places though, with how the snow had fallen.

She had gone a number of miles driving really slowly because the road was so icy, when suddenly she was sure she saw her narrow lane in the distance with the oak tree on the corner it was such a relief, she was nearly home. Which some would say was a lonely place, but she was used to it. As she got nearer she saw the sign on the corner of the lane, which was partly covered with snow, but she knew she was in Rush Moor Lane with the help of a low moon, thank goodness. It was necessary to keep going and not to stall the engine just to accelerate up the hill as she didn't want the car to get stuck again so she had to keep moving. If this man woke beside her he probably wouldn't have much energy to help her, she thought, taking a quick glance in his direction.

Jess had noticed whilst coming along the road, there had been only two other cars she'd seen, in the last hour. So there would be no such help from anyone. When all of a sudden she began to feel very cold, because the heater had cut out in the car again and the windows were steamed up from the man's wet clothes. Still she loved her old Citroen. Wiping the windows inside she took another look at her passenger seeing he was still fast asleep. Putting her foot down she pressed hard on the accelerator again. When all of a sudden the wheels of the car started spinning. "Oh no!" She cried out, in panic, accidently waking the man up.

"What's the matter?" Jake asked her in a confused manner wiping his eyes as he stared out through the window, because they weren't moving. "Where are we?"

"Well as you were asleep you didn't exactly tell me where you were heading. So I decided to bring you here to my home until the snow lets up. Was that ok?" She asked him.

"Perfect! No that's very good of you, thank you."

"But now the car is stuck and I can't move it," she told him crashing the gears. It's difficult to hold it, as we keep slipping back down the hill because I can't keep the revs up. So the engine cuts out."

Dare she ask? 'Do you think you could find the energy to give me a push, then I can perhaps get the car started once more, because we haven't too far to go now? My cottage is directly round that bend there," she pointed.

"Well I'll try," he told her. Pulling his coat round him and getting out of the car feeling a little more rested. Going to the back, he shouted: "Into first gear, now give it some wellie and I'll heave with my shoulder."

"It's moving," she cried .

"I DID REALISE THAT?" He yelled out!!

"Oh sorry."

"It's alright, I didn't mean to shout at you, it's the feeling of being so cold, it gets to you." "Steer it away from the patches of ice."

"Oh ok, I can't stop as it will probably cut out again. So you'll have to walk up to my cottage," She called waving through the open window.

"See you in a minute," he shouted, puffed out, as he also waved his arm in the air.

She hadn't really got a good look at him, only having taken side glances, but she had noticed one thing he was quite dishevelled and looked as though he'd been walking for some time.

Chapter 4

Jake began battling his way up the hill, the snow hitting him in the face now. This must be the worst weather conditions ever, he began thinking. He'd been lucky though because thankfully he got away from the prison and hadn't been caught. When Luke had told him one day that snow was on its way, they had both thought that it couldn't have come at a better time to escape the prison. But never in his wildest dreams had he expected anything as bad or good as this. In fact he was sure the police and prison authorities would have given up looking for him, due to this weather.

As he turned the corner he saw her car was parked next to a cottage, which looked lovely in the moonlight with the snow surrounding it. He was now intrigued to see what was up the lane further, it looked as though it was leading up to the moors, but it was difficult to see properly. Ah well there was no one around so he felt quite safe at that moment. The lights were on in the house which made it look cosy. And as he reached the front door it swung open. Jake prayed there was no other person around, say a Mr Somebody. Ah well he had to take that chance.

"There you are? She smiled. Are you okay?"

"I'm fine now," he smiled back.

"Come in! Come in! She opened the door wider. Come into the kitchen, I've lit the stove and it will be lovely and warm in a few minutes."

"This is very kind of you to give a complete stranger a lift and bring him to your home. I could have been a dangerous person who might have harmed you," he told her, trying to sound natural.

"Don't worry, that had crossed my mind," she smiled at him. "If you'd wanted to harm me, you would have done it in the car". Taking her duffel coat off, she hung it on the back of the chair, before staring at the man in front of her, as she told him. "I'm so pleased I was able to give you a lift, because there was no knowing what might have happened to you, with the weather so dreadful. We haven't had it as bad as this for some years and it can last for days, and weeks, especially out this way, because it's so bleak. All that's around here are moors as far as the eye can see."

Oh great Jake thought staring at her. She was a fine-looking woman, not really pretty, but very attractive, she had a round smiley face which gave off an interesting look. The small mole on her cheek was endearing and her eyes were the brownest he'd ever seen, they were beautiful. As she stared at him he felt warmth, in her friendly presence. Her auburn hair, looked naturally curly, though a little unruly through the snow, the woman wasn't tall, probably round about 5ft, and slim, in fact he thought, she could do with a little more weight on her.

Feeling embarrassed now by the situation, she began to speak a little hurried. "By the way my names Jess Sinclair."

Jake faltered for a moment, also feeling rather awkward, until he told her after a little thought. And I'm John Turner!" (Where did that name come from?)

She held out her hand smiling. "Please to meet you John."

"And you Jess," he answered, thinking that her name really suited her.

As they both shook hands, she sensed his were rather rough. "Here let me take your jacket it's soaking wet." She was thinking it was a tatty jean jacket most uninteresting, perhaps a working coat, well she didn't like his choice. Where had he come from? She shook the jacket and thought where was he going to at this time of night and in this dreadful weather? Still that could wait, questions later. She hung his jacket on the back of the other kitchen chair, where it dripped away, torn on the pocket.

"Sorry about the mess on your kitchen floor, Jess."

"Oh it's only water." She began to think though. He was a little untidy looking, well he would be, walking for so long in this weather. However she liked what she saw in this man, he was different, with a strong face and attractive stubble look. The sea-blue eyes and mop of black and grey hair impressed her. But what a boring T-shirt he had on. 'Rock my world' Whoever chose his clothes? But he was solid muscle, probably been working out in a gym somewhere. He was very tall towering over her. Smiling she told him. "I expect you could do with a cup of tea."

"You're right there thank you." He was beginning to think this was fate her coming along in her car. You could say it was a bonus for him too, that she was a lovely person and that she lived in such a remote area. He looked scruffy he knew, but he had been walking for some time. He decided to try something out on her. "I don't want to be a nuisance to you, but if I can rest here for a while, then I'll be on my way. Of course if that's alright with you?"

She had a wedding ring on, but where was he?

"No that's fine you can't go out in this weather, it's freezing. You would probably die in this cold. That's why I brought you here."

He turned to her. "What will your husband say? Bringing a complete stranger home to your house like this. Will he mind?"

"I shouldn't think so, as he died four years ago."

"Oh, I'm sorry."

"Thank you John. She looked him up and down before saying, "I see you haven't much with you, there can't be any clothes in that duffle bag it's too small," she pointed and smiled. "Well I was just thinking that up in the loft, I have a case with some clothes in. So many times I've meant to get rid of them, but never have, they were my husbands. I'll see if there is something which might fit you in there, would that be okay with you?"

"Would it? Thank you Jess, I really appreciate that".

"Don't thank me yet, you see he was a bit shorter than you and thinner. Still there might be some item of clothing you could pop on. As you must get out of those wet clothes?"

"That's very kind of you. His hands were warming now, as he stood by the roaring wood-burning stove. But his trousers were sticking to him and he felt so uncomfortable. It would be so nice to have something dry to put on, he couldn't believe his luck. Getting away from the prison, the hut and being given a lift then ending up here waiting to get some dry clothes. Somebody up there was looking after him, but he was wondering if the officers from the prison and the police were

26

on his track, he hoped not. He was feeling so much safer here away from everyone and was thankful as it looked the perfect place to hide out. What made Jess live here though? He wondered, cut off from the world and this wonderful human being was such a trusting person. He was now leaning against the sink staring round the kitchen. When he saw a photo of a little girl in a beautiful mother of pearl frame. Who was she?

"It seems very quiet here with no other properties or people around," he said smiling.

"It is, there are a few walkers who come from the moors and sometimes get lost and they knock on my door, to ask the way, wherever, but it's always nice to have a chat. I see the postman and my main friends but that's all. This cottage is well off the beaten track. 'Why did she say that to a perfect stranger?' He had noticed the hesitation in her voice.

"It's okay Jess you can trust me."

"Sorry but I do have to be careful because after all, I am on my own here, but, you see it's such a lovely place to live. Although I am wary sometimes, as you might guess."

He nodded.

It was funny but she trusted this person in front of her, as she carried on talking. "It is very quiet at this time of year, especially in weather like this and pointed towards the window. Nobody relishes coming up to the cottage, it's so out of the way. You see it can be quite dangerous to live here too. As I've found out in the past." She suddenly went into her shell. Had she told this man too much? When after all she didn't even know him, but she liked him.

"Jess what's the matter?" He asked.

"I'm alright but I was just thinking back."

"You looked so unhappy just then, what is it?"

After a pause she explained: "I had a beautiful little daughter once."

He was surprised by this statement: "Is that her in the photograph?"

"Yes that's her, she was just perfect?"

"Was?"

A few moments went by, tears flowed from her eyes as she began to explain. "She was killed!"

John suddenly felt sick to his stomach "How?"

"It happened six years ago when Becky was playing outside in the front garden, with her dolls. She went through the garden gate and down towards the moors, wheeling her dollies pram. The awful thing was I was trying to empty my washing machine at the time, as it went wrong and there was water everywhere. It could only have been a few minutes, which had passed, when I looked out of the window and couldn't see Becky anywhere. It was then that I realised she'd opened the gate and simply wandered off. It was a terrible shock, when I had been checking her every few minutes. I couldn't believe she'd gone, it was all so quick she literally disappeared into thin air that day, the next few days were a total nightmare, as my husband, the police, and I searched, in all the most unusual places where she might be on the moor. Jess's tears were flowing down onto her cheeks now as she tried to compose herself. The police found her … two miles away in some gorse bushes, she'd been murdered. I still find it hard to believe after all these years. She was shaking uncontrollably. My husband and I were devastated. She was four."

"Oh Jess I am so sorry," John told her. "Who for goodness sake could do such a terrible deed, to a little girl who was just starting her life and hadn't hurt anyone?"

"Yes you're right, apparently this individual had been walking across the fells when he came across my Becky, who was lost and he took her with him to where he later killed her. He didn't seem to have any remorse for what he'd done. It was said that he had a disturbed mind. So he went into a lock-up hospital, but when the case came to court, it was said he knew exactly what he was doing. So he was sent to prison. I just hope the authorities never release him. If it was left to me he'd rot in hell. I just couldn't come to terms with what he'd done to my little girl."

John was stunned by the whole story and found himself in an uncouth position. However he would be on his way tomorrow, weather permitting. Because if Jess ever found out that he'd killed his wife, he was sure she would go spare. Also that he'd been living for the past few years with these vile men in prison.

"I suppose you think I'm mad living here. After all that's happened."

Jake shook his shoulders.

"Well, after our daughter was killed, my husband's character changed. He became a really snappy, argumentative person and we didn't get on at all well, but we tolerated each other. Then he became ill with cancer and I did all I could for him, until he died. It was then I had to reassess my own life. You see I missed Becky more than anything and felt she was still with me, at times. So my decision was I couldn't leave here because of her, even though she'd gone, I feel she knows I'm with her, and so I've made my life here but it's hard sometimes. Still life goes on doesn't it?" She was looking at him. Who was this man in front of her? Why was she telling him all her secrets? Thinking back now she realized she'd made a silly move, giving him a lift, he could have been anybody even a murderer, she thought shivering. (Now she was being foolish.) John knew what was in her mind.

"Please don't worry Jess I know what you are thinking. As I told you I won't hurt you." He wanted to put his arm around her, to comfort her, but he mustn't.

"Sorry John I shouldn't have told you," she was now wiping her eyes as she rose from the chair, placing her hankie into her trouser pocket and staring at him, before saying. "I don't know why, but I'm not frightened of you. After all if you had wanted to hurt me, you could have done it a long time ago. Well let's make that tea?" She smiled, turning her back on him, and putting the kettle on again, before reaching for the mugs. Feeling a little better now after giving vent to her pent-up feelings.

"Yes, thank you, that would be lovely." He was so looking forward to this warm tea, but having had to wait while she told him about her little girl Becky and her husband! Which he had felt so sad for her. But now she was over her sadness and was handing him the long-awaited mug of tea. Having the hot brown liquid in his hand now, he drank and it went down quicker than he intended. It's certainly warming me up," he told her.

"Careful John it's rather hot."

He knew that, but it went down a treat. He was now having a job keeping his eyes open, at different intervals feeling very tired, having sat down by this wonderful log burner in this big old comfortable armchair, which had seen better days. When he heard her say…?

"I am sorry, when I talk about Becky but to me it's what keeps her with me always. Even though I get terribly upset, please forgive me?"

"Don't worry about that, I'm just so sad for you. That person whoever it was, had to be punished. I'm so sorry to think you lost your dear little daughter, Jess."

"That was such a nice thing to say," she said staring at him before adding. "What possesses people to do these vicious crimes."

"Circumstances I suppose."

"Circumstances! What circumstances?" She asked sharply.

"Well in your daughter's case, the murderers state of mind and his family background."

"I'll never forgive this man," She told him. "Whatever situation, they must be punished for their crime. that's life." She eyed the man in front of her, who was speaking and had sensed something in his voice. Dropping the subject she said. "John I won't be a minute."

On his own now, he began thinking about his time in prison. His cell hadn't been the best accommodation he'd ever had. Still he'd tried to make it comfortable, with the items he'd got. Which wasn't a lot. He had a bed, sink, and also a toilet. His pictures on the walls were from magazines which the guard George Trent gave him, one was a beautiful mysterious moors scene he remembered. Staring round this kitchen now he felt comfortable in the big armchair he was sitting in, it was old though. In the middle of the room there were four small chairs which had seen better days and a round table. On one wall stood a large cupboard with its holding knob hanging off. That needs a bit of renovating he thought and the old sink had seen

30

better days. Also the inside door to the kitchen needed painting. He got the impression this woman was a little hard up, to say the least and couldn't do DIY. He closed his eyes, when all of sudden he stirred heard a creak on the stairs. Turning his head he saw Jess walk into the kitchen, carrying some clothes on both arms. She looked very different now, having changed into a black jumper and leggings and her hair was neatly combed, her wavy chestnut curls hung in clusters onto her shoulders.

"You look nice," he told her. As she dumped her wet clothes in a basket ready to be washed.

"Thank you! It's lovely to be dry. Look I've sorted these out for you, she was saying, handing him a pair of tracksuit bottoms and a crew neck navy jumper, she wasn't going any further about underclothes. Anyway ... I was wondering if you would like to have a bath, as the water is hot now, it would warm you up. You must be uncomfortable in those wet clothes you've got on, they look as though there stuck to you and to my chair. If you like they can go in the washing machine after mine, how's that?" But she didn't intend to do it for him, after all she didn't really know this man. It was strange that he didn't have a case, which would have been difficult to carry in this weather anyway, he only had a duffle bag which looked as though there was hardly anything in it, as it lay on the floor.

"Great Jess I appreciate it, sorry about your chair I hope it dries out okay? Also many thanks I would love a bath."

"Good! And don't worry about the chair, it's my fault I should have put an old cover on it before you sat down. I think it has seen better days anyway," she laughed.

"Now you just point the way and I'll go and make myself clean and tidy. This is very kind, of you when you don't even know me!"

"Well that's the least I can do, you did push my car. Right, well the bathroom is just at the top of the stairs, on the left. I've put a clean towel in there and an electric razor, which I found in the case up in the loft. Thought you might need it?"

"I WONT NEED A RAZOR! I'M GROWING A BEARD," he answered briskly, finishing the last drop of tea in his mug.

"Oh!! Well as I said the bathroom is on the left at the top of the stairs."

"I'm sorry Jess I didn't mean to be so abrupt, that's the second time I have spoken to you like that and after you have been so kind and all. Forgive me will you? Put it down to my being wet and tired."

"Of course," came her reply, but she was taken aback a bit by his attitude. Changing the subject now she looked at her watch. "It's 8.30 I will cook us both something to eat when your nearly ready, alright?"

"That would be lovely."

She stared through the kitchen window, as the huge snowdrift continued. when her thoughts flew back to John. It was nice having a man about the place again, but she hadn't expected it to happen like this. Where had he come from? Where was he going to tonight? She wondered.

Jake climbed the stairs with his dry jumper and tracksuit trousers over his arm, thanks to her husband. Suddenly he noticed different things on his way up. Seeing torn wallpaper and frayed stair-carpet. You could tell that there hadn't been a man here for some time who could do all these repairs. He turned and walked into the bathroom. A slightly discoloured avocado bath greeted him with a detachable plug, lying on the side. The sink was chipped and the toilet still had an old green cistern, with an old chain hanging down. John went over to the bath and turned on the hot and cold tap and let it trickle in. His dry clothes were on the chair. as he removed his saturated ones from his body, the clean towel was hanging behind the door. Jess had thought of everything.

He was so looking forward to relaxing in the bath, but noticed as he stepped into it rust coloured water. He didn't give a toss about that, in fact that was least of his worries. The feeling of being warm was wonderful, as he relaxed and started to soak his weary body. What bliss! Not having been able to wash for some time. he had at one point entirely forgotten what he'd been through, over the last couple of days. Not forgetting his luck about Jess motoring on that lonely road and picking him up. He slid right down in the bath, and suddenly wondered what had happened after his escape from the prison? And were whoever hot on his trail? Surely they would give up tonight, what with the awful weather conditions. which had been his saviour. Anyway his tracks would be wiped out he knew that, thank goodness. Jess did him another favour by telling him, not many people paid visits to this cottage, that was what he really wanted to hear. She must have trusted him to part with this piece of information, so he felt quite safe here for the time being, as the cottage was well away from the road. Best to relax now and worry about that in the morning.

He could hear Jess in the kitchen downstairs, she was so nice but then he did at that moment think of his own wife. Ever since Kate's accident, he felt it had been his fault. Well it was in a way. But he'd never wanted to harm her. Sadly it had all gone wrong. She and Matt had been seen together many times by the publican and him feeling dreadful that he'd had to tell (Jake) about this. As he eventually got out the bath, he picked up the towel drying his well-toned body.

Then beginning to think again about his punishment for the crime he'd committed, manslaughter, was hard to take, as he'd never hurt anybody in his life before. But the six years he got in prison seemed so harsh. He had completed four, but he didn't know how? Because he hated every moment of his time in there, feeling very depressed. That's why he went for Luke's plan. He had heard that Matt had left town after Jakes conviction and his mother had moved through no fault of her own. So he had to do his six in prison, even though he didn't feel it was his fault. It was an accident. Then this opportunity came along to escape, so he did and was now hoping he wouldn't get caught; well time would tell. Shaking his head now he began to put the jumper and tracksuit bottoms on that Jess had given him, they didn't look too bad either, even without underclothes … As he then picked up the towel which was on the floor and began to tidy the bathroom. After all one thing they taught him inside was discipline. When all was done, he made his way downstairs feeling a different man. Not a convict.

Chapter 5

"Ah, there you are, you're looking a lot better now and more relaxed," she smiled. "Come and sit down? I put a cover on the chair as you can see?"

"Thank you Jess, sorry about making the chair slightly damp. I do feel much more refreshed though, having had a bath and putting dry clothes on, thanks to your generosity." He stared at her but could see she had become slightly embarrassed by the situation.

"That's okay." Thinking now whatever possessed her to bring a total stranger into her house, even though the weather had been a strong contributor? She stared at him liking at that moment what she saw. His hair was quite long, but it suited him and the dark stubble on his chin seemed right. Also on top of that he looked very fit as he stood tall in her kitchen, he certainly was interesting. This man was different to the usual type of men in the past that she'd known. He was an eye catcher and attractive, in a rough sort of way. She was embarrassed to think she was smitten with him. What was the matter with her she hadn't felt like this in years about a man? Wow!!

John also was eyeing the woman up opposite him, she was not very tall but well endowed. The wooden clip looked lovely holding her lustrous hair. Her whole appearance was beautiful, especially when she smiled at him, how lucky was he? As he took a longer look in her direction.

"I know why your staring at me it's because of my very large jumper. It was my husbands. I thought I might as well get some use out of it, having found it when I was looking for the clothes for you to wear, when I was in the loft. I probably look awful in it?"

"Well if I was staring? It was because it suits you," he told her.

A smile crossed her face at his remark: "So tell me, why were you out on a night like this?"

He didn't know why? Or how? But lies began to pore out of his mouth, as he began to explain things, without any trouble at all, he'd learnt to do that in prison. Otherwise you'd always be in trouble. He carried on with his made-up story feeling so guilty now though, as he told it without a flinch. Well he certainly couldn't tell her the truth.

"You see I have a brother Joe and a sister-in-law Margaret. She is about twenty years older than my brother. That was a good lie to start with he thought, where the hell did those names come from? Anyway I used to live with them."

"So you're not married then?" Jess asked him smiling.

"Eh, No! Well anyway, my sister-in-law didn't like me very much and we used to argue about anything and everything, when we were together. Joe married the wrong woman I have to say. She had a vindictive tongue and aired it on so many people, me included, until I couldn't stand being any longer in the house with her and we had a terrible bust up. I told her exactly what I thought of her and she told me to go. I blame Joe for marrying such a scheming woman. I did no more but got up and walked out of the house very quickly, as she began shouting abuse at me. Would you believe without my money and cards which I'd left on the bedside table? Stupid I know that now, but in the heat of the moment you do silly things. My brother will be surprised that I have gone, as I didn't even take my clothes which I had there, I just wanted to get away. I thought I would go back later to get everything, but I certainly didn't need another ear bashing." Would she believe this story? "Well I got about half a mile down the road not knowing where I was going. And suddenly realized the snow conditions were getting worse. Really, she pushed me to the limit, so I decided not to go back to the house. I just had to cool down, so to speak, that was funny what with this weather though."

"Then as the horrendous blizzard worsened, I began to think I'll pay my mother a visit for a while, as I haven't seen her for ages. Plus I have clothes at her house, (That should do it.) She would explain all to my brother in a letter for me later, when I tell her what happened. He didn't like bringing her into it though, still he had too. But she would never have interfered with Joes choice." He told Jess. (Had she bought it?)

35

She nodded.

"You see I thought I might be able to get a lift from someone if they passed by, because the buses and taxis had all stopped. He stared as she shuffled about in her chair now. Did she believe him? Or not? Anyway, that's when you came along in your car," he smiled. Would she buy the lie? "It's not often I raise my voice but my sister-in-law is a total nightmare". Going back again to this awful lie he said. "My brothers alright, but he's just hen-pecked and wouldn't argue against her. Well he didn't actually see me go, he was working when all this was going on."

"Would he have stuck up for you?" Jessie asked.

"Oh, I expect so, he's a good sort and will be surprised about all this especially when he finds I've gone. I'll ring him sometime. Anyway, that's enough about me. What were you doing out there on a night like this?"

"Well…" she leaned over and poured him another mug of tea.

"Thank you."

"I'd been staying with a friend of mine for a few days, three actually, her name is Stephanie. But this morning I felt I'd been at her place long enough, even though her partner Nathan never minded me staying, as he told me many times. Well anyway I decided to return home. I hasten to add my friend wasn't happy about this and tried to persuade me not to go. Simply because of the dreadful weather, which got decidedly worse. Bless her she was worried about my safety too. That's me though, I make a decision and that's it I follow it through. Anyway I don't like leaving the cottage for too long without someone being here. Do you know it took me three hours to get home, when I usually do it in an hour? Looking up at the clock she said: "It's 9 30 already?" He was still staring at her. "Is there something wrong?"

"Oh no! I felt so comfortable in your presence I was concentrating on what you were saying." He hadn't lost all of his manners in prison. He was so pleased she'd come along that road, he thought, in more ways than one. And felt safe here in the cottage it was well off the beaten track.

"Let's get this meal or we will never have it at this rate. Jess got up from her armchair. "How does bacon and eggs sound? You must be starving?" She looked across at him just as the phone rang. That will be Stephanie. wondering if I got home all right, I won't be a minute." She told him, putting the bacon down on the side, before turning the light off under the grill.

"I wouldn't tell her that you picked me up, if I were you." He said walking close behind her, before she entered the hall.
"Why not?"
"I just wouldn't!" He was looking round the kitchen door at her.
"Right! Okay, if that's what you want?"
"I do!" He was quite adamant at that point.
She looked in his direction as she picked up the phone. "Hello!"
"Hello yourself. You got home okay then?" My friend Stephanie asked.
"Yes fine, but I had to take it slowly as the roads were treacherous."
"I told you not to go didn't I? Still as long as you're all right that's the main thing, only you never know who's about at that time of night, do you?"
"No! No! You don't. Anyway thanks for having me. I'll see you when the weather gets better. She noticed Jake was listening through the crack in the door, to their conversation. How dare he! She thought. Well I must go now and thank you and Nathan of course, for putting up with me. I was going to ring you but you beat me to it, speak to you soon." She stood there twirling the phone cord around her hand, wanting to end this call
"You were very welcome, it was lovely to have you. Yes until our next chat take care. Bye."
"Bye Steph." Turning round she stared crossly at him. "Why did you do that?"
"Do what?"
"Stand at the door, when I was speaking to my friend."
"I'm sorry Jess. I thought you might tell her about me."
"I told you, I wouldn't."

37

"Well I thought your friend would think it funny, you bringing me back here, feeding me and giving me clothes. She might put two and two together."

"Two and two I don't know why? There's nothing going on," she told him calming down. He was quite right though when she thought about it, that wasn't the thing to do. When she had told her friend just before she'd left her. 'Don't worry I won't pick anyone up.'

After they both walked back into the kitchen. He suddenly realised that he'd gone too far, it was the tiredness which had taken over. The warmth from the open fire was wonderful, he'd missed these home comforts, being in prison. Smiling he put his hands up in the air. "Sorry Jess, I had no right to tell you what to do."

She was now smiling at him. "Good, it's forgotten," the moment had gone.

John sat in the old armchair watching her as she turned towards the cooker, putting the bacon under the grill. He was starving, which he must not show too much when eating his meal. He was so tired though and could hardly keep his eyes open. However, thinking deeply now and putting the food into the back of his mind, he suddenly realised he was totally besotted by this woman. He'd never met such a kind and interesting person, who had such a lovely nature. Kate had never been like that. Her character had been rather coarse at times, towards things that happened in life. That's why he could see Jess was so different. She had time for people he could tell. Well him as it happened.

When at that moment she turned round and pointed to the chair: "Is it dry now?"

"Yes it is, I will take this cover off for you," he smiled back. "Sorry!" He said putting it on the vacant chair, thinking he shouldn't have said, what he did to her just now. Sitting down again his eyes began to slowly close, through the heat of the fire. He'd had two dreadful days. but felt relaxed for the first time in ages and was soon fast asleep…until he felt his arm being tapped.

She watched him stir, his strong muscles protruding, bringing to light her inner feelings. This man was something else, rugged, attractive, and a mystery. Who was he? She shook her head. "Wake up John the meal's ready." She was glad now that she'd picked up some odd groceries from Steph's local shop nearby, before she left, bread, butter, teabags, eggs and bacon. At least they had a meal.

As he woke he said. " I'm sorry again Jess. I was so tired. I suppose all that walking in the snow did that and what with this wonderful fire, I couldn't keep my eyes open."

Now he could smell the aroma of the fry up, it was everything he'd dreamed of when he was in prison. The meals he and the inmates had inside were awful, bacon and egg would be swimming in fat. Jess grilled the bacon he noticed and boiled water to put the egg in with a little vinegar; all healthy. He watched as she got the large loaf cutting a number of slices. Placing the butter dish on the table he stood up and walked towards it, as he then gave a fleeting glance out of the kitchen window. Thankfully It was still snowing, which made him feel happier, nobody would be out in this weather, he was sure about that. But then he began to wonder would she turn him out when he'd eaten? Time would tell.

As it happened she did notice John was eating ravenously (which wasn't meant to happen.) As for the sister-in-law situation, she wasn't totally convinced by what he'd told her. Surely he wouldn't have left his money and clothes behind? Nobody could drive you to that situation, no matter who it was. She began to think though because he was so hungry, did his sister-in-law not feed him? For him to turn out on a night like this. And you would certainly take what was yours before leaving. No something was not quite right. Still it was nothing to do with her. She had only given him hospitality from her end. But fancy going out in this kind of weather? Why hadn't he told his sister-in-law, he'd leave when the snow cleared a bit? She was now thinking of the jean jacket he was wearing, T-shirt, his trainers weren't too bad, but certainly not right, for this type of weather. No this man was a mystery. Stephanie had been so worried about her returning home on her own, and because of the terrible weather conditions, but more importantly whom she might meet on such a night and she had been right, believe it or not.

It was a strange feeling, but she did feel safe as she'd thought before, with him around. However he was a complete stranger. These last five years had been hard and she had never fancied anyone since Alex demise. Of course their marriage hadn't been the best, but they had both tried hard to have a good life, although it wasn't to be and went downhill rather quickly. Especially when Becky their daughter was killed. As they began to argue and argue and just didn't get on. They both got irritated with one another, it had been an horrific time, which she'd rather forget, but she knew she never would. Jess was now very tired, but she couldn't go to bed and leave this total stranger on his own in her home.

"You're tired," he told her noticing her yawning. "Jess would you mind if I stayed and rested in this chair just for tonight? Then I'll go in the morning." But he didn't know where?

"Well I'm not turning you out in this weather. No way! You can stay here of course until morning. Okay? And yes you're welcome to sit in the chair all night if you want? But I will get you a cover."

"Thank you, that's so kind of you, as I don't fancy going out in this." Never in his wildest dreams did he ever think it would snow as it had. He saw she was looking rather thoughtful at that moment, as though she was about to say something else.

"I was just thinking, you could use the spare bedroom if you want, I've just got to make it up?"

"Well if you're really sure I'm not putting you out. That would be great thank you." Then in the next breath. "Here let me help with the washing up?" He leaned over and grabbed the tea towel. "You know what? That was a lovely meal, thank you Jess."

"It wasn't that exciting, but it was better than nothing until I can manage to go shopping properly and you're not putting me out." Then for the next half an hour the two chatted away, comfortable in each other's company.

He was so tired now, after the long day of breaking out of prison and walking for nearly two days. It was a good job he had had a rest overnight in the hut. Then by luck Jess had picked him up this evening his second day of walking in deep snow, but this was wonderful here, and a good hiding place. Also being here with Jess at this particular time, it couldn't be any better. But the meal he'd just had, really had made him very tired. He felt totally wacked. Nevertheless he decided, there and then, that he would try to make an early start in the morning, weather permitting. "It's been a long day."

"It certainly has," she said staring at the man in front of her. "I'm feeling rather weary, having driven through that white blanket of snow." It was funny really, she always used to be shy with people she didn't know; why? But John was different. She never felt nervous at all with him. Here he was a total stranger, going up to bed in her house and she didn't mind.

"I do appreciate you letting me stay here Jess and as soon as I possibly can I'll leave," he told her.

"Well let's see what the weather is like in the morning, shall we?"

It was a big cottage with a large kitchen; living-room, dining-room, then upstairs on the next landing, were three bedrooms and a bathroom. She put the lights out, feeling slightly embarrassed at that moment, as he followed her up the stairs, which were creaking as usual. Reaching the top, she then opened a cupboard door, and took out a pair of sheets, pillow cases and a blanket. Then turning she entered a small bedroom, with John close behind her. Where they both set to, making up the single bed.

He thought at that moment as he watched her, he really fancied this woman like crazy. But didn't know much about women, after losing Kate four years ago. So he had to be careful not to blow everything, her kindness was second to none, she'd been so sweet throughout.

Chapter 6

Jess threw the sheet across the bed to him, she took particular notice of his strong hands when he took the end, tucking it in roughly. Throwing the blanket over she said. "You should be warm enough,"

"Thank you, I'm sure I shall. Goodnight Jess he called out as she reached the door and thanks for everything."

"You're welcome," she smiled, as she began to close it.

"If you don't mind, you can leave that!!" he told her brusquely. Never wanting to be shut in ever again.

She tossed her auburn hair. "Oh Okay! Goodnight! Hope you sleep well?" Jess wasn't happy that his door was open, after all he was a complete stranger. Walking across to her room now, she didn't know why? But she did sort of trust him, after all she could be running a bed and breakfast accommodation. Mind you they wouldn't leave their door open, she was sure about that. That's if she ever did bed and breakfast, which she definitely didn't intend to do. This was a one off, but all of a sudden Jess felt rather anxious. She must stop being silly, or was it because she was too trusting? She kept thinking about what happened to her young daughter and became sad at that moment. It was hard at times.

Thank you Jess I'm sure I shall, he shouted back." Prison seemed a long way off now, as he settled down into the crisp cotton sheets, he was exhausted, but his mind was all over the place and he knew it would be impossible to sleep. What a day it had been, but, on the other hand what luck meeting Jess. His life was in such a turmoil, but he never regretted escaping from the prison, well not yet. Being with hardened criminals, rapist, abusers, etc. He hated being there. No the outside was the best, especially now. Then he tried to get his head together planning what he should do next. Had the police given up the search in these conditions? He hoped so. Suddenly Jake heard the floorboards creak, as Jess had been in the bathroom, making her way to her bedroom. He was very curious at that moment, dare he look? Yes he must ... so he got out of bed, and peeked through the crack in his door, noticing hers was ajar, he began to open his wider knowing he shouldn't, but he was curious as he slowly walked across the landing towards her room. The leg of the chair was against the door on Jess's side, she was probably a little nervous by his presence, after all his door was open and he was a complete stranger. He was doing something he shouldn't and might blow everything by this actions but he couldn't help himself. He hadn't seen a woman like this for so long. After all he was a man and they needed love and attention. It was then that he noticed through the crack of her door, she was undressing. Transfixed, he stared well and truly, what was the matter with him? But at that moment, he did feel she wanted him to look. He was sure she knew he was there, being watched as she took off her bulky jumper and jeans. Then methodically she removed her panties and lastly her bra until she was naked. John was in a total hypnotic state by this time. Jess was something else. She was sexy, and very voluptuous. He was now feeling very excited and weak in the legs, as he put his hand round her door to remove the chair He was beginning to feel the vibes that she wanted him too. Never telling him to go, when he suddenly pushed hard moving the chair and opened the door wider. He shouldn't have done this, because he might have blown everything.

Jess was feeling slightly embarrassed as she looked at the most muscle toned body she had ever seen, who was now totally in the nude. She reached out for her dressing gown to cover her own modesty, waiting for what she felt was to be the inevitable.

Jake wasn't worried by his nudity, because that's what they did all the time in prison, however he had always worked out in the gym, that's why his body was so toned. He meandered over towards her, watching as he saw her looking him up and down. His vital part began to react, he was thinking this was wrong, but he couldn't help it, he fancied this woman like mad. Still he shouldn't take advantage of her after her being so kind to him. This would probably be it and she wouldn't want him after this. He wanted her even though it wasn't right, so he slowly turned to go back to his bedroom. He couldn't do it. But how he'd missed this side of his life in prison.

43

"Don't go!!" She told him in a quiet voice. Feeling mesmerized by this man. She began to stare at him again, as he walked towards her. She gasped as she took in his naked body, which was so impressive. How did he get like this? What was happening to her? She knew she wasn't able to control her feelings, because she wanted and needed this man. By the look of him he also needed her, badly! It was wrong she knew, but couldn't help her feelings at this particular moment. The thing was he was somebody she didn't know, what was the matter with her? It was funny but ever since she'd met this man, from nowhere, she liked him and more.

John stared at her, lust within him was working overtime. Grabbing her roughly he began pulling her dressing gown off. Throwing it down on the floor. The burning desire between the two was intensifying. He couldn't brush this situation aside. As she and he fell onto the bed she wrapped her legs around him, as he began to melt. His masculinity was second to none. As he then held her in his arms and began to explore her body, moving from one position to another. Kissing her full lips with a fiery passion. He never stopped, as he caressed her body. But he tended to be rough with his actions at times and aggressive. The frustration came out, but she seemed to love it, responding to his every need and desire.

Jess couldn't believe what was happening. What was she thinking getting into this situation? She had been a long time without a man and did need affection. Lust was good. John had a fantastic body, he was big and solid all over.

They both clung to each other enjoying every moment and then when it was over, he fell to the side. Turning slowly to her he noticed the sheer look of contentment on her face, then he realised he'd pleased her and felt thankful for the moments they'd shared. He rested his elbow on the pillow, stroking her long auburn hair, which was so beautiful. She opened her eyes and smiled at him, but not a word was uttered as they embraced each other, before falling asleep. (He was running, as the weather conditions got worse, it was freezing, he would die if he didn't find somewhere warm. Reaching a rough unmade road, he felt a hand on his shoulder.)

Chapter 7

"John! John! Wake up! Wake up!"

He stirred. "What is it? What is it? Oh it's you Jess."

"Of course it's me, who did you think it was? I've brought you a cup of tea."

"Oh I was dreaming," suddenly he felt very awkward, I'm sorry about last night Jess taking advantage of you, but you did get under my skin so much, I had to have you."

"Well I was as much to blame," she told him as she sat on the edge of the bed, handing him his mug of tea.

"Did you enjoy what we did last night?" He asked cheekily.

"Yes of course, but with a total stranger? What was I thinking of?"

He couldn't help himself as he slowly looked her up and down in her silk dressing gown. "You were lonely and so was I, it just happened Jess. It's nobody's fault. We needed one another and the snow brought us together. it was fantastic."

"When was the last time you had a woman?" She asked staring into his face.

"Not for a long time, in fact I can't remember just how long. You see I didn't want to get involved with anyone, after my last relationship failed, it was too painful," he told her. It was yet another lie, 'how he desperately wanted to kiss her now,' still the moment had gone. There was no reaction from her, after his confession.

Now as she looked at him still lying there completely nude. She said: "I can't believe what I did last night and with someone I know nothing about." He, was not looking at all worried, as he stared at her. What a good-looking man he was in a rough sort of way. As she began thinking, but, who was he really? Because she felt that he wasn't telling her the whole truth. As the lines on his face said something else, so did those large well-worn hands. She watched as he put his mug on the small table, then after a minute he reached out to pull her down, but she slipped out of his grasp. "John you hurt my wrist then?"

"Sorry Jess, you know I've never met anyone as lovely as you are. That was such a wonderful night for me and I hope it was for you too?" He eyed her up and down and realised she was having doubts now. So he thought he'd better tread lightly. "You were lonely Jess, you needed someone to be close to and I filled that gap. Don't feel guilty. What we had was good, better than good, and we've got nobody to answer to."

"Yes you're right, it was good," she smiled.

"The way it all happened, I was meant to meet you, we just hit it off from the start. Life is too short to worry about this happening. I fancied you and I think you me. Okay we had sex, well we're fully grown adults. Please Jess don't upset yourself. It was the snow which played a big part in all this wasn't it?" Suddenly Jake sat up and looked through the window. It had stopped snowing so he must get ready, it's time he went on his way, he began thinking. The powers that be, would be looking out for him, once conditions were better.

"I suppose so, and as you said we are adults and yes it was good; better than good," she smiled, going out of the room and into the bathroom.

Jake got up sighing, it was all so confusing. What was he thinking to have had sex with this woman, who was a total stranger and him, a wanted prisoner? Life was so complicated. But Jess didn't seem like a stranger, he felt as though he'd known her forever. She was a delight to be with, but he had to think of the future if there was one. Lots to do now as he began to wonder how all this would end? He had to get away from here, for a while anyway! The prison authorities must be searching different areas, so it was vital he moved on.

It was later when Jess began to feel embarrassed by what had happened last night but tried to act naturally as she looked at John who was sitting in the kitchen now. Looking quite neat and tidy with his own clothes on, which weren't that good, but clean. She in the end had washed and dried them for him. Now moving forward she picked up a box of eggs. Scrambled that's what she'd make for him, well there wasn't much else. However the weather looked a little better this morning, it had stopped snowing. Perhaps she would be able to go into town and get some more groceries. As her supplies were going down pretty quickly, having an extra person to feed. She began to wonder would her dishy lodger be going today. He had said he would, but who knows? He was sitting comfortable in the big arm chair again and she felt his eyes burning into the back of her. Jess placed the two plates down, with the piled up scrambled egg on top of the toast. This was so embarrassing after last night. She didn't want to meet his eyes, which incidentally were rather a lovely sea blue, but underneath them she felt they were concealing something,

"That's lovely Jess, thank you, I must hurry up and eat this, because I have to get on my way." More walking! He would go and see his mother, she lived quite a few miles further on, he knew.

Jess felt at that moment, he seemed to be in a terrible hurry, all of a sudden she said. "I'm going into the town after breakfast, if you would like a lift I'd be happy to take you. That's if the car starts and the roads are ok."

"That would be great many thanks," he said. Forgetting his manners at that moment as he pushed a heaped forkful of egg into his mouth, she didn't see as she was busy making the teas.

"Where are you heading?"

"Well as I mentioned before, I will go and see my mother for a few days. Then after I've sorted myself out. Who knows?" He never brought up about last night, but if only things were different and he'd met Jess first, none of this would have happened. Then his wife would still be alive. But what would the outcome be now? So much had happened, where would it end? He only knew he just couldn't dismiss Jess from his life, after what they had experienced together, never seeing her again, wasn't a question. But when?

She was now thinking, it probably meant nothing to him what they did last night, she had been lonely and he was there that's all, but she did fancy him and wished he wasn't going. She would love to have a man in her life and also have a family again. But this time be really in love, which she hadn't been, not really with Alex. Then there was her dear little Becky who would always be her dearest love, she would never forget her.

"Jess that breakfast was great thank you.

"So pleased you enjoyed it." She reached across the table for his empty plate, when the phone rang. Putting the plates down she made her way out to the hall.

He followed her nervously: "Who's that?" He felt very agitated.

"I don't know till I answer it, do I? Probably Stephanie again."

"What are you going to tell her? He asked abruptly. Nothing about me I hope?"

His manner had changed again he was brusque. Looking at him from the hall she moved towards the phone. "Don't worry I won't say anything about you or last night. Alright?"

John realized at that moment he'd gone too far and the phone was still ringing. "It's only that our meeting should be kept quiet. Now answer that phone," he smiled, she noticed the anger had gone from him suddenly, so she reached out and closed the kitchen door. Didn't want him to listen into her conversation with Stephanie because he wouldn't be happy.

He gazed out of the window in the kitchen. The weather had eased but the ground was still covered in deep snow, as were the trees and bushes, which were bending over from the heavy falls. Staring across the white blanket of snow on the ground he felt safe, because he was sure the police wouldn't venture up to this spot. He really hoped not. In fact they probably didn't even know there was a cottage up here. He couldn't believe what he was seeing at that moment. It was coming over dark again, when suddenly the heavens opened up once more. It's no good he would have to persuade Jess somehow that they shouldn't go out today, but perhaps stay here. Another day would be good to lay low. He escaped on the Saturday it was Monday now, three days since his left that dreadful place. Prison!!

Chapter 8

"Hi! Stephanie's voice echoed down the line.

"Not you again," Jess laughed.

"Yes it is. I can't help worrying about you in that lonely spot, you should never have gone home, well not until this weather had calmed down."

"Stop worrying, I'm a big girl now and I would have had to come back here sometime wouldn't I? As this weather might go on for days and you know that I couldn't leave this old cottage without any heating for too long, you see I do not want any burst pipes."

"No of course you don't, I do see that. You know I've had a job to get to the hospital, these last few days. I couldn't take the car out because it's too slippery. Also the bus takes an age to get there, so I walked in the end, but got in late a couple of times. I needed to be there though. You can't hold these babies back when they're ready to be born. Oh sorry!"

"Don't be silly Steph I've told you before not to worry about talking of children. It happened and life has to go on."

Stephanie loved being a nurse and had delivered Becky all those years ago, that's why she didn't really like to bring the subject up too much to Jess, it was very painful for her, but things came out without realising.

Jess remembered the excitement among her friends, when her daughter was born. And how devastated they were when Becky was killed at the age of four.

"Well I was going to try and get into the town, but I don't think I should now, because looking out of the window in the hall I see it's snowing very heavily here again, I have never known a winter like it have you?"

"No I haven't. Do you have enough food?" Stephanie asked.

"Yes for a few more days." Better not mention how low she really was on commodities, she didn't want her friend to start worrying and so, she had to finish this conversation. "Well I have to go now, lots of washing up to do, no dish washer," she laughed. What did she say that for?

"You can't have that much Jess with only you there?"

She was quick with her answer. "Ah yes, well I didn't wash up last night and I had a big breakfast this morning, and I've been baking too." She had to end this conversation because she was on the verge of tripping herself up. Knowing John was probably hovering in the kitchen, waiting for her to finish.

"Goodness you have been busy. I'll ring you next week then."

"No, I'll ring you," Jess replied," cheerio for now."

"Bye, then. Don't do anything I wouldn't do!"

"Right. Ha! Ha! You know me?"

"Do I?" Then she was gone.

Good! She was making Jess nervous, knowing John wasn't that far away, and probably listening, as she casually walked into the kitchen.

"Jess it wouldn't be wise to go out today, as it's snowing again. Would you mind if I stayed for one more day?" (He wouldn't mention the phone call.)

She glanced outside "Well actually I was just thinking the same, when I noticed what it was like out there, she said staring through the window I think your right, we shouldn't venture out today it would be silly. And of course you can stay another night"

He breathed a sigh of relief.

And she dreaded the thought of him leaving anyway.

"Well I was thinking if we went into town and I left you, then you might have trouble getting back, with this weather with no one to help you, if there's another blizzard. Also you never know, you might meet some awful character on the road." A smile came to her face. He saw she was suddenly thoughtful. "Don't worry Jess it won't be a repeat of last night."

Relieved, but also a little worried. "The only thing is, I'm running rather low on food."

"Never mind I'm sure you'll manage, I'd like to pay you, but I haven't any money yet. But I would like to do a few jobs around the house for you, though."

"Please don't worry John."

"No I want too, as I've seen a few things that need attention," he told her. She had been so kind to him about

50

everything, actually in more ways than one, which was now on his mind. Later he got stuck in as he put the knob back on the cupboard door, and sorted the hinge out on the kitchen unit door, made the stair carpet secure which was frayed, he was doing whatever she wanted him to do and he began to feel a lot better. But he kept thinking about last night when she was in his arms, he noticed she kept staring at him. It was probably on her mind too. Anyway he was feeling happier now forgetting other things.

She noticed he was looking out the window again. "I don't think anyone will come up here for a few days. You're not hiding from someone are you?"

"Don't be silly Jess I don't think my sister-in-law is likely to walk up here do you?" (Keep it light.) He smiled. "No I'm just interested in this weather and wondering how much longer we're going to have to put up with it." He wanted to get on the move as soon as possible to see his mother, then he could sort himself out. She'd only visited him twice at the prison, it had been far too stressful for her. The day went by quickly when Jake realised that as much as he liked being with Jess he had to move on. Although he knew in his mind, he wanted to come back here just to be with her again. Holding his hand out, he took the steaming hot cup of chocolate from her, which was wonderful. The two sat staring into the wood burning stove, in front of them, lost in their day dreams

Dare she say it? "This is so cosy, I like having you here John."

"You know what? I like being here with you Jess," he smiled. She looked especially pretty today he thought. Her beautiful auburn hair as usual was cascading over her shoulder in small waves. He knew she had washed it this morning, because he had seen her coming out of the bathroom with wet hair.

"Thank you for doing all those jobs for me today. That is what I've missed, a man about the house. It's strange but it was as though we were meant to meet one another, don't you think?" She asked him, having forgotten their small disagreement when she was talking to *Stephanie*.

51

"I have to say it does seem funny, and I feel that I've known you for ages." If only circumstances were different, he would love this woman to be his wife. Ah well … such is life. He leaned towards her and gently kissed her full lips, she didn't pull away either. Later that evening they had a make do meal and at 10.30pm went to bed. Both in their separate rooms. Jake had felt he shouldn't push his intentions on her, in time he felt they would be together again one day, he was sure of that.

Next morning Jess felt sad that John was about to leave her as she said to him. "Whenever you're around these parts, will you come and see me again?"

"You know I will," he told her, as they walked across the drive." The snowstorm having eased up. Both had got up early for the trip to town, now they were nearly at the car which stood a little skewwhiff where she'd parked it two nights ago. "Mind how you go because it's very slippery in parts, come here?" He told her, grabbing her arm.

The warmth from him was comforting, as was her warm jacket which she needed today, it was an icy cold wind, although John seemed in a hurry to get away, which was a shame. Given more time, Jess could well have got to like having John around and her mind was running wild now.

Opening the door of the snow-covered car, he then began to clear the roof and bonnet. "Give me your keys Jess and I'll see if it starts?" He said.

"Thank you."

After what seemed ages the engine spluttered into life.

"Thank goodness for that," he told her. "You get in the driver's seat and I'll clear the windows."

She thought at that moment: "Can you drive John?"

"Yes of course, I had my own car but it was old, so I got rid of it and thought I would get another when I could afford it, but it hasn't happened yet." He looked at her, all these lies, he really hated himself for telling them. Once you tell one it grows into a bigger one, but he had to do it. Thinking now how Kate had spent his money, but he mustn't mention this to Jess.

She smiled and nodded as she got into the driver's seat. Ten minutes later they were on their way down the narrow lane to the main road, which was rather slushy, but easier to get along than the other night.

John was getting very agitated. He was hoping they wouldn't bump into the police on the way.

"You okay?" She asked him.

"Yes I'm fine. What makes you think I'm not?" But his character was certainly changing again he realised.

"Oh it's just that you seem on edge," she answered.

"WELL I'M NOT!! I'm thinking about what I have to do." That wasn't nice he thought, to talk to her in that tone of voice. "Sorry Jess."

She overlooked his outcry, as she said: "Well, we're nearly into the town, do you know Ferris Town John?"

"A little, he lied, as he watched one or two cars on the wet road. And then his gaze took in the scene across the fields as the white blanket had surrounded the country side. He sensed what she was thinking.

"How beautiful is this?"

"Yes, when you're indoors," he managed a laugh.

She felt a little down now that he was leaving and she might never see him again. Arriving in the small town she pulled up outside Boots. When suddenly she turned to him: "I must tell you before you go, I don't usually make a habit of picking people up and doing what we did the other night."

"I'm sure you don't Jess, Let's put it down to two lonely people needing affection at that particular moment in time. It's forgotten okay?" He knew in his heart of hearts that it never would be, because he actually had fallen in love with her. He wondered if she possibly had fallen for him too? She was everything he ever wanted in his life, how was this situation going to end? He a prisoner! Un-be-knowing to her.

Jess began to think what they had that night would never be forgotten. "Alright," she smiled. She was going to miss him, even with his attitude problem. But she was still wondering who this man was? And what was the real story? Because what he had told her didn't ring true.

"Thanks for this big warm jacket he pointed, which was a tweed coat she had bought for her husband, but he never wore it because he began to lose weight, as he became ill. Well believe it or not, it fitted quite well although slightly tight. She'd made him take it because his coat had seen better days. "Do you know your husbands clothes have saved the day for me?" he smiled, "thank you. They have been a godsend especially when I was so wet through the other evening. So … I'm sorry I should have asked you if you'll be alright going back home?" He looked up at the sky. I would hurry up and get your groceries and head back quick, or else you won't make it up that lane. I think we're in for another snowy day."

"Yes you're right. As for the clothes my husband doesn't need them now so I've put them to good use so your welcome." Then in the next breath she said, "I'll probably never see you again, will I?"

"As I mentioned before. You will!"

There was a quick intake of breath from Jess when she informed him "I could take you to wherever you want to go, if it's not too far?"

"No, I'm okay thanks, the walk and fresh air will do me good."

"Hope you enjoy your time with your mother?"

"Thank you." He stared at her face which was rosy and bright. Reaching for his duffle bag, he told her. "My life is about to change I hope."

"If that's what you want, I hope it does too. Good luck. I did you a couple of slices of bread and jam," she smiled getting it out of her shopping bag, "that's all I had in the cupboard; here!" She passed the well-wrapped up bundle towards him and watched as he put it into his duffle bag.

"You're too good to me Jess. I'm going to miss you," and he knew he certainly would. "It seems as though we were meant to meet on that awful night, fate brought us together." When suddenly he stopped talking, as he saw a policeman heading towards them. Panic! "Whatever is this about?" He said out loud.

Jess looked up hearing a bang on her window and seeing a constable standing there beside the car. Winding it down, (these old cars.) She smiled.

"Excuse me madam, the uniformed man said. I must ask you to move along if you will? You're obstructing the flow of traffic."

She smiled at him. "I am sorry officer, I was dropping my friend off, but I'll be going now."

On a freezing cold day Jake's hands were sweating. He felt a nervous wreck as the man stared at him, before walking off down the road ... Jake hadn't been recognised.

"Well I'd better move on, or I'll have that policeman after me." Jess laughed. I must go and get those groceries first and stock up my cupboard. Sorry John what were you saying?"

"Oh, only that it was fate that brought us together, but, I feel really dreadful that you used your food on me. I'll make it up to you one day."

"Don't worry about that, it's just having the company more than anything that made me feel good." She looked in a shy way at him before adding: "and everything else that happened. In answer to your question, you're right it was fate us meeting that evening. Anyway good luck I do hope things work out for you. See you again sometime."

"You can bet on it," he smiled. Kissing her cheek now. "Bye and thanks for everything," he enthused getting out of the car and throwing his duffle bag over his shoulder. "Remember what I said, you be careful you hear."

"I will. Bye! See you John Turner" she laughed, as she headed the car in the direction of the supermarket.

"Bye Jess Sinclair he said." Waving his hand.

Chapter 9

As she also gave him a quick wave back, then she was gone. He didn't know why but Jake began thinking how lucky he was. Incidents kept happening in his favour, because Jess's television hadn't been working at home – the set had broken down a few days before, he came on the scene. He could have looked at it himself, but made an excuse he wasn't very good with televisions, another lie. Hopefully there would be nothing about him on there now, but you never know. Funny but that wasn't all, Jess's radio had a dreadful crackle, but she never bothered him, to ask if he would look at it. So neither of them had heard the news on the radio at all. He was now thinking his escape from prison must have been on there; or perhaps not? He was now thinking how he and Jess had chatted with one another around the cosy fire. Him telling her how much he'd enjoyed their time together. And she had agreed too.

So now he was making his way along the footpath as fast as he could, but it was rather difficult to walk in this weather with the ice under foot, also the slushy piles of snow which made it slippery for him. His one thought after Jess went was he had to get away from the town as quick as he could, in case that policeman suddenly came too who he was. Looking behind him he felt easier and not quite so worried seeing nobody following him. The traffic was moving slowly now due to the weather conditions. He was so pleased he'd changed his look and attire. Jake was hungry as he walked along, so reaching into his wet, sodden, duffle bag, he pulled out the jam sandwich and smiled to himself, thankfully they hadn't got wet, Jess having wrapped them in tin foil. He ate while he walked in – between the snow flurries – because he was getting hungry and so his energy levels had dropped, which wasn't good, he hadn't realised it was so far. This sandwich would make him feel a little better he thought. It was so kind of Jess to have made them. Where would this end? He hoped it wasn't much further to his mother's place, being the first time he'd ever been in this district.

Popping the last bit of the sandwich into his mouth, he reached into his pocket, pulling out a piece of paper, his mother had written her new address on, when she told him that after he'd finished his sentence and he was out, he must come and see her. Well he was out! His poor mum had to move after his conviction as people where she lived, became very hostile towards her. He remembered her telling him it was all because of his confession, which was interpreted as wrong, he had a moment of anger but he hadn't hit his wife, he had just pushed her, not for one-minute thinking she would trip and fall. So his mother had been distraught about the whole incident and couldn't wait to get away from where she lived. So she moved a distance renting a flat in an old property, miles away from the last house, which was where he was making for now. She had written to him saying she was much happier because nobody knew about her and (Jake) in this new place. Like him his mum renamed herself Amy Shaw. He now felt the atmosphere made everything seem calm, apart from the odd car and lorry on the open road, as he trudged along treading the deep snow but it was getting hard though, because of the blizzard which had started again, twice as bad as the last one. He really hadn't seen such weather even as a child. Good job he had this warm coat on that Jess had given him. That brought her to his mind, as he was now wondering if she had arrived home yet without any problems? His feelings were so strong for this amazing woman, whom he'd only known for a short time, but she wouldn't want him, if she knew he'd killed his wife and into the bargain had escaped from prison. Life was a bitch at times! He suddenly began to envy people in their warm homes.

Now he definitely needed some warmth himself. Jess had given him three pounds which she had put in his pocket. He hadn't told her, but he still had his three pounds from the prison, so now he had six pounds. He would one day pay back everything he owed Jess however he didn't know how. All of a sudden he spotted in the distance a public house, dare he venture into it? He slowed his step and looked at the address his mother had sent to him. He mustn't get this too wet because she had drawn a map. He began thinking he would never have found her house off his own back, in this weather. He carefully covered his hand over it, looking in what he hoped was the right direction, but he was certain he had a way to go yet and it was getting decidedly colder.

A few cars passed but he kept his head down and struggled on. He'd been walking for what seemed like at least an hour perhaps longer, he didn't really know because he didn't have his watch, it was being kept for him by the prison authorities. Well he wasn't bothered if he never saw it ever again. He was wondering what the reception would be like when his mother saw him, but he was looking forward to seeing her, she was the only one that had really stood by him. Now he was looking at 'The Old Oak Pub' which had come into view in front of his eyes. Dare he? Yes he'd chance it, as he felt so cold and thirsty he needed to get into the warm for a while, but he knew he had to be careful. Walking up to the porch he kicked the snow from his shoes, and opened the door into a lovely atmosphere, where a roaring fire greeted him. There were a few people in there as he walked up to the bar.

A man with a cheery round face asked: "Yes sir, what can I get you?"

"Pint of larger please." So far so good.

"Terrible weather isn't it? I'm wondering when this snow is going to stop." He pulled the pint and handed it to Jake who didn't get much change from four pound.

Jake was about to say, that's gone up a bit, but he bit his tongue.

"Haven't seen you round these parts before?" The man was saying pleasantly.

"Ah no!" He hoped he wouldn't be recognised. because in just a few days his persona had changed a little. He was now hoping there hadn't been a picture on television of him. As he carried on the conversation he told the man: "No you wouldn't have. I'm just visiting." That should satisfy him. He put the long-awaited glass to his lips and drank the cold larger, enjoying every bit of hops that went into it. It had been so long since he'd had anything this good. It was worth the money even though it was flipping cold.

"My goodness not a day for visiting is it?" The publican in front of him said. "You look as though you've come a long way?"

When a scruffy man from the corner of the bar sidled up to where he stood staring at him. He wished this nosy parker would disappear Jake pulled his wet coat collar up. Hoping to blot the man out. "Well sort of," he answered the publican."

"Are you from these parts?" the annoying individual asked him. Coughing!!

Jake dared to stare at the annoying little person. (Must keep my cool.) "Actually no, I'm on a visit, but not the best of days to come," he smiled. Before lifting his glass of larger to his lips again.

"Who would come out in weather like this, if they didn't have to?" The thin bald man was saying with the irritating cough.

"You did!"

"Ah, but I only live over the road."

Why doesn't he go? "Well I'm going to see someone whose ill. I didn't bring the car, because the weather is so bad and I thought I might get stuck in the snow." 'Why should I have to explain to this interfering individual' Jake was thinking, as he nodded to the barman and walked away from the two. Looking over to a quiet corner where a middle-aged woman was sitting near the roaring log fire.

"Do you mind if I sit here?" he asked. She shook her head at him smiling. It was great to feel that wonderful warmth from the fire after the extreme cold outside.

Then the woman put her newspaper down. "No you sit and warm yourself and take no notice of him she pointed. He's like that with everyone and wants to know all their business."

"No I won't," he smiled. After half an hour John decided to make a move, he'd been in the pub long enough. And the nosy man was talking to the publican now having forgotten John for the moment, which was good. The lady hadn't bothered him too much either, she was more interested in her newspaper and what looked like her gin and tonic beside her. But as he got up to go he heard her say. "Best of luck in getting to wherever you're going. Hope it stops snowing for you. But I have a feeling this snows in for the day."

"Yes, I think you're right. Well cheerio!" He nodded. Walking towards the door. The barman waved, as the nosy man shouted something, which Jake wasn't bothered to hear. He made his way along the main road again, looking at different properties to the left and right of him, it was sometime later when he thought he must be nearly at his mother's. Then all of a sudden he saw a long sign in front of him, but he couldn't read it properly because it was covered in snow, so when he reached it, he ran his sleeve along knocking the heavy snow off and saw it read 'Deer Lane.

Turning left he began to walk down the long path, the silence became deafening, having left the traffic behind him. It had been a totally different noise as the slush of melting snow and ice got caught up in the lorries wheels as they went past. The rough path he was on now, led to an avenue of trees swaying from side to side and it was difficult to see where he was going. He was now wondering was this going to be the right place. His mother had explained at the time, that the house was at the end of a lane, but it was a long walk through the line of trees. He was now hoping she would be home. And what would her reaction, be, to his escape? Which she must have heard by now. At that moment he stopped as two deer's disappeared into the dense wood. Looking up he felt the gust of wind and snow hit him straight in the face. When he turned a bend in the lane he was surprised to see a huge house in front of him. Was he pleased? Or what? It was such a welcoming sight, as he had begun to think that he would never reach here and would be picked up before he did. Standing now in the deep snow, in front of the huge front door he began to bang on it with his fist, but then stopped, as he noticed a bell on the side of the wall. So this was where his mother lived? It was quiet! In fact noiseless. Desolate! Fantastic! How had his mother found such an out of the way place? Surely someone else lived here. Well if anybody was behind those windows they might have seen him by now. When he realised his dark figure must have stood out in the snow. But no, all was well luck was on his side again. But suddenly he felt very cold and tired. Even that little break in the pub wasn't enough for his worn-out body, he was wacked. When he heard a sound.

"Who's there?"

He recognised his mums voice. "It's only me mum. Jake."

"It can't be," she shouted out.

"Well mum it is, it's me, open the door?" As she gently opened it, he was confronted by his mother.

"Oh my God Jake it really is you?"

"Yes mum it's me." He noticed from the bright light in the hall that her hair was very grey now, but with another quick glance he saw she was still underneath it all an attractive woman. Even with the few lines on her face, as it all of a sudden, drained of colour.

"Jake! I hardly recognised you with that beard. What are you doing on my doorstep?"

"That's a nice welcome I must say. Have you got anybody else here?"

"No I'm on my own."

"Perfect!!! Can I come in then? He asked her.

She stood to one side. "Of course you can." She watched as he banged his shoes one at a time on the wall outside. And shook his coat. She was not able to take in that her son was standing in front of her. When he should be miles away in prison. Going into a bit of a daze, she pointed to another door, "this way," she said, flummoxed by the situation.

He followed his mother through the hall into a very large kitchen. It was like being with Jess in hers, however this room was twice the size, but again lovely and warm. It was great to see his mum again, he'd always been very close to her, often spoilt by her, as he grew up as an only child. He put his arms around her and cuddled her into him, kissing her cheek. "Don't worry mum, nobody knows I'm here. Yet!"

Chapter 10

"Jake what on earth are you doing here? You look awful and you're soaked through," she kept staring at him enquiringly. "Here give me that wet coat," she said, helping him off with it, which looked as though it was stuck to his body. "I think you need a hot drink, let me make you a cup of tea. After putting the kettle on she turned to her son, "Jake what have you done?"

"Make that tea first and I will tell you everything mum."

Not listening she asked: "Why aren't you in prison? Oh my goodness I fear I'm not going to be happy, when I hear this explanation?" Turning round she began to warm the pot before putting the hot water into it then handed the tea to him. Whilst he began to explain everything, not that memorable night though. (This was like history repeating itself.)

"They never mentioned anything about a man escaping from prison on television, or on the radio did they mum?"

She now looked thoughtful: "Well I haven't heard anything because I haven't felt so good lately, having caught a nasty cold. It's this weather which has caused it. So I have been in bed for a few days. The only thing I've listened to are my CD's with my ear plugs. So you see I've not had the radio on, or watched television and I haven't been out for a paper either, so I don't know Jake. However you look so different now with that rough beard look, almost unrecognisable. Please don't tell me you escaped from prison?"

She was amazed when he nodded.

"Whatever possessed you to do such a thing? You only had another two years to go. I can't believe this is happening. What if the police come here? Mind you it will take a while for them to find out, where I live now."

"Mum sit down, stop worrying. I'm the one that's in trouble not you". Jake couldn't believe how lucky he'd been so far. "The police will come here, when they find out where you live. I'm sure they will put two and two together and realise, I would have made my way to you." Jake then told his mother all that had happened to him and his friendship with Jess. Of course leaving out how friendly they really had become. "So you see mum, since I broke out from prison ... and then being with Jess I made my way here to see you. But don't worry, I won't be staying long, but I had to see you, as it's been such a long time since your visit to me at the prison four years ago now."

"His mother looked thoughtful for a moment. Yes I'm so sorry about that I hated going in there with those horrible prisoners about. So Jake what about this woman? Surely she'll give you away?"

"No mum she won't. She doesn't know who I am."

"Didn't she hear the news at all, well that's if it was on the radio or television about you?"

"As it happened she didn't! Because we've not had any radio or television on, because, would you believe, neither of them are working at her house? She lives near the moors and there was no chance of even getting a newspaper. So you see as far as I know not much, or if anything has been said about my escape. And she's never mentioned about a prison break."

"Jake you should never have done this, you caused a terrible accident and you have to do your time, that is how life is. Your punishment was six years in prison, whether you like it or not. You must go back you know, they will get you in the end." She began to feel very tired now.

"I hope not, well so far so good." Then in the next breath he asked. "Does anyone else live around here?"

"It's strange you should ask that, because in a few weeks' time the builders are coming in, to renovate the house and make them into separate flats. They won't be for rent, I have to buy, but that's okay. There used to be another person here but she moved out a few days ago. She was a lovely pleasant lady, but she has gone into a home now. Then there's Mr and Mrs Jackman in the bungalow which you might have seen when you made your way down the lane, they're very nice people. They own this property and decided to sell it to these builders who will renovate it. Anyway I haven't got to know many people in the district, as I mainly keep myself to myself," she said. "So it will be nice having someone around in here eventually. Being virtually on your own isn't so good and I do miss Mrs Franklin, she was so friendly and we had lots of chats together."

"I didn't really notice the bungalow as I made my way here, what with this blizzard hitting me in the face, I had my head down and coat collar up as I made my way to this property. You know it's all my fault, losing your friends and having to move here because of me. Still I must say this is a wonderful hideout for me for a while. It's just like where Jess lives that was lonely too. Terrific, now I've hit on another quiet place, can you put me up for perhaps two days mum?" He smiled

"Well you should give yourself up, but yes, of course you can stay as long as the police don't come, she told him with a serious face, this is not the thing to do, it will not work out, you take my word for it. Nevertheless you're my son and I will stand by you. You see I do think the judge was harsh giving you six years when it was an accident.

"Thanks mum and sorry, but I won't give myself up."

She sat there shaking her head.

Jake was beginning to think his mum had lost a small spark in her character, she seemed more serious. It was such a shame because she had always been a hands-on mum when he was young, and the two always laughed a lot. Now she looked tired, but perhaps it was the ending of the cold and she was trying to get back to her old self. What had he done to her, over these last few years with his situation?

"You've lost a lot of weight since I last saw you. Are you eating properly?"

"Oh I'm okay, but sitting here day after day worrying about you in prison hasn't helped. Then of course I've had this nasty cold, which went to my chest and it's taking me a while to get back to normal. Anyway you don't look that good yourself Jake."

"Look I've just broken out of prison and have walked miles to see you, in this unbelievable weather. So this is why I'm not my bright self and looking a bit bedraggled I know. But I have to tell you this, I have taken another name now. It's John Turner." He watched as the colour drained from her face.

"So I've got a new son have I? Well I prefer Jake! For goodness sake what will they do to you if you're caught?" She asked feeling sick with worry, for him.

"I don't know and I don't want to know, because I don't intend to be caught mum. You are funny because I'm still your son Jake," he told her. "One day I hope all this will be behind us and we'll be back to normal."

Jake … John you pushed Kate and you have to serve your time, that's the law." She was surprised as to how much prison had changed her son. He had a hard streak in him now, she could see and hear that in his voice. It was to be expected, being with such a mixture of violent people.

"Yes but I didn't mean to hurt her. Surely you can imagine my distress of finding out my wife was having this affair with my best friend. Who we said could stay with us after his break up from his wife."

"I suppose I do and I know you would not have hurt her intentionally."

"No I wouldn't, although I can say this now, we had our ups and downs in our marriage, but everyone does and it wasn't a real love affair between us, but we were happy."

"I had noticed that at times, when I stayed with you both and you had a few spats, but, I thought everyone has difficult times in marriage. Then a while later, you both seemed fine," pausing, she then said. "Look I just want to put a few more vegetables in this pot, for the two of us, but personally I'm not very hungry now, seeing you standing on the doorstep, that was a shock to my system."

There was plenty of stewing steak in the saucepan with a few carrots, onions, sweet potato and parsnips, but she added more, it would be perfect for the two, it looked a lovely tasty stew to have on a very cold day. She had a feeling John (that was difficult) would be hungry. Perhaps when it was cooked, she too would enjoy a plateful. That was how she saved money by buying meat and vegetables, making stews and freezing them for whenever.

Later as they sat at the table about to eat, he leaned across the table and asked. "Do you really like living here mum? Only it's such an out of the way place for you."

65

He looked around now, the kitchen did remind him of Jess's place. His mother's electric fire made the room very comfortable and warm. In fact the room was boiling hot now after having the gas cooker on with the dinner bubbling away. When his mother walked across the room and turned the fire off, probably noticing he was hot too now.

"You know Jake when you were arrested, I was pointed out as a murderer's mother. Which was so hurtful, because all my so-called friends went against me. It wasn't easy living where I did. Until one day I happened to see this advertisement in our local newspaper it said. 'Flat for rent.' So I applied and blow me I got it, yes I like living here. nobody bothers me, well not much. All I have for company at times are the deer," she said, "they're lovely and come right up close to the house. As I think I told you when I came to the prison to see you a couple of times, I had only just moved then. Anyway I did say it was off the beaten track, however the summer months are lovely here it's so peaceful. You know I'm very careful with my money John, and manage very well always pay my bills on time, so that's the main thing. But I'm very frugal with what I spend my money on. You know I also have a new name as I told you in my letters didn't I? Amy Shaw seems to suit me."

She saw him smile. So I have a whole new identity. You know your father would have been devastated if he'd known what had happened to you and where you have ended up and my situation."

"Yes I know Amy" … he smiled squeezing her hand, "he would." Then in the next breath he said: "Now we both have new identities, but not through choice mum. Yes I feel as though I've done my time and paid my penance, nevertheless I'm really sorry for everything that has happened," he explained bowing his head.

His mother stared at him also feeling sorry for her son and the position he was in. "But you shouldn't have pushed her in the first place, your father and I never brought you up to be violent." Staring at him now she stopped talking, as he went very quiet, stunned by her outspoken words. All of a sudden the atmosphere improved as she began to dish the meal up, placing his dinner on the table, both forgetting the moment for a while as they chatted between mouthfuls, she having a small plateful in the end.

As he went to move his mum told him: "It's okay I don't need any help, it won't take me long to wash these few plates up."

He was looking very tired she noticed.

It was at that moment he decided to tell her everything as he sat there. "It was one of those evenings when I popped into the pub for a pint after work. hearing two men discussing my wife and it wasn't good, what I heard. I just exploded when I got home. You didn't know all this mum, so now I have explained it to you I hope you can understand how I felt by all the secret things that had been happening under my nose and behind my back too, between Kate and that slime ball Matt.

She sighed: "Thank you for telling me John, however this is such a nightmare. You'll be safe here though for a while."

She was wiping the sink down. "Still with all of it, it's so nice to see you, but I know I shouldn't say that, with what's happening?"

There was no feedback from him. When she turned round she saw that he was fast asleep in her not so comfortable chair with the wooden arms He evidently had flaked out in the chair after that confession. She could see how tired he had been especially after all that walking. Amy stared down at her bedraggled son, he should have taken his wet tee shirt off though, mind you it was probably dry by now from the warmth of his body she thought, they'd both been talking for so long. She was now on her way upstairs to get him a blanket. The motherly instinct came out a few minutes later as she covered him over, just like she had done when he was a boy, all those years ago. He never stirred in the chair, his shoes were beside him. No matter what he'd done, he was her son and she naturally would give him a mother's support, good or bad.

Now as she climbed the stairs again a pain distorted her face, as she looked down at her poorly hands, her rheumatism was getting so much worse, because her fingers were so painful now. She knew the cold weather wasn't helping her and being in this old flat, and having no central heating. Amy was excited about the new place. The builders were due to come in April, then she would be lovely and warm indoors. In the meantime she had to put up with the cold. Holding the banisters tight she climbed the rickety stairs. She was now so looking forward to having a heating system. It would be a wonderful day, no more feeling cold, warmth would be in every room. That would be so good for her aching bones. Still not to think about that now, that was least of her worries when she had so many other things on her mind.

Chapter 11

When Jake woke up, he looked at the clock on the wall, it was six o'clock in the morning, he began rolling his head in rotating circles, until his stiff neck felt easier. Thinking back now, he began to remember that he'd been so tired last night he'd dropped off to sleep in the chair. It wasn't a good atmosphere in the kitchen at the moment, in fact it was very cold, so he pulled the blanket round him and began to smile as he thought, his mother must have covered him up, she had always been such a good mum and very caring. However he couldn't laze here all morning, there were things to be done. Getting to his feet he pulled back the curtain, and stared outside at the deep snow, which had once again lain. This was insane, never in his wildest dreams could he have visualised weather that was so uncontrollable. It was as though somebody up there, was looking after him and giving him the break he needed, because he wasn't a murderer, but a man that had been devastated by an awful accident. Thinking deeply how his world had crumbled. Well he could hear no movement from his mother's room above, which he'd noticed when he went to use the bathroom. So, she must still be asleep. 'breakfast in bed would be a treat for her,' it would be something she never gets, living on her own. He would surprise her. Finding a tray he put two plates and an egg cup on one, before, putting the electric kettle on for a cup of tea. Then he picked the biggest egg he could find in the fridge and placed it carefully in boiling water. Whilst he made some toast; all was ready now, marmalade as well. Making his way up the stairs to his mother's room, he pushed her door open. "Morning mum!"

She was awake. "Oh morning John." She would never get used to that name. She frowned, when she saw the tray. "What have you been up too?" she asked him, pulling herself up and pumping the pillows behind her as she did it.

"I've made you some breakfast."

"Yes I can see that. This is a treat for me."

He laid the tray on her lap and then went to pull the curtains back wide. The morning sun filtered through the huge windows, which drew him onto the scene outside. The crisp white snow dominating everywhere it had now stopped snowing, which made everything around look so lovely and fresh. As he stared into space he was thinking life was so good on the outside. He would never have seen this beautiful scene in prison. There was no movement not a soul around. Turning back to his mother, he watched as she tucked into the lovely egg and he smiled. He really must try not to worry her too much.

"John that was a lovely thing you did, your father used to do the same many years ago. It has been such a long time since I have had breakfast in bed. Thank you son your spoiling me. This is so good after a restless night worrying about you. She put down her teaspoon and turned to him. Now you really should start thinking of yourself and what you're going to do next," she told him.

"Eat up mum, we'll talk about that later. Now would it be okay if I have a bath?"

She nodded.

"Wish I had some clean underwear though?"

"Well your old case is in the other bedroom under the bed, there might just be some in there." Then in the next breath. "This is a lovely egg."

"Best in the fridge," he laughed. "Now enjoy it because you deserve it. I forgot I asked you to take care of my case when I went into prison. Also thank you for covering me up, when I was asleep in your chair last night."

"You're welcome, hope you're feeling better after a good night's sleep," she was saying, dipping her toast into her boiled egg.

"As a matter of fact, I do, feel fine now."

"Good! But you know I still can't get over the shock of seeing you on the doorstep."

"Yes I suppose that was a bit of a shock?" He watched as she nodded, enjoying her breakfast.

It was a while later, after having a lovely bath and putting on clean underclothes which were in the case, he was now making his way downstairs, wearing the black T-shirt Jess had given him from her husband's case in the loft, he felt a lot better. This was such a funny situation everything being repeated. Now as he made himself a couple of pieces of toast, his mother walked through the door with the tray in her hands. He reached out and took it from her, looking at her dressing gown, which had definitely seen better days. If he had the money he would have bought her one. He would one day perhaps? She looked pale and thin, what had he done to her?

"That was lovely, thank you dear. Oh my it's cold in here," she told him. Plugging the electric fire in.

"Sorry mum I didn't like to put it on as I don't want you getting a huge bill."

"Well we can't sit in the cold Jake and I've used all my logs up for a fire. Anyway enough about that, I keep trying to put your whole situation to the back of my mind, but still I can't help worrying about you. I do wish that you'd finished your time in prison and not done this silly thing." She sat at the table, "especially when you didn't have long to go. I would never have thought that you would break out of prison."

Jake had a smile on his face as he heard his mum say, breakout, it seemed so unreal.

"I had to get out as I told you last night. You have no idea what it's like in there? I despised the inmates and especially the perverted ones, always making it hard for me to live from day to day. They pestered me the whole time, wanting me to do dreadful things. Which I wouldn't do."

He now began thinking of Luke whom he detested and who was a violent individual. He hated him, but at the time had to stick with him, because he had been his meal ticket to get out. Also he had got the cutters, which they couldn't have made the break without. But John hated him to such a degree, he never wanted to see him ever again, now that he was out. But he was wondering if Luke had told them all at the prison now about their planned escape. Ah well Jake had been the lucky one getting away and the other man was back in prison, thank goodness.

He looked back at his mother: "So you see it's unbelievable what goes on behind prison doors, you've no idea mum, I had to get away. Can you understand?"

She nodded. What was happening to her? She'd just got her life back and was almost happy, knowing that possibly two years or even less with good behaviour and Jake would have left prison. Now if he was caught he would have to serve a longer sentence, this situation was disastrous but she didn't want to say too much.

John knew what his mother was thinking, she had always been a good woman and had protected him through his school years. That was until he went to college. Something that he'd always wanted to do was forestry, so she and his dad had given him backing for this move as much as they possibly could. But in the end he'd failed his exams and never wanted to take them again. So he had decided to become something entirely different. having liked tinkering with cars he decided he would be a garage mechanic instead. Never fulfilling his real dream.

Being married to Katie was good and they were happy, so he thought, but had never been madly in love with her, like he is with Jess. Still it worked and his job had made him contented. He just needed another car because his was so old. So that's why he did lots of overtime at Murphy's Garage. Then on a Friday evenings he would hand his pay packet over to his wife, after first taking a little for himself to see him through the week. Whereby she always put it into their joint bank account as he thought, but he found out later that she had been delving into the money they had and it was all gone. He couldn't believe it. Then he heard from her on that dreadful night when it all came out, that she and Matt were going away together, that weekend. It was devastating for him. The house had been a tied one it came with the job. That was the other perk which had pleased them both at first when they married. The two had been living happily there for a number of years, then Matt came along and everything fell apart.

Since the accident he'd heard the chap had moved to another district after the court case was over, being terribly upset at losing Kate. As he had loved her at the time. Looking up he saw his mother who had been sitting quietly, whilst he went into his own world, she looked so sad.

"You know I wish none of this had happened and we could get our lives back to how they were?" She was saying as they both looked at one another.

"So do I Mum. You know I didn't kill Kate on purpose, as I've told you. Still it was called involuntary manslaughter as you may remember?"

"Yes," She was wondering what her husband would have said? Having died of a heart attack before the verdict came up; literally days before. Jake had been so terribly upset about this at the time, thinking it might have been his fault that caused him to have this heart attack, with all the stress, he never forgave himself for that. However his father had had a bad heart for many years.

"What will you do now? She said quietly, "there will be no life for you John. It can only go from bad to worse, when the powers that be catch up with you."

"I just wanted to see you Mum and explain to you why I did what I did. Anyway it's only a matter of time before the police or prison authorities find out where you live and I don't want you involved. I'll leave here very soon, but I just need some time to sort out what I am going to do next, okay?"

"Please give yourself up John. I know you've made a mistake escaping, but perhaps they will be lenient with you."

"Sorry but I can't, I won't go back to that place. I intend to try and start a new life somehow."

"You only had two more years to do, then you would have come out putting everything behind you. As it is now you will always be looking over your shoulder, surely you don't want that? You accidently caused Kate's death and so you have to pay, John, to free your mind of this terrible deed. I still can't believe you're a murderer. Not my son, not my flesh and blood!!" Thinking now she had become quite fond of John's wife, over the years, never believing she could do what she did. It had been a disastrous thing to happen and that her son had caused it.

He watched his mother, as she wrung her hands. "Please Mum don't get upset. I made a decision to escape from the prison because if I hadn't I would have topped myself. Many times I've wanted to end my life."

"Oh no!" His mother cried out. "Please don't do anything silly, promise me?"

"I promise; not now I'm out," he said kneeling in front of his mother. As he kissed the top of her head. "Come on now I'll make you another cup of tea. It's good for the nerves," he smiled. "Look I will be safe here for a couple of days. In a way it's good that you moved," he smiled. "However if this snow eases up the powers that be will probably be down on us like a ton of bricks. So let's hope it starts up again."

"One more thing John, are you sorry that you accidentally killed Kate?"

"More than I can say, but it's too late now isn't it? My life at the time crumbled around me. Now I'm going to build it up again whatever way I can. He placed the mug in front of her. So drink that tea mum and then go and get dressed and I'll wash up, then we'll sort out what to do next."

Ten minutes later she stood up. Now I must go and get ready won't be long, glad you slept alright last night in that chair?"

"Yes it was fine, it's quite comfortable, you know?" He didn't tell her about his aching neck, which was going off a bit now, thank goodness.

"That's good, but I'll make a bed up for you in the small bedroom for tonight." She was saying.

"Thanks Mum," John shouted out to her as she walked up the stairs now, "it won't be for long as I told you."

He switched the radio on listening to *'Fire It Up'* by Joe Cocker as he cleared the dishes away. This was great, he'd missed hearing music from a good player whilst in prison. His little radio in his cell, crackled the whole time. Now he was trying to put the last few days out of his mind, but, it was so hard to brush Jess aside as he now wondered what she was doing? Was she as lonely as him? Again what would she do if she knew what he'd done and that he'd escaped from prison? When a sudden feeling of doom and gloom come over him. What was he going to do? When all of a sudden the kitchen door opened and in came his mother, looking a lot brighter and smarter. In a grey jumper and black skirt, she certainly looked a lot better than she had last night. He realised that it had been a shock for her, seeing him standing there on the doorstep.

"Your bed is made up John, under different circumstances it would be lovely that you've come to stay with me."

"Great, well as much as I wanted to come and see you, if it hadn't been for the snow, I probably wouldn't be here. Thankfully due to the weather, I'm sure it's been difficult to track me down."

"Did that woman know where you came from?"

"No! I made up a story as to why I was out in this weather, and I think she believed me." He told his mother. Telling her the story about his sister-in-law and the clothes and money situation.

"Jake how could you? That poor girl."

"I know! I know! I don't like myself at times. Anyway she didn't query it too much and she let me stay the night, in fact, I stayed two nights. His face never changed. She has a lovely cottage on the moors as I told you. It's very lonely but for me, the perfect hideaway, nobody would have come up the narrow lane in this diabolical weather. I was lucky."

"You were," she was reading the vibes coming across the room from her son. "Was she nice Jake?"

"Very," came his reply.

"Do you hope to see her again?"

"Yes I do Mum, although it's going to be awkward because there are so many big problems ahead. But I don't suppose she would want me if she finds out what I've done, do you?"

"No, I don't son because she sounds a lovely trusting person. Perhaps if you gave yourself up things could work out for you. Even though you will have to do a longer sentence now."

"Well I'm not going back there not if I can help it, to that dreadful place," as he then took a deep breath. "There is one very big problem though." He watched as his mother sat up firmer in her chair, before carrying on with what he was saying. "Her little daughter was murdered on the moors, she was only four years old. So you see she would be horrified if she knew about me and what I'd done."

"Oh my God that's terrible. Tell me?"

So he did.

"But in your case you didn't really kill your wife, it was an accident, as you've always said."

He saw his mother was getting upset now so he would end this.

She was now trying to forget the last bit of the conversation for the moment. "It's amazing how many of your so-called friends stick by you in times of trouble. I was called names for having a son ... as ... a ... murderer. A lot of them knew you and the kind of man you were, but no they wouldn't change their minds, it was your fault, sorry John!"

"I'm the one whose sorry Mum, for putting you in this position. What can I say?" He got up from his chair and went across to his mother, putting his arms around her, as she did him.

"Don't you worry son I'm tough I can cope alright."

"Well I'm not a very good son am I?"

"Don't say that, it was the happiest day of our lives when you were born and you were a good man once you can be again J-o-h-n."

"I sincerely hope so Mum, my life is depending on it."

Changing the subject, she asked. "What do you think of my big garden? Mr and Mrs Jackman let the two flats out in the house. But the other lady of course has gone now, so there's only me, I pay my rent and that's it. I'm so lucky to have found this place its perfect," and in the next breath, she said. "I love watching the deer which appear here from time to time. You must have seen them as you made your way down to this property? They're always about you know. It's such a peaceful place to live, but lonely – however, I have joined a club, which I go to once a week and enjoy. I do know two or three people in the area. Still I'm pleased I live here as it's right out of the way you see this lane leads to nowhere."

John had taken that in the night before, how big the house was, as he stared out of the window. "It's like looking at a postcard out there," he said. "Yes I did see the deer as I made my way here, they looked fantastic as they took flight through the woods. Anyway I'm happy that you have some sort of outlet." He looked at her but she seemed deep in thought.

"Yes ... but that's not all," she replied, going suddenly silent.

"What's the matter Mum you seem troubled?"

"John I forgot to mention that ... I have met a very nice gentleman at the club."

"Well what's wrong with that? he asked her. "You don't have to tell me about what you do in your private life that's your own business," he told her. You only get one stab at life so you go for it. Now you look worried what's the problem?"

"The problem is he's just retired from ..."

"Yes? John asked'

"From ..." she looked down at her hands, which had become very hot now. 'Slate Moors Prison' You see he was a prison guard there. Oh John I'm so sorry."

"What!!!" ... Shouted her son. "What's his name?"

"You don't think you'll know him do you?"

"The prison is very big so I might not, we have many officers or guards as there called sometimes. But I have this awful feeling and I hope it's not who I think it might be. Tell me quick Mum?"

Chapter 12

"It's Trent, George Trent," she answered him.

"I don't believe this, Trent? ..."

She looked at her son: "Do you know him?" Being totally frightened of the reply and that John had gone very quiet. He's such a lovely man and we get on so well. I really like him. I shouldn't have got too friendly with him, because of your situation. But now I have the name of Amy Shaw he won't find out that you're my son. But he told me he had worked for the prison authorities for twenty-five years and is retiring this Saturday. Did you know that John?" She asked him.

"Yes I do know him, but I'd forgotten about his retirement what with everything going on. In fact we used to get on really well, I can see why you like him. You're not going to believe this, but he was sort of guarding me and others when I escaped. Also it's through him I got away, because we were joking together and so he forgot to search me properly. Which nearly always happened when we left the prison for some reason. The thing is I had the cutters strapped to my leg, which of course he didn't find. John strode up and down the kitchen now agitated, as his hand went through his hair. This is something I hadn't expected though," he told his worried Mum.

"What do you mean?"

"This man trusted me and I let him down, but it's backfired now you being friendly with him."

"How unbelievable is all of this?" She was saying.

"You're right there Mum, we used to have a laugh at times. But he must have been so angered by my escape from prison, especially when he was in charge of all of the prisoners and he trusted me. And what did I do? Let him down. This is really weird that he's become your friend now."

"Oh goodness I hate that word prisoners!"

"Well that's what we were Mum. Prisoners."

"You know I would never have told him anything about you? But how it all happened was, we met at the club and our friendship has grown. He told me he lost his wife ten years ago.

Anyway he always liked this area and thought he would move here when he retired, So he has moved to a little one bedroom flat in the district, and this is his last few days at the prison, he didn't seem to mind coming backwards and forwards to the club, which is some distance away from where he used to live; actually thirty miles. Well you see I was thinking I'd better not get too friendly with him, after finding out what his job was, but I thought perhaps you wouldn't know him anyway because, it's a big prison. I do like talking to him, because he does make me laugh at times. He seems quite interested in me. I don't know why?"

"I do Mum, because you're a lovely person, that's why." She looked very pale now, he noticed. He must not give her all these worries. It was his problem, he was the guilty one. She liked her new found friend and she needed someone, but why George Trent of all people? "Well as long as you're happy? However you know what will happen if he finds out about me don't you?"

She nodded.

He then noticed her face getting very anxious again.

She was frightened to tell him, as she slumped down onto the chair.

"Whatever's the matter Mum? You look terrible."

"I've just thought … he's going to pay me a visit." Amy was twisting her hands together as she glanced at John.

"When?" He asked.

"Today!!

"Great, well I will have to hide," he smiled, looking out of the window. "I shouldn't think he will come in this weather would you?"

"Well yes I would, because apparently he doesn't live too far away now, so it won't take him long walking, or if the weather permits by car. He told me two days ago on the phone that he's so pleased he moved here, because he could see me more often," she told her son, smiling.

"Did he now? Do you know, I remember that he mentioned that he intended to move when he retired, but not where. Well anyway what time did he say he was coming?"

"11 0'clock, his mother answered, beginning to get flustered again. If he finds you here there's no knowing what he might do."

"Let's face that when it comes, shall we?" He said grabbing the tea towel and thinking back to Jess. "History repeating itself. I'm getting used to this situation," he smiled, thinking back to Jess's friend.

"They chatted away leaving everything clean and tidy. Right I'll take that blanket upstairs, that you had last night," she told him, moving towards the item.

"No you won't, I will."

"Thank you love. Do you know it's so good to have you here, but I wish it was under different circumstances."

"So do I," he said stroking his chin, so we've got half an hour before 11 o'clock. I'll just take this up to the bedroom then." He told her picking the blanket up.

"Where will you hide?" she asked, him.

"Don't you worry, I'll wait upstairs in one of the bedrooms, till he goes."

"I'm really sorry about all of this."

"It's not your fault. I'm the one that's brought disgrace into the family. You didn't know that I would break free from prison. Now we haven't much time, George Trent is always on time, that I do know. Listen? What's that?" He said, with one finger in the air.

She looked into the hall at the front door and saw the shadow through the bevelled glass. "Oh no, it's George! He's come early."

"Don't worry Mum. Leave it a minute, before you answer the door." He told her.

"Alright!" She suddenly felt sick, this was dreadful as she saw John hurry as quick as he could up the stairs.

Throwing the blanket onto the bed in his mother's room. Hearing her opening the large front door downstairs, and his mother say "Hello George."

Chapter 13

"Hello Amy. He looked up towards the sky, "my goodness it's just started again, is this ever going to go away?" he said, brushing his coat with his hand. "That's why I came early to try and beat it, which I've done just, hope you don't mind Amy?"

"No of course not, come in George. Let's go into the kitchen where it's lovely and warm, shall we? You'll soon dry off in there. She watched as he wiped his boots on the door mat. Why have you come out on a day like this?" She asked him.

"I promised to come and see you on my day off and I always keep my promises."

She smiled a little nervously. Entering he kitchen she said: "Here give me your coat?" And helped him off with it, hanging it on the back of the chair. Feeling glad at that moment that she'd hidden Johns coat and haversack, having been dried out thoroughly.

"There, that will be a little dryer by the time you go home. This electric fire gives out a lot of warmth to the kitchen. But as you know I don't have it on all the time, because of the expense." Stumped at that moment for words she said to him. "I didn't think you'd turn up in this weather." Why was she rabbiting on?

"You know me?" He looked round the kitchen. "My goodness it's lovely and warm in here."

"But that sky out there still looks full of it," she remarked, peering through the window. "Here sit down by the fire and warm yourself, George," she told him. "Would you like a cup of coffee?"

"I'd love one Amy?"

It did seem funny him calling her by her new name.

"So how have you been then?" He asked her.

"Not so bad, the arthritis gets me down at times, but still I'm not the only one to suffer from that complaint. Anyway how are you?"

"Me! oh I'm fine, apart from my eyes. I'll be glad when I get this cataract done. You know I wasn't looking forward to leaving the prison, because I'd been there twenty-five years as a warder. But I'm sure I will enjoy the next stage of my life, doing what I want to do. Once I get used to it, only a few more days."

He watched her making the coffee. She was a lovely lady and he felt so lucky to have met her, particularly at this stressful time as she came across the kitchen with his drink, being careful not to spill it, when she heard him say.

"Only thing is I'm not too happy at the moment, you see something happened which I didn't tell you about. One of the prisoners escaped, his name is Jake Farrendon." ... The mug Amy was carrying crashed to the floor and she felt her face drain of blood.

"Don't be frightened."

"I'm ... not! The mug just slipped out of my hand it's the arthritis."

"Oh that's rotten and it can be very painful. Here let me clear that up for you?"

"No don't worry I'll do it, thank you George."
Flustered she cleared the broken bits up and wiped the floor, before bringing him another cup of coffee.

"Come and sit down Amy?" He smiled.

What was he going to say? Being aware he was staring at her now. Amy felt at that moment as though she was going to burst into a ball of fire, with this situation. So bending down she turned the fire off saying. "My it's so hot in here, isn't it?" Anything to take his mind off the subject of her son.

"Yes you're right, I'm also lovely and warm now. Anyway what was I saying? Ah yes ... well going back to this prisoner I was telling you about." He bowed his head. "I think it was my fault! You see I didn't search him like I do the other prisoners, I just liked the bloke, he'd had a raw deal, it's a long story. There were times when we used to joke with one another a lot, before going out on work duty. For some unknown reason I always trusted Jake. Knowing the full story and that his wife's accident was just that. So this was a big surprise to me when he escaped from prison, whilst working outside on a dreadful snowy day like today. Basically it's my fault as the governor told me in no uncertain terms. So I'll be glad when he's caught and I can get on with my life again. Are you alright Amy?"

"Of course, why?" She wished she'd said that a bit nicer to him.

"It's just that you look so hot, you haven't got a temperature have you? Perhaps your cold is still with you?"

"Oh no I'm fine, just got a bit overheated that's all. I was just thinking that this Jake is somebody's son and what a worry it must be, for his family. Still they commit a crime so they have to take the consequences, however bad it is, don't they?" She told him nervously, knowing she had to say the right thing.

"Yes I know. Do you think you'll be going to the club on Saturday that's if you're okay?" Because we can celebrate my retirement day.

"Oh yes I'm sure I'll be fine, can't miss your special day," she smiled.

"You know I'll escort you and bring you back home."
She smiled. "Thank you George." When suddenly there was such an almighty bang that she nearly dropped her own mug.

Jumping up from his seat, George looked up at the ceiling, before looking at her. "Whatever was that?" he asked her.

"I think I know, sorry I jumped, I always do when there's a bang, it just frightened me, she told him. The cat must have knocked something off my dressing table, which he's always doing, he's a little devil."

But he had noticed her shaking. "You know I shouldn't have told you about that prisoner escaping, I think it's unsettled you? I'll just go upstairs and check it out, if you don't mind. I don't want you worrying."

"NO DON'T DO THAT!! It's nothing," she replied.

"Look, don't you worry, nobody will hurt you, not while I'm here." With that, he got up and walked out the kitchen, making his way up the stairs.

She hurriedly following close behind. Amy's legs were feeling like lumps of lead now. As she also began to think where the devil was John?

Him realizing he'd caused a commotion, by knocking the vase off the dressing table. So he had to think quickly. He knew

George Trent would come up and check it out because, that's the sort of person he was. When he heard his mother talking to the man, as they both climbed the stairs.

As George suddenly pushed the bedroom door open. The blanket was lying on the bed where Jake had put it. The vase which had been on a dressing - table was on the floor now, broken into a few pieces.

John watched through the crack, seeing his mother standing there in the doorway, shaking.

Where was her son? She wondered, not worrying about the vase, but what George was about to say?

"Funny I don't see the cat anywhere?"

"He shot out from under the bed, when you were looking at the broken vase on the floor," she told him. This was a nightmare situation. "He will have disappeared into the house somewhere. He's just a stray that comes round and I feed him, which I suppose I shouldn't, because he keeps paying me a visit", she half smiled. "He must have gone through the cat flap." Thank goodness there was one in the kitchen, which the last people living there must have had put in for their cat. She had never sealed it up.

"Not to worry it wasn't an expensive vase anyway." She noticed George had already picked most of the bits up off the wooden floor. "This was a day for breakages Let me help you," she said, wanting to get back downstairs.

"No it's okay, there are only a few more pieces over here, he pointed picking them up. So what I will do is to take your vase home and mend it for you. Then It will be as good as new. So if I were you I'd shut these doors when he's around. What's this cats name?"

Oh no! She thought quickly. "Well I don't really know it's not on his collar, but I call him a little Tinker!"

"That's a good name, for him."

"I thought so!" Little did he know she didn't have a cat!

"That's very kind of you to try and mend my vase George. Now let's go downstairs shall we?" After Jake had knocked the vase over, he must have gone into the other bedroom across the hall, she thought.

"Not before I look in the other rooms, you never know."

84

She suddenly felt so sick at that moment, and told him in not so many words.

"You don't have to do that, after all it was only the cat."

"So you say, but I want to make perfectly sure that you're safe. He was carrying the broken china, but then gave the object to her. Just hold that for a second please Amy? but be careful you don't cut yourself," squeezing past her before opening the other bedroom door.

Amy knew her face must look like a beetroot. The room was empty! But where was John?

George walked out onto the landing, where she was standing. As he then went to check the bathroom next door.

She stood hovering, waiting for him to say. 'What the blazes are you doing here?' But it didn't happen.

"Right now, everything's fine the portly man with the smiley face said, taking the broken pieces from her. My goodness Amy I've never seen you with such a high colour before I think you've still got that bug in you."

"I hope not." That was close, but where was her son?

Now in the kitchen George began to finish his coffee as he chatted to Amy and it seemed like an eternity before he told her. "Well I must go now, got to pick a loaf up at the local shop. Can I get you anything there? Don't want you going out in this awful weather if you don't have too, do we?"

"No I'm okay George for bread, and got plenty of food in the freezer." Even if she didn't have, she didn't want him to know that.

He was staring out of the window now, shaking his head before he turned to her. "I say could you give me a carrier for this vase Amy?"

"Yes of course, thank you for your help today. He put the pieces in a plastic bag from the cupboard. It's very good of you George to take this home to mend."

"It's not too bad hopefully I'll have it back to you as good as new, in no time. Shame I couldn't mend your mug. You could say you've had a smashing time today," "And stop feeding that cat, or else you'll never get rid of him and you won't have any items left in the house," he laughed loudly.

"You're right there," she smiled, feeling awful that she had lied to him but she had no choice.

George began to put his overcoat on. "So you look after yourself because this Jake Farrendon whose on the loose could be in the area. But I have to say he never appeared dangerous to me. Still you never know if he was put in a corner he might retaliate, but I found him quite a nice bloke, still I have to say I'm disappointed in him. I suppose him spending time in prison, probably took its toll. You see he certainly wasn't like the other inmates. That's why he escaped I suppose. Silly fellow! We think he was escaping with one of our most dangerous prisoners we have, but don't know why yet? But thankfully this man was caught we think he organised the break. So they have to watch this person more, because the prison authorities believe he will try to escape again. How Jake ever palled up with this man is beyond me. Both were so different."

Please hurry up and go she thought, she didn't want to hear all this about her son and the other prisoner.

"Bye George be careful, thanks for coming."

"Well thank you for the coffee, probably see you on Saturday then." He pulled his coat around him placing the warm trilby hat on his head and picked up the carrier bag, with the broken vase inside. Hope you will feel better by then. Give me a ring and I will come and pick you up and also see you home after the club as I said."

"Thank you you're too kind." She pulled open the door, "I bet you wished you'd brought the car now, being so cold outside?"

"Well I thought I might get stuck, which could have happened. But if the weather is still bad on Saturday I will pick you up in the car. Mind you if the snow is deep I won't, as we'd better not go. I don't want you catching another chill and having to walk in this. Just ring me, or I will you; okay?" In the next breath he said. "It's so quiet here."

"It is and thank you George. You're ever the gentlemen."

"He laughed, try to be, thank you Amy." Bye!

In the next breath she shouted: "It won't be quiet when they start re-building," "Bye!" Seeing him raise his arm to her. Now to find her John.

Going quickly up the stairs, she shouted out. "Where the devil are you John?" When she heard a noise come from her bedroom.

"Here!"

"Where?"

Chapter 14

"In the wardrobe!"

"What?"

She walked into the room and opened the wardrobe door wide and there was her son crouched on the floor amongst her shoe's. "What an earth are you doing in there?" She asked him laughing now, but feeling very relieved.

"It was the only place I could find."

"Well it's a good job George didn't look in there, he would have had a heart attack if you had jumped out on him. I suppose you found out once you were in, that it was difficult to get out. There's only one catch on the outside with these old wardrobes, good job the back is coming apart, so you were able to get some air."

"You're right there, but I was fine, just a little cramped. Help me get out please?"

She gave him her hand, as he said. "Sorry I broke your lovely vase, you see I was looking through the window at the weather, when my elbow knocked it on the dressing -table and bang it slipped onto your wooden floor."

"Not to worry it wasn't the real thing anyway. Still it was a shame my small rug wasn't in that spot" she said, "it then wouldn't have broken. Do you know I thought George would never go, especially when he heard the bang, I was blaming the cat; but I haven't got one! You know that man is so kind and spoke so well of you. Even though you did what you did."

"Well I gained his trust and now I've let him down." He suddenly felt so miserable. Pulling himself together he said to his mother, that cat thing was quick thinking. Putting his arm around her shoulders. Sorry for giving you all this worry."

She stared into his face: "Whatever you've done and of course I'm certainly not happy that you escaped from prison, but you're still my son and I'm here for you."

"Look I will move on as soon as the thaw sets in," He said to her, once they had walked back down the stairs into the kitchen.

"She clasped her hands together. "Where will you go?"

"I don't know yet and perhaps it's best you don't either, because if you're ever asked by the police, where would I have gone? You can honestly say you've no idea, that puts you in the clear, doesn't it?"

His mother nodded. "I suppose!" She stared at him. "What are you going to do with that beard?" She pointed.

"Keep it, it's a good disguise don't you think? I had stubble on my face before I left the prison, but now my salt and pepper beard has grown so quickly, even after four days. As you can see my hair is going very grey as well," he smiled. "So I'm beginning to look a different sort of person."

"Your right there, but she wasn't happy with his look. I wish you'd give yourself up."

"No way Mum, I'm out now and that's where I'm going to stay, if I can."

"Well you could do with a new pair of jeans. Going to her bag she got out fifty pounds and handed it to him. Here take this!"

"Mum I can't."

"Take it, I cannot see you walking around like a tramp," she said. "I drew it out the bank the other day, to buy a new bedside light, because my old one won't work."

"Oh that's a shame, I will look at that for you, but I don't want this money. So take this back and get your new bedside light."

"No I want you to have this."

"Oh … what can I say? Thank you, I will pay you back one day, you can be sure of that, but I really don't like taking this from you. However my jeans are terrible I agree."

"Well you get yourself a new pair quickly because the ones you have on look as though they're on their last legs. That was funny! Anyway going back to the money, I don't go far, or spend much but I save my pension if there's something I need. Oh and I do sewing for people who wish me to and advertise in our grocer's shop window: anyway would you mind taking a look at my old lamp for me, I would appreciate it?"

"Lead me to it," he said. Putting his hand on her shoulder.

"I'll make this money up and get another lamp in time, so don't worry," She held the £50 note out to him again.

As he slowly took it from his mother. "Thank you. I know it's not a good situation, but I'm out of prison and that's where I intend to stay."

She raised her voice. "I know Jake, but in the eyes of the law you shouldn't have done what you did, so you have to serve your time. We don't make these laws the government does. If only Kate hadn't lost her balance. It was such an unfortunate accident to happen I know, but now you've made it a hundred times worse for yourself do you realise that?" Tears were trickling down her face, as he gently put his arm around her, when she suddenly pulled herself together. "Heaven knows I don't want you to go back to prison. The trouble is now you will get a longer sentence, making it so much worse for yourself."

John knew his mother was right. "I just don't see it as murder. Yes," he carried on, "I might have been out early, but it would probably have been another two years I would have had to serve. Well I couldn't stand it in there any longer, or I might have done something to myself in desperation."

"NO JAKE!!!" (She forgot.) That would have been such a terrible thing to do."

"I hated it and everyone in there, apart from George," he smiled. "So that's why, do you understand mum?" The stress was beginning to show on his face, as beads of perspiration started to appear when he thought back. He was now rubbing his hands together, over and over again but he stopped suddenly when he saw his mothers face. "Don't worry, I feel better now he said calming himself down, but I really shouldn't have palled up with that terrible con. You see I don't know what he was in for but it wasn't good I feel? My one aim was to get away from prison and I did." His mother was still staring at him, so he stopped what he was talking about and became calm again. "I'm here for a day or two, so I will do those jobs for you." Thinking now of the things he did for Jess whilst he was with her and he turned towards his mother. "Don't worry I don't feel suicidal anymore. I have a life!!" But please say if you would rather me go?"

"You are of my flesh and blood and I love you dearly, you know that. You have taken this decision to do what you did, even though I feel it isn't the right thing. Still I will always stand by you, you know I will John?"

He nodded, before saying to her. "What a lot of worry I've put on your shoulders I'm so sorry for everything, whichever way it turns out." He bent and kissed this sweet natured woman on the cheek, he didn't deserve such an understanding mother. "Bless you. I will always treasure those words you have just said to me. Forever…"

"Right now the only thing that does worry me is someone might come to my door. It could be the milkman or the postman who sometimes has a cup of tea with me, before he goes on his rounds."

"Oh I see, quite popular are we?" He laughed.
She hit him with the tea cloth she had in her hand and laughed out loud. "Listen my son? Don't you go getting any ideas that your mother is flirting or a loose woman."

"Would I do that?"

"Yes you would." They were laughing so much now putting everything bad behind them, as the laughter increased. It was just like old times, but not so!! As she began thinking about years ago the banter between them used to be such fun.

"Mr and Mrs Jackman sometimes pop in to see me, but not very often, no problem now as they're visiting their daughter for a few days."

"Oh well, I don't have to worry then Mum, however I will be very careful not to be seen and it won't be long before I'll be leaving you, as the police will be on the ball really soon, looking for me. But I don't think this weather is helping much."

"Well Jake I expect they'll have a job finding me! What with my new name and new address, but I'm sure they will whittle it down eventually. So do you think we'd better get started?" She smiled at him, hope I'm not being too bossy?

"No I'll forgive you, we must get these jobs done." He was only too happy to help her because she couldn't do them. "Now what's first?" He asked.

Amy smiled "Well could you check some of my plugs, and that stubborn table lamp in the bedroom which won't work?" She asked him.

"Well let's hope I can mend it. I am sorry that now you have to save up again, what with me taking your money."

"Don't worry I'd rather you have it."

"Thanks Mum. Now lead me to the lamp, Genie?"

"You twerp," she joked! With every awful thing that was going on they were still able to bring a little humour into it.

"Tools are in that cupboard over there," she pointed. But suddenly her thoughts were of Kate and she felt guilty. She had always got on well with her when she was alive. But there hadn't been the rapport she always wanted to have with a daughter-in-law. The younger woman had never been over friendly and always argued over different situations when (Laura as she was named then) popped into see them both. But Jake and Kate seemed to tolerate each other but she always seemed jealous when she his mother, joked with her son. However what happened to that young woman should never have.

Chapter 15

Amy was busy getting on with all her jobs, when John joined her.

"All done and I mended your lamp. Do you know this is what I did at Jess's, repair things, as she hasn't had anyone do that in years," he smiled?

"Ah, well you're spreading yourself around she laughed, thank you."

"No it's me that should be thanking you for everything, Mum. I'll definitely get those new jeans before these drop off me." He smiled, but I don't know where yet? Or when?

"Well yes that will be a problem I know, but I'm sure you'll find a way."

As he gazed out the window now, he noticed there was a barn at the back of the house, but the snow was still coming down thick and laying again. "Would you like me to chop some logs for you?" He asked his mother.

"Would you? Mr Jackman lets me use the barn. So that would be brilliant if you would do that? Then I can have a fire in the living room and that will make the place lovely and warm. I light the fire in there now and again when its bitterly cold, but I run out of logs and I haven't got around to ordering any since being poorly. It does save my electric fire burning, so yes that would be a boon, if you would do that for me. There's plenty of wood in there to saw up, from fallen down branches which Mr Jackman put there. He knows I will get somebody to saw them up for me. You!! I'm glad they're away though."

Jake was so very pleased to do something for his mother. Minutes later he was thinking of Jess and decided that he would make his way back to her. Missing her so much he was now wondering, did she miss him? After all they hadn't known each other long, but would she really be happy to see him again? Well he hoped so, because where she lived was the perfect spot, right off the beaten track and he felt so safe there. He would love to make a life with Jess, but, would she with him?

Not if she found out about his past. He thought it had been such unusual circumstances when they first met on that snowy night. This kept coming back into his mind but then he suddenly thought of Kate who had been an only child. her mother and father had died years ago, that was a blessing really, as they would have been devastated by what had happened to their daughter. Anyway he had to get on. "Have you got a saw by any chance? It does help?" He laughed.

"Well there is one in the barn hanging up with lots of other tools out there. Your father used to collect tools, so I brought some of them here when I moved. Would you believe a couple of them have come in really handy at times? You probably remember he used to hoard them? Like I collect knitting wool," she smiled.

"Yes, I do remember the things dad did." It made him feel so sad at that moment as he thought of him now with such fondness. That's why his mother had become so important to him, after all, she's all he had and vice versa. Well he would always be there for her if he could. She was so important to him. John had had the most doting parents anyone could ever have, when he was growing up. How could he have made such a mess of his life?

"Well mum I'd better get on," he told her. He was glad he'd checked all her plugs, because a lot of them were faulty, also the lamp was downright dangerous, so he was more than glad to fix it. Well he would make perfectly sure, that his mother was going to be alright before he left the house and that all of her jobs would be done.

"Thank you Jake I appreciate what you're doing for me, especially with all your other worries."

"I'm only too happy to do these different jobs for you Mum, but you know I'm surprised that George has never offered?"

"Well I never asked him, because I didn't want him to find out too much about me, or to get too comfortable here, don't forget I've only known him a short while, but thought what a nice kind person he was and liked him instantly, that's how we became friends. Anyway do not stay out in that barn too long, it's very cold again today, and you never know, the police might turn up."

"I hope not." John walked out of the back door, treading the deep snow and kicking it in front of him.

Before she pulled the door too, she suddenly shouted to him. "John!! I forgot to say, the postman might come in for a cup of tea today, as it's so cold and he'll be here any minute. Look if he comes I will take the pot of flowers off the kitchen window sill, and when he goes I'll put them back up. So keep watching," she saw him nod and put his thumb in the air. At that moment she decided to make a chocolate cake, which her son had always loved. She couldn't see John now through the window, but he must be sawing away.

It was sometime later when the cake was cooking and the wonderful baking smell filled the house, she heard a knock at the door.

'Oh no! It must be Tim?' Well she had to answer it, because if it was him, he would come round the back, having done that many times. Not wanting to miss his chat with her and his mug of tea. Well any other time would have been fine, but not today, as he might see Jake in the barn.

Oh please stay where you are she thought, walking quickly over to the sink and taking the flowers off the window sill, before going to answer the door.

"Morning Amy."

"Morning Tim," she smiled, opening the door wider. "How are you today? Coming in or not?"

"Oh Amy I'd love a cuppa to warm me up, if you don't mind?"

She couldn't say no, because she nearly always gave him a drink when it was cold. The only worry was he was a very nosy sort of person, and was constantly trying to find out what people in the village were up to.

"No that's fine, come in? I bet you're having a difficult time getting around today, with all this snow?"

"I am, it's so dreadful out here," he told her stepping inside. Could you get me a cloth please Amy? As I've made a mess in your hall," he was dripping all over the floor, even though he'd wiped his boots on the mat. I'm sorry about the mess on the floor."

"That's okay Tim, I'll get a cloth and wipe it up."

The poor devil looked frozen she thought hurrying to the kitchen to get the floor cloth out from under the sink. Thinking she wished he hadn't always expected to come in every time. Well she certainly didn't want his company not today.

"Here give me that cloth you're not doing that, he told her." She handed it to him as he bent down and wiped the puddles up, there that's better. Now for my cup of tea, I really need one this morning Amy. It's so flipping cold out there, I wonder when these conditions are going to get better. The temperature seems to have dropped again."

It did feel cold when the front door was open.

"Come through Tim," she said, a little on edge, as she told him, "I'll just put the kettle on."

"Thanks, my goodness, it's so cosy in here. What have you been up to Amy?" As he began to warm his hands by the electric fire.

"What? WHAT DO YOU MEAN, WHAT HAVE I BEEN UP TOO?" She knew she had been a little sharp with her response, as she stared at the man in front of her with the uniform on. He'd been a postman for fifteen years and was a pleasant enough person, all but for that one thing that was annoying. She hoped he hadn't noticed her tone of voice. But he had!

"I was just wondering really how your week has gone, sorry I didn't mean to pry?" (not true.)

"No! No! Tim I'm sorry to have answered you so brusquely, I think this weather's getting me down, because I haven't been able to go far."

What came to her mind again was John. She was glad she told him about the postman, he would probably be there for twenty minutes, having his drink. She stood leaning on the sink talking to him but began to shake when she heard the noise of John sawing, acting quickly, she turned the small radio up to stifle the bangs or whatever.

"I love this tune 'Smile', she told him nervously, as she bent down to get the cake out of the oven. (Jake wasn't watching the kitchen window evidently.)

Tim looked flummoxed for a moment. "Yes! Yes! It's nice. YOU KNOW WHAT THERES AN ESCAPED CONVICT ON THE RUN." He shouted, but only a small piece in the paper.

She felt ill at that moment, but she did turn the radio down a bit.

That cake smells lovely. "Anyway as I was saying, this prisoner could be around this area, so the police think. There was a tiny bit in the paper this morning and evidently has been on the run a few days," he told her casually.

She swallowed hard. "Really! Well I'm not nervous. she told him, looking outside now, as I'm in an out of the way spot here."

"That's why I mentioned it, because of you living here, it's very lonely don't you think? Just what an escaped prisoner would like. Well I hope the police catch him soon, so that we can all sleep well in our beds at night," he told her.

She could just hear Jake sawing again. Why? Because the flowers were still NOT on the window sill, which would have told her son the man hadn't gone yet. Mind you he wasn't visible thank goodness. Her guess was that he thought he couldn't be heard. So she turned the radio up again. She could tell Tim looked really fed up with all the noise now, as he pulled a face.

"I love my music," Amy said smiling, with Frank Sinatra now on in the background. Doing it his way.

"Well I'm not that bothered," the postman told her, "I can take it or leave it. Oh I nearly forgot," he shouted over the music. "HERE'S YOUR POST," he said loudly pulling two letters out and handing them to Amy.

"Thank you Tim, it's probably more rubbish. She stared at the letters in her hand now. One was a boring flyer and the second one looked like a bill. Nothing exciting, she told him, laying them on the table.

"I must go now, lots to do. THANKS FOR THE TEA AMY." He said loudly getting up from the chair.

"No thank you, for my mail. She couldn't wait for him to go. Here's your coat, I hope it doesn't get any worse out there. Oh I am sorry I never offered you a piece of cake."

"Well I wouldn't want any Amy as I'm trying not to have anything too sweet, I've got to lose a bit of weight," he told her, patting his stomach, "but thank you that was very kind of you to offer."

"You're welcome," when suddenly there was a bang. He stood up listening! "Did you hear that?" He said walking towards the window.

She grabbed his arm, "I never heard anything, just your imagination Tim," she told him, steering him towards the front door just wanting him to go.

He couldn't wait to get away from all that noise on the radio, "You certainly like your music. Amy? Well I wouldn't go out today if I were you." He was saying opening the door, as once again snow drifted in.

"Don't worry I'm not, it's warmer indoors. Bye!" Sorry about my loud music," she laughed, thank goodness he was going. Then he raised his hand in the air and to her horror turned and walked in the direction of the noise that had occurred. What was this man going to do? She ran towards the kitchen window. Seeing him heading for the barn. 'OH NO!' He mustn't find John. What should she do?

She opened the window in desperation. "Tim! Tim!" She called out. "Where are you going?"

"Just checking on that noise," he yelled.

"Don't worry I'm sure there's no problem," she shouted back. But he took no notice of her, as he walked into the barn. "Oh please keep out of sight Jake," she whispered to herself. When all of a sudden she felt relief as the postman came walking out after a few minutes.

"Everything's fine, he shouted!! The only situation I could find was a nail fell out the wall and the saw was on the ground. Somebody over the back there must have been banging."

"Thank you for checking." Now feeling quite sick at that precise moment. She waved goodbye to him as he went on his way and she pulled the window too. She couldn't take much more of this worry. Jake must leave soon, she thought, where was he?

Amy placed the plant back on the shelf to let her son know that the postman had really gone now.

"That was close," John told his mother as he walked into the kitchen with an armful of logs, which were to go into the other room.

She gave him a weak smile. "You think people don't care about you, but there are some that do, he was trying to protect me saying there is an escaped convict in the area. Sorry Jake evidently there was a small piece in the paper, she nervously told him."

"Oh great, that was probably a few days ago he read it! So I just have to be careful, he brushed it aside now for his mums sake. Looking at her he said in a lighter tone of voice, please don't tell me somebody else is going to come to the house today? You know I might have to leave earlier than I said I would. He noticed the relief on his mother's face. There are plenty of logs outside now, which should see you okay for a while."

"Thank you, and no there isn't anyone else coming she smiled. Where were you in the barn by the way?

"Behind that old cart you have in there, I heard you shout to him, so I moved quickly having finished the job, placing the saw on the nail, but it fell out and the saw crashed to the ground. Well the postman came in picked it up off the floor, pushed the nail back into the wall and placed it back, then walked out. But I thought he had spotted me at one time, looking straight in my direction, thankfully no he didn't."

She stared at Jake. "I said I would put the flowers back when he went, you nearly blew it. My son who we brought up to be good and kind to everyone, is now being hunted down as a murderer. Do you know I wish we could go back and start all over again," she said sadly. "Anyway John come and have this leak and potato soup I've made for you. It will warm you up. And I've made you a chocolate cake too which you used to love."

He looked across to where it stood. "Wow! Thanks mum it looks lovely, he told her taking his coat off. What had he done to her? "Sorry about my mistake, you know I got so into sawing I forgot the flowers," he smiled. His life was such a mess, perhaps he should give himself up to the police for her sake, she was such a good woman. She didn't deserve this.

As the two sat at the table later, she began thinking about when her husband was with them and how the three used to chat away together, over different things, they were such wonderful memories, laughing at this and that. Now her son was in deep trouble, in a way it was a good thing her husband wasn't alive to hear all this. John being hunted by the police. She suddenly thought it must be awful, being with villain's, murderers, rapists, etc.

"Penny for them" he said, as he pushed his empty bowl of soup aside. seeing the worried look on her face. "Don't worry Mum I'll be ok."

"How can I not worry about you? You're my son whom I always want to be there for. As you do for me. In the next breath. Here try my cake." She laughed.

"Thank you," he said taking a bite, "it's just as I remember that cake, great, your such a good cook. Anyway Mum I'll be going very soon, but I feel a lot happier now I've seen you and know you have made a life here and have friends. One person I wish you hadn't made friends with though was George, even though he is a good chap."

"He is, but thankfully he doesn't know the real me! You know what John. I'm getting used to having you around.

"Well I'm getting used to being around," he smiled brushing his hand across his beard.

"I bet that itches?" she laughed. For the moment forgetting all of her and John's worries.

"It does but I have to have it. It changes my whole appearance. At the prison they will have an old photo of me, which probably is in the paper."

"Your hairs long too … But do you know, I quite like it?"

"Oh thanks mum, so does Jess!"

He saw her smile,

"Do you think you will get away with this?" She asked him.

"Well I'm going to give it a damn good try. Now I'm out of that prison I'm going to do my best to stay out. You don't know what I had to go through in there. Some of the inmates pick on you, calling you names, getting you into trouble, perverts everywhere, playing up to you, it's sick, it really is. So I had to get out you must see that?"

"It was a very silly thing to do though," seeing at that moment he looked very annoyed with her now, as he told her.

"IT MIGHT SEEM SILLY TO YOU MUM BUT I DON'T THINK YOU'D FIND IT SO IF YOU KNEW EVERYTHING THAT GOES ON THERE. I know it's totally my fault, I shouldn't have done what I did."

She had upset him! "Sorry son I didn't think, this is getting on top of me."

"Oh, it's ok mum and that wasn't nice of me, to shout at you." Putting his arm around her, noticing he'd nearly reduced her to tears.

She'd never been spoken to like that before, and it hurt, especially from her own son.

"Let's try to forget about what we've both said shall we?"

This was the son she had known, kind, and caring. The woman nodded, feeling, almost like crying. She began thinking back, when her husband and herself had bought Jake his first bike, how thrilled he'd been at the time. His father had worked all hours in the factory to pay for that bike, wanting to surprise his son. He hadn't been disappointed. Jake had been thrilled to bits with his new bike at the time.

"What are you thinking about mum?"

"Your dad."

"Well I too, often think about him."

"John   stop blaming   yourself   he was ill before your situation arose with Kate."

"Yes I know, but I can't help thinking he would have been devastated to hear about what's been happening to me. Just then his mind took in other things when he looked at that snow outside, well anyway he pointed, this has given me a breathing space, to think about what I shall do tomorrow at least."

She sighed!

Chapter 16

Next morning his mother nearly had a fit when she looked out the window, horrified. "Charging up the stairs she yelled, John! John!" Feeling hot and flustered as she entered his bedroom.

He opened his eyes and yawned, pulling his bed covers up which were strewn everywhere. "What's the matter?" He asked her, propping himself up on his elbows. Noticing how distraught his mother was now. "It's not the police is it?"

"No! no!" But it could be soon."

"What's that noise then that I can hear?"

She pulled back the curtain. "It's rain! The snow is melting fast."

John was out of bed quicker than when he got in last night, as he wrapped the blanket around himself and walked over to the window, staring at the torrential rain which had taken them both by surprise. He felt that the police would soon be paying a visit to his mother, once they could get round better. This could be the day when they found out where she moved to. Having waited for the weather to change, then they would be looking for him.

"I have to get washed and dressed," he told her.

"I'll get breakfast while you're doing that. Then what's going to happen?" She asked.

"I have to leave Mum, because eventually the powers that be will whittle down your whereabouts and I can't let you take these risks for me."

"Alright son," she turned and went slowly down the stairs. Putting the bread in the toaster before making a ham sandwich for him to take with him. Ten minutes later he jumped down the stairs, two at a time. Pushing the door open to the kitchen, as his mother stared at him.

"Here eat this, she was saying as she leaned over passing the hot buttered toast on the plate to him. "Where will you go?" She asked feeling very worried for her son now and what might happen in the next few hours.

"I don't know yet mum, but don't you worry I'll be okay."

"Well I have to admit you do look quite different now. More like a hippy in those tatty jeans, she smiled. And that thick hair looks clean and neat even though it's long, not at all like a rough looking convict!"

"Thanks Mum for those few kind words!" He was eating his toast as though there was no tomorrow.

"If they catch you, you'll be back in prison again John, but now I'm wondering how long for?"

"I don't know Mum, I have thought about that, but they've got to catch me first and I don't intend to make it easy for them. You know I was happy with Jess when she took me in. I think that I will try and get back to her somehow. Of course she knows nothing about my situation. So I will have to live my lie again."

"You sound as though you're very fond of this woman. Is that fair to be so deceitful towards her? To what sounds like a very nice lady."

"Well you're right she is nice, better than that she's lovely. I've not known her that long but I have grown very fond of her. Of course she knows nothing about my past and that's the way it's got to be. Funny but I thought I was in love with Kate all those years ago. However Jess is something quite different. I love everything about her however, I must go Mum."

When suddenly the phone rang. "I wonder who that is?"

"Answer it! He told her, trying not to sound too sharp."

"Hello!"

"Hello Amy, it's me George."

"Oh! Oh! Hello George."

"You sounded startled, anything the matter?"

"No, I was polishing the furniture and on my knees when I heard the ring and I ran into the hall to pick the phone up, I'm just puffed."

"I see, you're a busy lady."

"What did you want George?" She asked getting a little tetchy now.

"Only to check to see if you are coming to the club tonight, because the snowy weather seems to be on its way out. As I told you I want to celebrate my retirement day with you." He laughed.

"Yes that would be nice, I look forward to it. And you can tell me how your last day went? Thankfully I feel a lot better now, see you later." She turned looking at an agitated John. When she heard George say down the line.

"But we will have a drink, at The Old Oak Pub first?"

"Okay that would be nice."

"Good, see you then, say about 7 30 okay?"

"That's fine," she told him.

"I'll come and pick you up in the car. Bye!"

"Thank you George. I'll be ready," she said. "Bye!"

As the woman replaced the receiver she looked up at her son. who had been pacing backwards and forwards: "That was George," she added.

"I gathered that, You're going out with him then?"

"Yes, she smiled we're going to The Old Oak Pub, and then to our club. But I won't meet him if you don't want me to"

Now, thinking of the prison situation and Jake knowing him, he saw the look on his mother's face, she liked this man. Who was he to say who she could go out with? Even though it was one of the prison officers who he had got on so well with. What a strange world this was that his mother met this man and had since developed a strong friendship with him. It was unbelievable that from all the men in the world it had to be him. "Mum you go out with him, he's a good bloke. You know that's the pub where I chanced having a pint on my way here. Thanks for everything you've done for me. I'm truly sorry I have put you in this awkward position. If the police come – let me rephrase that – when the police come and you can be sure they will, I do hope you'll be able to get through the questioning."

"Don't worry I won't mention that you've been here, she smiled."

"You're a diamond Mum He kissed her on both cheeks, and look after that arthritis."

"You look after yourself, as I don't know where this will end and I'm very worried for you."

"Don't be, you have your life to live and heaven knows I have ruined so much of it. I just pray that you don't have too many more problems, with me being your son." As she seemed very keen on George he would hate to spoil that friendship. His attention was now focusing on the window when he heard a car and people shouting. Hearing the intake of breath from his mother as she stood next to him following his gaze.

"JOHN IT'S THE POLICE I BET. Give yourself up?"

"Never! They've found out where you live mum, now the snows going." He grabbed his duffle bag and coat.

"Where are you going?" She asked before he made his way to the back door.

"I don't know yet but don't worry about me. Bang! Bang! They'll knock that door down in a minute. Give me two minutes then go and answer it okay? But keep them talking and then they won't see me slip out the back."

He noticed the worried look on her face, as he walked across to her side putting his arm round her shoulders and kissing her cheek before saying, "I will be alright, stop worrying and I'll write as soon as I can."

The banging on the door continued.

"I'm off mum, bye, thanks for everything."

"Bye John, take care." She was finding it hard to stop the tears from coming, that would never do.

The heavy rain continued as he waved to his mum and ran through the wood the snow was melting rapidly. In a few hours you would never know there had ever been any. He hurried in haste, looking back from time to time he couldn't see anyone following though. His mother was evidently doing as he had said and was keeping the police talking until he was out of sight. The density of the wood helped him to trudge along and lose himself in there. Thank goodness he'd not been spotted as he came to a clearing in front of him where stood a bungalow, what must be Mr and Mrs Jackman's who owned the land. He sneaked around it glad they were away as his mum had told him. He was off the beaten track a little but had a feeling it wasn't much further to the road, when suddenly he approached the slushy, water logged lane where he first started out. There was the huge tree which he'd passed as he'd entered. The snow had gone from it now so it looked a little crestfallen. When he heard something. What was it? It sounded like a dog barking and someone was talking. He suddenly realized the police were in the wood. Running like mad now he knew he had to get away quick.

Thinking they couldn't have believed his mother's story, because surely they wouldn't have come through the wood so soon. John was puffing like mad. He had to see Jess he would be safe there at the cottage, if he could only get out of this situation. He ran along the lane until he eventually joined the roadway walking quickly. as traffic past him at high speed, he had to do it. So he put his thumb up in the air, please stop someone he thought, he must get away from here fast. When a screech of breaks made him turn around, it was a huge articulated lorry and it was pulling up beside him. John stared at the person when he put his window down.

The rough looking man inside said. "Want a lift mate?"

"Yes, yes, thank you. I want to go to Luvington?" He told him.

"Going right past there, hop in." He pointed to the passenger side.

"Thanks a lot," John said to him, slipping his wet coat off as he put it on his lap. He must look like a drowned rat. But thankfully he was in a warm cab now, shooting out onto the main highway. Well away from the police, he hoped; everything was happening so fast though.

The driver often picked hitch hikers up when he was travelling, he met some nice guys on the road. "Rough old day isn't it?" he said.

"You're right there, it's rain and slush now. John turned and stared at the man alongside him. He was a big chap but had a pleasant face. How far are you going?" John asked him.

"Well a lot further than you. The Medway."

John didn't want the man to know that he would pass right by the lane that he wanted. So he chose the village before, which wasn't too far from Jess's lane. " Okay?"

"Well we might as well be on first names, for we've got a few miles to go. My names Hal."

"Hi Hal! Mine's ... John, (he'd better keep to his made-up name.) Now to make up a good story. I'm on leave from the Navy at the moment. You know how it is? Us sailors get through our money so quickly. So that when we want to visit our families we're broke, when we're on leave. It's not the thing to do, I know"

"Well we all do things we shouldn't so I can see that, you've got to have some relaxation at times, when you've been on ship for a few months. Money doesn't go far old chum. How long are you home for?"

"Oh, a couple of weeks before we go back to sea."

"Where are you off to next then?"

"Not sure yet, could be anywhere. As you can imagine we get to see lots of different countries." The lies just flowed out of John's mouth. It was funny really, because there were times when he wanted to join the Navy. But that dream went.

"Where have you been before?" The lorry driver asked.

"China, Korea, Australia, oh and many more." Had to get off this subject.

"Are you married?" Hal asked.

"No!"

"You?"

"No, not yet, I like my freedom too much, no ties that's me. Anyway women want lots of attention and I'd never be at home. My driving job takes me all over the country."

"Oh I see, well I expect you'll marry one day."

"Perhaps. What about you? He smiled. Although you know what they say about sailors. They have a girl in every port?"

"Well not every!" John told him. "It's a shame we can't wear the navy uniform out now though, too dangerous in many respects. A long time ago they didn't have these problems, you would see in Plymouth near the Hoe hundreds of naval ratings walking around. My parents told me many years ago, that it was a lovely sight to see sailors with their girlfriends on their arm when they were on leave. Things have changed now we're not allowed to wear our uniforms out, it might be because some bolshie individual will pick on you, well that's what I think anyway" He really wasn't telling a lie for once, his parents had talked about such things, but the words seemed to flow out of his mouth. Well this man didn't know him from Adam so he felt safe what he said.

When all of a sudden Hal said. "Well I'm older than you and yes I can remember that time."

"Well that's amazing." John looked over his shoulder to see if any police were around.

"Looking for somebody mate?"

"No! No! Just wondering how much traffic there was on the road."

"It's not too bad today, but usually there's a long queue on this road. So where are you going to then?" The driver asked.

"Oh my brother and his wife are putting me up for a few days." That was it, John didn't want to explain anymore. "I think I'll have a nap now if you don't mind?"

"No that's ok you go ahead," Hal seemed to be thinking now. "Look I forgot to mention John that I need to stop at the motorway restaurant for a while I have to see someone. We could have a meal or a coffee. Is that okay with you? I bet you could do with a bit of sustenance by then, I know I could?" He noticed the other man's reaction to that statement.

"Thank you, yes I could," but was worried about the money when he heard.

"Don't worry my treat, I've had a good week," Hal told him.

John raised his thumb. "Thanks!!"

All he wanted to do was to see Jess again. Closing his eyes, he began to think of all that had happened in the last few days. The prison, Jess, the people in the pub, his mother and now this man. He wasn't tired after a good sleep at his mother's, but he pretended to doze off not wanting to talk.

'Blimey that was quick,' Hal thought. Well they were nearly there at the service station, when he pulled the wheel over expertly to avoid a car. He had to be careful on the road because it was still a little icy, being very cold, although the snow was almost gone. He had a full load today washing machines and dryers. A quarter of an hour later he turned quickly to see John stir. Hal knocked his arm: "Want a fag mate? He nudged him. "I guarantee you'll enjoy it." He winked.

Pretending to yawn John stretched: "Thanks, but no thanks, I'm not into that stuff, you shouldn't be either, driving this rig. You could lose your job."

Amazingly he was giving this man advice. Perhaps he could change and there was hope for him yet?

Cheeky bugger! Who the f- - - was he to tell him what he could do?

John opened the window slightly, as the man puffed away on his cigarette. He had to tread lightly because this man was going to pay for his meal. "Sorry I didn't mean to be rude." He said.

"That's okay mate, I know what your saying is true, but that's my life."

Chapter 17

Meanwhile ... "No! No! I didn't know of my sons escape from prison."

"Well Mrs Farrendon," The two policemen were now sitting in her kitchen. "It's taken us a few days to find out where you were living." DC Bob Slater pointed out, "as you're now going under the name of Amy Shaw. Am I right?" He watched her closely as she nodded and carried on saying. "The snow has also held us up a great deal, you see we would have been here a lot sooner, but for the weather conditions."

"As I told you officer I didn't know, I haven't seen my son," she lied and stood up from her chair explaining why she was living under an assumed name, (like her Jake she was now telling lies.)

"Right, well I'm sorry to have brought you this news about your son," he was saying. "But if you don't mind we'll just look around the back. Take Bruce with you just in case there's any trouble," he told one of his men. The Alsatian dog was invaluable to the force as he had done some good work, finding whoever in the past.

"I'll search through the wood?" The police officer said.

"Yes you do that! Sorry it's not that we don't trust what you say Mrs Farrendon. But Jake could have been coming to see you and is hiding around here."

"I haven't seen my son. I can't believe he's escaped from prison I don't condone it at all." Did she sound genuine? Well the young man seemed quite satisfied.

"If you do will you please give us a ring? We have to find him as soon as possible. After all he is a convicted murderer."

"Wrong officer, my boy is not a murderer. It was an accident!"

"Anyway don't forget what I've said. We have to catch him with or without your help."

"Of course!" Pigs might fly. She wouldn't give her son away, ever!

Coming back a while later with the dog, the policeman said. "I really thought I saw someone in the wood," then he smiled. "I was wrong it was a tree bending over."

"You'd better get some glasses," Bob Slater said to the young officer with a smirk. "Well thank you for your help Mrs Farrendon. Don't forget to let us know if your son should get in touch."

She smiled. "It's Mrs Shaw now officer, but that's okay. As to your question, well of course, I can't believe it." She showed him to the front door, hoping her Jake was well away by now, probably on his way to see this Jess. He had sounded besotted with her but was this woman feeling the same? Amy was now thinking what would happen when she found out what he'd done? Would there ever be any future for them? I doubt it, this Jess wouldn't want someone who'd committed murder. Then there was George who to her horror had been a prison warder and had befriended Jake. It was an unbelievable coincidence. Well she had to get herself ready now, because she was going out with George this evening, she enjoyed her Saturdays with him. Amy put the sandwiches back in the fridge, which John had forgotten to take in his hurry. She would eat those tomorrow. She'd never get used to that name.

John began to think of his poor mother now, hoping she had got rid of the police. He felt so guilty at bringing the whole situation to her doorstep. He shouldn't have gone there, but he did want to see her, as he hadn't done for some time, years in fact. After keep nodding off and on he looked around and asked in an anxious tone. "Where are we?"

"Service station and restaurant," Hal told him.

"Oh great," he said but began to feel a little nervous now. Would somebody recognise him? John hadn't eaten since breakfast, his mum had made him a sandwich but with all the rushing off when the police came, he'd left it on the kitchen table. Anyway now he was wondering, who Hal was going to see? John was getting really worried about being with lots of people and was hoping there weren't any pictures of him in the newspaper's. Jumping down from the cab, he walked around to the driver's side. Putting on his jacket they both strolled into the restaurant.

"Boy this smells good doesn't it?" Hal was saying sniffing the air.

"It sure does." He had the money his mother had given him, if push came to shove, bless her, but he didn't want to spend it here, only on a pair of jeans.

Hal saw his look. "Don't worry John as I said I'll pay."

"Thank you but I really should have treated you, as you gave me a lift."

"That's okay I've got more money than you. They do a mean Lasagne here. It's my favourite place when I'm on the M25 route."

"Well I must try it." John told him, as both picked up their full plates as well as the desert of apple pie and custard. Hal then got the coffees. Nobody was taking any notice of the two men as they headed for a table in the corner.

"This meal is pucker," The man commented. Pushing the hot food into his mouth and not looking up until he'd finished his desert, As John did. "Well I can see you've enjoyed it too?" He said to him. "Don't they feed you on those ships?"

"Yes of course, all that you can eat, but I was feeling very hungry today, I don't know why? Like you. It's probably the cold weather."

A coach load of people came through the doors and they rushed to get into the queue. The assistant looked a bit fraught pushing her hair back from her face now. When all of a sudden John noticed a man staring at their table which made him very edgy. Had he been recognised? He'd take a chance and tell Hal who had his back to him. "That man over there keeps staring at us."

Hal turned round and acknowledged the man, with a lift of the chin and began to get up from the table. "He's looking for me I won't be a minute John." He carried his head low as he made his way over to the chap.

"Okay," John thought the man looked rough with his pony tail, earing's, horrible old trainers, torn jeans and worn jacket, he looked like an overgrown hippy. He watched as Hal

112

placed his hand on the other man's shoulder and they headed outside.

John thought it was quite obvious what they were up too. He'd seen enough drug problems in prison, it was running rife. That was one thing he wouldn't get involved in, he'd seen what it can do to a person. He'd got enough worries of his own without worrying about them. Drinking his coffee now he began to feel warmer and wasn't thinking too much about his situation, in fact he felt quite relaxed, nobody seemed bothered about him. That was until Hal came tearing over, pushing chairs out of his way, as he reached their table. "Quick we've got to get out of here?"

John began to put on his damp coat and followed Hal out of the building. "What's the matter?" He asked

"Well I'd just got what I wanted from Harry and I think you know what that was?"

John nodded, beginning to put two and two together. "Yes, and what happened?"

"As Harry was leaving the car park a police car drew up and picked him up, somebody must have told on him. So we've got to get out of here pronto. Because no way do I want to get caught with what I've got on me. So let's go and stop looking at me like that, you knew what I was up to, you're a man of the world, aren't you?"

John nodded he was also starting to panic. "Surely your friend Harry will tell them about you receiving and that is exactly what you're doing isn't it?"

"Yes. No he won't tell them about me. Yet!"

John was panicking. "I think I'll make my own way now."

"You don't have to. I can still drop you off."

"Thanks but no thanks I can't get involved in this sort of thing. Not being in the Navy and all. By the way don't mention me, if you're ever picked up."

"Of course not! I've got to get going now, it's been nice knowing you John. Good luck on your travels."

"Thanks. You know what? You're very silly to take these drugs. If I were you I'd stop it right here and now, because like I told you before, you'll lose your job if you get caught."

"Well that's the chance I've got to take and you aren't me, mate. I've been taking them for too long now and I can't do without them. But thanks for your concern," and he walked off towards his lorry.

John shouted out. "Oh, but thank you for the meal." He saw the other man wave, and was relieved not to be with him anymore, as he watched him pulling his vehicle out onto the open road. Driving at a steady speed probably not wanting to draw attention to himself. He himself certainly didn't want to get involved with all this, he'd got enough troubles of his own. Now to thumb another lift, it wasn't too far, from what he could remember of the route when he was with Jess. Even though Hal had taken the motorway and then had joined the small roads when he John was asleep.

His mum began thinking about her son now, he must be well away. She was hoping and wondering if he'd managed to get a lift to this woman's cottage. She sounded very nice, but dreaded to think what would happen, when she found out. Thank goodness the police had seemed satisfied with what she had just told them, that she didn't know where he was. They also understood why she had taken another name. Her hands suddenly felt painful from the arthritis, as she rubbed them together; such pain, the cold always did that to her. It was the damp conditions too; not good for this complaint. She would be so much better in the summer, hopefully. But when the house was renovated and radiators were put in, how lovely and warm she would be then, in the winter? She couldn't wait, but had too.

To think that George had worked at the prison and had actually got on well with John was amazing. The awful thing was he was guarding him and the group, when her son got away. It was a small world, but she dreaded to think what would have happened, if he had found Jake hiding? Looking at her wristwatch now she decided to get ready for when George would pick her up for their evening at the club.

It was 7 pm when Amy walked down the stair's feeling a little brighter, especially now she had smartened herself up, but she had to try and put her son out of her mind for a few hours at least. No way did she want to let anything out about him, when she was with George, especially the police paying a visit, that was definitely a No! No! However, it had been an awful shock when he had turned up on her doorstep. Suddenly she heard a loud knock at the door, taking a deep breath she walked towards it opening it wide hoping it was who she thought it was.

"Hello George, I'm ready, I'll just get my coat and handbag."

"Look at this Amy he waved his arm I can't believe the snows almost gone," he said staring at her, "I say you look very nice?"

"Thank you George for the compliment, but it's only my old skirt and jacket I've had them such a long time. Anyway you too look good and very smart yourself," she told him, having noticed the tweed jacket under his overcoat and his very nice blue shirt and tie. "Yes I'm also glad the snow has gone; but was she?"

"Well thanks but my clothes are old too. Now it's time for the oldies to enjoy themselves," he laughed. let's get going then. My new car awaits you." He waved his arm pointing in the direction of the shiny new white Nissan vehicle. She slid into the seat beside him, pulling her seat belt across herself.

"This is nice George are you pleased with it?"

"I'll say I am, my last little car wouldn't have lasted much longer. Having retired I thought it was about time I bought myself a decent one. It was a lot of money, still what the heck you can't take it with you and you can't buy a new jacket either"

She laughed "you're right there."

They pulled into the pub car park a little later. "It's busy tonight George isn't it?" Noticing all the cars parked.

"It's a popular pub," he told her, helping her out of the car, as he then went onto say. "I think you'll enjoy this evening at the club, as I think there's to be a jazz band playing. So we'll have a quick drink here, before going on."

"That will be nice George," she smiled. Anything to take her mind off John.

Now they were making their way into the brightly lit public house, when the barman called out. "Hello there George. What can I get you?"

He looked behind him. "Amy?"

"Sherry please!"

"Also an alcohol-free lager for me, Stan please."

"Right you are, coming up."

"There's a table over there Amy you'd better grab it before somebody else does," George told her.

"Okay." She began to walk over to the corner when she heard …

"I bet you were surprised to hear about that prisoner escaping George?"

Stan didn't know that it was him who had been looking after the prisoners, on that disastrous day. He had to answer this chap though and make it sound normal. At that moment he wished he hadn't told the bloke anything about his job. "You're right there, it was one of those things that happen from time to time. But I'm sure everything is being done to look for him."

He then turned and walked towards Amy. She felt sick as she listened to what was being said. That was her son they were talking about. George especially had no idea of the fact, as the barman didn't realise of course. John had been in this pub he'd told her. She was trying so hard to forget everything, just for one evening.

George was feeling somewhat embarrassed by what had been said. He'd liked Jake Farrendon. Always thinking, that he shouldn't have been serving a long prison sentence, with his particular situation. That's why he had taken to the fellow and had trusted him. After all who wouldn't be cross and upset hearing your wife was having an affair, right under your nose? George put the two drinks down on the table. He thought he wouldn't say too much to her, because he didn't want to frighten her.

Amy stared at him and noticed he looked really pale at that precise moment. She hadn't known it was George who was looking after the prisoners, until John told her, when he had arrived at her home. So she knew what he was thinking, she had to try and take his mind off it now.

116

"I like this pub George. I say are you okay, because you don't look so good?"

"No! No! I'm fine, it was just something Stan said." He was hoping she hadn't heard the conversation up at the bar, he didn't want to worry her, because she lived on her own. "Nothing important, let's enjoy our time together, before we go to the club shall we?"

Poor George. She suddenly felt sick she must get off the subject. Going out with him was more like going out on a date, which she hadn't been on for years; when she first went to the club she'd been drawn into company that he was in, when they were there. Then after that he had started to pop and see her at home, that's when their friendship had grown. So she decided at that moment to try and enjoy their time together tonight. When she reached into her bag and pulled out a card for him "Happy Retirement George." As she handed it to him.

"Thank you Amy I expect there will be a few of my pals there tonight from the prison."

"Great!!" As it turned out it was a good evening at the club and George seemed to really enjoy it.

John had managed to get himself a lift in another lorry but this man wasn't quite so friendly. He didn't want to talk much. That suited John and he began to wonder where Hal was now? Nice fellow, but silly! Very silly! Well hark at him when he was in a great deal of trouble himself. But he'd never succumb to drugs, although they were offered many times to him inside. He never really knew how these prisoners got them though, someone on the outside must have brought them in. All of a sudden he noticed in the headlights, the very old building on the corner with the scaffolding which he and Jess had passed when she took him into the town. It wasn't too far away from Rush Moor Lane perhaps a quarter of an hour. He didn't want the bloke to know too much though, as he told him, "This will be fine mate thanks."

"Alright if you say so, but it's blooming dark here and a bit of a dead place," he said, looking round. "Still if this is okay I will pull over?"

He wasn't such a bad bloke. "Thanks again for the lift, bye!!"

"Cheerio. Right soon I'm off to Scotland with this load, but I have other stops first."

"Well safe journey," Jake told him, jumping down from the lorry. And giving the man a thumbs up sign, as he watched the lorry pull away. John then started to walk fast.

Chapter 18

The weather had certainly changed in just a few hours, from horrendous snow conditions to a downpour of rain as he made his way along the main road, knowing it wasn't too far to go now. It was good that he had managed to get lifts and wasn't recognised. Thinking when he had walked to his mother's it must have been a few miles. It would probably take him about another ten minutes to get to Jess he judged and couldn't wait to see her again. Even though it had only been a couple of days.

How lonely he felt at that particular moment as the darkness enveloped him as he walked briskly, towards Rush Moor Lane. His heart pumping fast. What would she say to his coming back so quickly? Would she be pleased to see him; or not? She had said he was always welcome. With that twinkle in her eye. What they had had before been wonderful, well for him and also he hoped for her. Now he was wondering if she'd missed him, just a little. What he really wanted, was to stay with Jess indefinitely. This was just the place to do that, he thought quickening his step. 'Could he start a new life here?' He wondered? Or would the prison authorities and police always be looking for him?

This place was perfect for him. Perhaps he might even marry Jess one day if she'd have him. He had big hopes, he would just have to wait and see. This was it, as he stared in front of him which was difficult, how could Jess live here in such a lonely barren place on her own? he thought. Mind you he was really pleased that she did, as far as he was concerned. He had asked her before the very same question to which she answered, it was where she had her little girl and there were some happy memories of her here, even though she was killed on the moors. She told him she always felt that she was with her daughter every day. Poor Jess!

He thought if only he could be the man for her. That swine who killed her little girl should have been hung up. If only there was a life that they could have to be together, he'd always look after her. Then things might be a whole lot different if only he hadn't done what he did, but he thought he might never have met Jess either. The one thing he didn't want to be known as was a murderer. At that minute he hadn't noticed the uneven pothole in the lane and tripped, as he hurried along walking so fast, he couldn't wait to see her again. Remembering the night they first met on that terrible snowy evening and made love, which had been wonderful, she in his arms.

He stared with difficulty through the rain, as he walked up the lane. He didn't want to call that special time a one-night stand, it was more than that. The intimacy was wonderful between them, as they both needed comfort and loving. Not much further to go he began thinking. This was such an isolated place, but it was perfect, well for him anyway, with the fields and moors all around and its nooks and crannies which was unhappily near where little Becky was found. For him Rush Moor Lane was perfect to hide out, that's if Jess would let him stay there for however long? It was amazing that the snow had nearly diminished but unfortunately it was pouring with rain now. George Trent kept coming to his mind and he couldn't help feeling sorry for him. When the man trusted him John shook his head. He now hoped he wouldn't frighten her at this time of night as it was such a dark evening. He wished his mother had checked his pockets before she'd put his jacket in the washing machine, as it had Jess's telephone number on a piece of paper in there and he could have rung her. How sorry she'd been when it came out of washer in bits, because it had been ex-directory, so he couldn't get hold of Jess because he hadn't memorised her number. She'd had some dreadfully sick phone calls, after the death of her little girl, so that's why she changed her number, she'd been through so much. He began to feel sad at that point. He had to keep his identity as secret as possible, until the time was right to tell her. Suddenly he saw a light and curls of smoke escaping from the cottage's small chimney pot. She was in! Thank goodness! Then he stopped in his tracks, as there was a small mini car next to hers. He was now wondering who was with her? Well he wasn't turning back, he had to take a chance. Thankfully it wasn't a police car. He walked up to the front door and knocked the brass knocker.

Shaking the rain drops from his coat as he did so, when somebody shouted out. "Who is it?"

That wasn't Jess's voice, what should he do? Well he was here now. "I'm a friend of Jess's, would it be possible to speak to her, if she is in?" He yelled through the closed door, not feeling at all relaxed at that moment, if he ever could be, in fact he was worried, would she see him?"

When all of a sudden, he heard the bolts being slid back and a key being inserted. As the door opened and a chain was released, he was confronted by a tall, slim blonde-haired woman, who had big enquiring eyes. He began thinking, go careful. John! Feeling totally flummoxed he started to retreat back from the door. "Oh, I'm sorry to disturb you, but could I speak to Jess please? He asked again."

"I'll see, just a minute," the other woman told him.

"Who is it?"

He heard a voice which he knew so well, coming from inside.

"It's a chap who says he wants to speak to you."

"What's his name?" He heard Jess shout out.

He was beginning to wonder about this encounter as the door opened wider and he stared at the woman in front of him, who looked very on the ball. "John!"

"He said it's John."

"Oh, come in John, come in," he heard Jess call out from the kitchen.

"Sorry about this, but you can't be too careful what with this escaped prisoner about," the blonde woman told him.

He nodded. "Better to be safe than sorry," he answered in a natural voice.

"You'd better come in then from this awful weather, my goodness your soaked. Hang your coat on the hall stand there," she pointed. Going onto say, "Jess hasn't been too well,"

" Oh what's the matter with her?"

"She's unfortunately had a nasty bug and I have been looking after her for two days. You see that's all the time I could get off from the hospital, I'm a nurse. Anyway, I'm going in a while, because she told me I'm not to worry now, as she can manage."

Good! He began thinking! Nodding.

"If you would like to go through to the kitchen, she's sitting by a lovely fire, that way."

He turned and walked towards where she'd pointed, this was the place he knew so well but he was wondering? Did she know about him? Had Jess told her everything? He turned "Thank you."

She eyed him carefully. Not bad! This must be the man whom her friend had given a lift to and had helped her in the snowstorm, Jess had leaked it out when the two women were chatting together. Stephanie sensed her friend hadn't wanted to say too much about the incident, but she had pressed her so much that she had given in, disclosing what had happened. But she began to guess there were things that her friend hadn't wanted her to know, watching closely as he entered the kitchen. This had to be him?

Now as he entered the warm cosy room he remembered. He saw Jess sitting in the comfortable armchair, with a blanket over her legs, noticing the shallow look on her face. Her eyes looked tired and her beautiful auburn hair didn't have the same lustre it usually had.

"Hello, Jess what's all this about then?" Feeling very concerned now, as he took her hands in his.

"Hello, John what a surprise it's so nice to see you again," her palms were now very sweaty, and she knew it wasn't her bug which had caused that to happen. She didn't think he would ever come back again and he had and so soon. He looked good and his face was more rested she noticed.

"Your friend was saying you haven't been well Jess. How are you now?"

"Well I have been rather poorly these last couple of days." She put her hand through her hair feeling slightly embarrassed that he'd caught her looking like this. "I'm sorry I must look such a mess."

"Don't be silly you look lovely. He was kissing her cheek now, when he heard her whisper in his ear. "I began to feel ill the day I dropped you off in the town."

Stephanie was closing the kitchen door now, with her back to them. As Jess spoke louder, "I'm a lot better now having been to the doctors and with medication I'm picking up. My friend's nursing care is wonderful though and she came straight to my home to look after me."

Steph had joined them smiling as she stood back, taking in the scene in front of her, it looked a very cosy indeed.

"It's so nice to see you again John let me introduce you to my friend, this is Stephanie."

"Nice to meet you," he remarked, not even looking at the woman, but thinking this must be the one on the phone? As he then abruptly turned to look at his lovely Jess sitting in the chair.

'Well pardon me for being here,' Stephanie thought.
If looks could kill, she would have been dead by now, because she was still staring at him as Jess was, who also couldn't believe his attitude at times.

He now realised he'd been a little brusque, so he had to put that right. "Thank you for taking care of Jess Stephanie, it's a good job she had you," he smiled.
But she noticed that he couldn't take his eyes off Jess. "Well you've certainly cheered her up and that's no mistake."

John turned to Jess. "Yes, I do believe I have," he said, squeezing her hand.

She really didn't need the blanket on any more, she was hot enough but so pleased to see him. "Sit down John."

"Okay, thank you!"

The other woman turned to the two. "I'll make you both a cup of tea," she told them walking across the kitchen to fill the kettle.

"That would be lovely, thanks Steph," Jess was definitely feeling so much better now she had John back. "I think the medicine the doctor gave me is working, I should be back to normal in no time."

Steph looked at John as she passed his tea to him.

"Thank you," he answered, not holding the mug by the handle.

Jess now remarked "I can't say enough about Steph she's taken such good care of me. Making me lovely drinks and meals, but she has to go today. She's a nurse," she smiled

"Yes, she told me that," John answered her briefly.

"I wouldn't be as well as I am, if it wasn't for her nursing powers," Jess smiled.

He had to be nice to this woman, because he had a feeling she was now thinking. 'Who the hell was he?' Turning he said. "Thank you for taking such good care of Jess. You needn't worry anymore, she's got me now."

'I bet she has!' Steph thought. Jess had explained to her that John had left his sister-in-law's house, because he'd had an awful row with her. Which did seem rather a weak story. Would you turn out on such a night as it was at the time? Still her friend didn't seem worried, she was just happy to have him there now. But the way they had met did seem strange, when she'd said to her friend after her stay with her, "be careful on your way home as you don't know who's about." And what did she do? She picked this man up, not knowing who he was and where he'd come from.

Stephanie noticed that the rain was very heavy outside and windy, but the snow had completely gone. She was pleased she had now met John and it had been good of him to have helped Jess push her car up the lane? But she did think he was a little forthright with his words? "Well ... I must admit you look so much better now," she said, smiling at Jess. "I was quite worried about you at one time, still as long as you're okay now, I will go."

"Thanks for all you've done for me Stephanie, I will be okay."

"Yes she'll be fine, you go," he added. Wondering why had Jess told this woman about him? After he asked her not to say anything. Ah well! It was out now, best not say anymore.

'Cheeky devil! He'd certainly got his feet under this table.' Stephanie thought. 'His appearance wasn't that good either. Still ...

Jess suddenly felt embarrassed by his bossy attitude. He'd taken it for granted that he was staying. Well she had hoped he would of course. But he shouldn't dismiss her friend like that, after all she'd been so good to her. "You saw your mother?" She asked him, changing the subject.

"Yes I did and she's fine, thank you."

"Well I am pleased to see you John and it's only been two days since you went," Jess told him.

Time to disappear. "Well I'll go now Steph told them, you sure you'll be alright?" That was a stupid question to ask, seeing the cosy situation between the two in front of her.

"Of course she will," he answered. "Now I'm here to look after her. Let me see you to the door."

'Well,' Stephanie thought, planting a kiss on her friends cheek, after that blunt remark. "Take care won't you?"

"I will," Jess told her friend.

He noticed a bag by the kitchen door. "Is this your shopping bag?" He asked the woman.

"Yes it is, it's alright I can manage," she told him. "Bye Jess see you soon."

"Okay and thanks Steph for all your help. And you'll be home before it's too late." Jess was trying to ease the situation.

"Yes you're right, I will, and I won't pick anybody up either. Ha! Ha!"

'Very funny,' he thought. 'Go!!'

Then she turned to John. "Look after her?"

"You can bet on it."

She took one last look at her friend smiling and blew her a kiss then she was gone.

"Jess," he bent down and as she looked up, he kissed her passionately. The beautiful person he had come to love, when all of a sudden the door burst open!!

"It's pouring with rain out there. Oh!!" Stephanie's mouth was wide open now, when she was confronted by the scene in front of her. "I'm terribly sorry to intrude." The woman began to back out of the door. "It's just that I forgot to say I will ring you every day, okay?" She told Jess who's arms were wrapped around this man. How embarrassing damn! She shouldn't have gone back. "Bye." She turned and hurried out of the door, as the two heard it shut!

"Oh dear we were well and truly caught then," he said laughing.

"It's not funny John. We hardly waited until she'd gone, heaven knows what she's thinking?" But Jess also laughed out loud, "poor Stephanie. We're awful John."

He looked at her. "Well she can see we are fond of one another. If she doesn't like it, that's just too … "

"JOHN!! That's a little hard after all she's done for me." Why did he say things like that? She began thinking, he had quite an aggressive streak at times and she wondered why?

He knew he'd said the wrong thing. "Jess I'm sorry." What an idiot he was. He'd gone too far on his accusations about her friend, whom he knew she was very fond of, "I do apologise. I can't think of anyone else when you're around, you know your very precious to me. Or didn't I ever tell you that?" He asked smiling.

"Well no not in so many words." She was staring straight into his face. "We hardly know each other, how can you say that?"

Showing his true feelings now he said. "I feel as though I've known you all my life." As he pulled her closer to him, never wanting to let her go. His knees were aching now through all the walking he had done, so bending down was hard, still he didn't care at that moment, as that was least of his problems as he then began wishing he'd known her first, because he was really in love for the first time, if that was possible? Also only knowing each other for a few days. It wasn't ever like this with Kate, she had never shown much affection, well to him anyway. Now he began to wonder what was going to happen in the next few months; would he be caught? Not if he could help it. The one thing he did know he was going to enjoy their time together. And he was going to try and be the best he could towards this lovely woman. When his gaze took in her face next to him, he asked, "Jess you look so pale are you alright?"

"Yes of course I am," she smiled, just not completely back to normal yet. "Stop worrying, in fact you know what I'm going to do?"

"No!"

"I'm going to make us a sandwich," and she began to get out of the chair.

"No you're not, I'm in charge, I promised your friend. Now you just tell me what you fancy?" He was saying now having got up and was sitting on the arm of the old chair.

"Cheese!"

126

"Okay that's a cheese sandwich, coming up." He was so happy.

"John what made you come back again so quickly?" She asked him.

He was staring at her now taking her hands in his. "I simply couldn't get you out of my mind Jess. So I walked and hitch hiked to get here. I know this is stupid, but I think I'm in love with you."

She looked into his eyes as she said, "Well I think I'm in love with you too, silly isn't it? As I hardly know you, so there's a lot that I want to know about you." She saw a look cross his face at that moment.

"Well there's not much to tell so we'll talk about that some other time shall we?"

"Yes of course, if you want?"

"One sandwich coming up." He had totally forgotten prison for the moment, until suddenly it all came flooding back. Everything was such a nightmare. All he wanted was a life for him and Jess. But he knew it was putting their relationship in a difficult position, because she wouldn't want him, if she knew his circumstances. No he had to keep as quiet as he could about his life. He was going to have to make more lies up. But thought Jess didn't deserve this and her having her child murdered by a vicious know nothing madman. There had been lots of those in inside. Then he thought that if he hadn't broken out of there in that dreadful snowstorm, he would never have met Jess. No he would have been serving his time for another two years probably. But he just felt he couldn't have stood it for much longer. Now he was out and had to try and get a life going here, if he could. This was where he felt safe, but how long was he able to keep it from Jess about his past he didn't know ...

Chapter 19

A few weeks on and snowdrops began to show their pretty heads, followed by primroses peeking through clumps of tufted grass. The two were so happy together. Jess had persuaded John to stay for however long and of course he wanted to and intended too. He loved it at the cottage and felt safe. She had told him she hoped this situation would go on forever.

He did too, well time would tell. Although in his mind he should have gone miles away, if he didn't want to be caught by the police. However Jess had come into his life and he was happy as could be. There were times when the thought of not being with her, would be like losing a limb. Their relationship blossomed over the weeks and their lives together was a happy one. He did wonder if they were still out there looking for him? When one day she'd rung the newsagent shop and ordered the mirror to arrive every day and a local paper once a week for him, she thought he would like this, as he hardly ever went anywhere. However, she was surprised that he wasn't bothered to have one really, so she cancelled the order. Thank goodness! Jess herself was always on her sewing machine altering things, so she didn't have time to read much herself so she wasn't bothered about a paper.

Then one day something good happened they acquired a lovely dog. It was a present from John well the truth is … he had found him on the moors, when he was taking a walk and there wasn't a soul around, the dog was lost so he brought him home. Jess loved the large Labrador, which was light brown in colour. John hoped that nobody would ever want him back because he and she had become quite fond of him. The dog took to his new name really well, they didn't know how old he was, perhaps two? There was no disk around his neck. So that's why they named him Stamper, putting their own mark on him. How certain things happened seemed unbelievable, because she didn't have many visitors, and indoors she'd had a smart metre box installed which did all the readings for the gas and electricity. She really had thought of everything not to be disturbed by anyone she didn't want, so no hassle. This was an unbelievable place he thought.

Jess would usually go to the town in her little car to get food for her and John which was fine, then one particular day she went to a sports shop and bought his jeans which he wanted, finding out his size first, that was from his mother's money he had told her. No lie. They had now become a couple. Whilst she did what she had to do John was busy doing this and that. He didn't mind being left to do whatever indoors and he was happiest at the cottage. 'Why don't you come to the shops with me John?' She'd asked him often.

However he always had an answer, then one sunny day he saw an advert in their local paper, which he asked Jess to get, that help was needed with a small furniture concern. At the time he wondered how small. He felt more confident in himself having filled many hours working in her garden, seeing to all the plants and also the vegetable garden, which gave them all they ever needed in produce. So he had no weight problem and looked fit and healthy. He loved this new life, still he had to ask Jess. "Could I borrow your car for a while?"

"Yes of course, but why?"

"Well I'm good with my hands as you know?" he smiled. And there's a job going I saw in your local paper the other day, good job you got it. As I feel I really need to earn a bit of money. So I want to go after it."

She was surprised and happy he was going to get involved with something he was interested in. "Look I know the place so I'll take you. It's wooded which if you don't know it is difficult to find. And you shouldn't be driving my car anyway. You really must sort your driving licence out," she told him. But as usual he went off that subject.

"I will, but for now thank you."

Well, he met a Mr Clive Hammond who thankfully, was impressed by his skills and hired him, to make bamboo chairs. John had excelled in prison making different things, so this job would be easy. Mr Hammond showed him how and that was it. The best of it was he would deliver the wood and then John would work in the little shed at the bottom of the garden. He couldn't work with Mr Hammond there wasn't enough room for both of them in his workshop, which he didn't want to do anyway, so it all worked out well. He took a chance going to him, but he had to do it as he needed the money which helped with his keep. The man lived three miles away. Mr Hammond needed help badly as he was getting a lot of orders for this particular furniture. Thank goodness he seemed to take to John from the beginning and so it was just the two of them. He always gave John cash so it was perfect once more, how lucky was he? However he didn't earn that much, but it helped, telling John at the beginning we'll see how you get on first and go from there. Which was perfect, and it suited the younger man. but he knew that he might not be able to stay with Mr Hammond for too long. Still for the time being he was elated.

Then one Monday morning Jess looked at him and said. "Let's go to the town John?"

"Sorry Jess, I can't. I have three more chairs to do, then there's the garden." He told her.

"You've always got an excuse haven't you? She smiled. Don't you like going out?"

"Of course I do, but at the moment there's too much to be done with the work from Mr Hammond. After all we do need the money don't we?"

She nodded but didn't pursue the conversation, because she knew it annoyed him, so Jess kept quiet. She had told him about her husband and how they were never really in love, when suddenly she began to feel she hadn't liked him very much at all, because he always blamed her for Becky's death too, which was a terrible thing to say to her. Then after Becky and he had died she began thinking, would there ever be a time she would meet anyone else, or even get involved with someone again? She had, John he made her feel especially good by his words of love towards her, over the last few months. But Jess got tired of hearing from her friend that she should find out more about him, whenever she was on the phone, this did unsettle her, he would tell her in his own time. Then there was John who didn't want to be in Stephanie's company either. In fact her friend had kept well away since the last time they had met and they hadn't seen her for some time. So she really wished that John and her friend would get along with each other. It was so important to her. She enjoyed her shopping time but she always had John on her mind, wishing now he had been there with her today. Anyway, it was one of those days that she was glad he wasn't in a way. She had decided to do something that she needed to do. And had time to herself now she was wondering what his reaction would be? Putting the groceries on the kitchen table, she shouted out. "John?" Finding him just finishing off painting all the doors in rich brown paint. He had certainly improved her home so much. All the jobs that had been piling up before her eyes, were now going down fast, thank goodness.

"Hello there, did you have a nice shopping trip?" He said as she entered the living -room.

"Yes fine." What would he say? she wondered. "John would you come into the kitchen for a minute?"

He could tell there was a problem, something was wrong. Had she found out, about him?

Chapter 20

Jess began to make a cup of tea, before telling him in no uncertain terms. "I'm two months pregnant!"

"What? No! No! You can't be."

"Why can't I be? I'm pregnant!"

"How do you know this?" he asked the excited woman in front of him.

"Because I went to the Doctor's this morning, and he confirmed what I had been thinking. I'm two months pregnant. A woman knows these things. Aren't you happy with my news darling?"

Happy; he was numb. "Yes" He loved her and wanted her to have his child but not yet. Not with a prison sentence hanging over his head. After all there would be. Doctors! Nurses! Hospitals! People! Stephanie!

Suddenly she threw her arms around his neck. "You don't look pleased. Say you're pleased." Her auburn hair hung loose on her shoulders and her cheeks were now bright pink, she was so happy.

"Jess, I am pleased but our situation is not good at the moment. we're not married, also I don't earn a lot of money and my job is probably only for a short time." "And now to top it all I'm going to be a father." (he hadn't bargained on this, a baby and him a jailbird!)

"Well we can rectify that can't we? She was saying. You could get a better job, then you would have more money, so that we could get married," she told him excitedly. By the look on his face, he didn't look happy, she suddenly began to feel depressed. This was what she'd always wanted since Becky was taken from her, that one day she would meet the man she really loved and they would have a child. Well that time had come, she loved John and she knew he loved her. So what was the problem? She sat in the chair and put her face in her hands, as tears began to fall.

"Don't upset yourself Jess. You know I'm pleased? We always said one day we hoped that we would have a child together. It's just that I thought it wouldn't be yet. But you know I'm thrilled to bits, whether it's the wrong time or not."

"Are you John? Are you really?" Her smile got bigger as she began thinking, she didn't know much about this person in front of her. Except that she loved him.

"Yes really!" He told her, laughing, as he watched the excitement build up on her face.

She leaned into him again pulling his beard playfully. "That's made me happy," she told him, planting a kiss on his cheek, before picking up her tea cup. Who would have thought that after a chance meeting, our relationship would go this far? Here's to you, me and our baby then. You know I never thought I'd be pregnant again, I'm so thrilled. But I will never forget Becky. No never."

John had to admit she looked a picture now. He loved this woman very much and realized over the last few weeks of being with her. She was all he ever wanted and now of course their baby, whom he would protect with his life. What life? He was an offender, a jailbird, who had broken out of prison, he was in hiding and the police were looking for him and now this, he had a son or daughter on the way, where would this end? His life was a total mess. Jess was now staring at him.

"Please don't worry John, it's not as bad as it seems. We'll manage."

"Course we will, somehow," he told her, kissing her soft beautiful lips. He had noticed how she looked so healthy these days which was good. But he had no idea that she was pregnant, their one passionate night together was the culprit. They should have been more careful.

"It was a lucky day when you came into my life on that dreadful evening. I love you John. I never thought I would say that again. Now I'm pregnant my life is complete"

He bowed his head. "But Jess you know nothing about me, only the little bit I told you. Don't you think we're living in a fool's paradise?"

"No I don't know a lot about you, but when you're ready you will tell me more, I'm sure. That will be when you can confide in me totally. So until then, I'm happy as long as your by my side. You know my first marriage wasn't a happy one.

Then I lost my little daughter Becky, which was the most horrific thing that can happen to a person. She was my life and I loved her dearly, if I could go back and still have her here with me, I would. Life is strange sometimes, because I would probably never have met you if it hadn't been for that awful snowy night. I have been thinking lately that she sent me to you. Is that silly to say that?"

"I don't think so." How deceitful he had now become, to this woman who he loved. Without her he wouldn't want to live. Should he leave her? No he couldn't, not with the baby coming along, his baby which he'd always wanted. What would be the outcome of all this?

She leaned into him, giving a long lingering kiss.
Later it led them to the bedroom again, where all this had begun the very first time they had met. Receiving a little passion and petting from her John, whom she loved and was pleased to give whatever he needed of her, as she now lay in his arms feeling very content, after their gentle love making.

He looked down at Jess as her auburn hair splayed over the white pillowcase as usual, staring at the contour of her body which was pressed against his, so much so he could hardly breath, they were now one. He knew from that moment on, that he would stay with Jess forever, if that was possible? Their actual sex life was so good, if only he could start his life all over again. She would have been his one and only love he knew that now, she meant everything to him, he'd never had this feeling before, this was bliss. His life was good now in every way, he was so lucky to have met Jess who was a wonderful human being, but it was just a little bit too late. He began to think what was he going to do? As she slept, he wondered how close the police were in catching him? Then for the moment he smiled when he thought about her coming home with jeans, t-shirt and other things for him to wear when she was in the town. She was trying to smarten him up. She loved buying clothes for him, apart from the money he gave her from his mother's money for the jeans. There were times when he would try to make it up to her from his wage packet, but she really didn't want it, as she had money saved she told him, but she was appreciative when he forced her to take it. Then there was a time when he bought a bath, toilet and sink from Mr Hammond who had taken it out of his own place, because he'd got a new one. Jess hadn't minded that they had his old bathroom set, which was far better than their own one, well anything was better than what she had. The best of it was, it only cost John £30 and between Mr Hammond and himself they'd managed to sort the baths out, up and down the stairs, after struggling to get them on and off his van first, which was difficult. Still the two men weren't going to disappoint Jess by not putting Mr Hammonds bath in.

Jess had been thrilled to bits at the time, to have a much better bath than the one she already had, avocado, a bit of an old-fashioned colour. She loved having the white one.

Clive Hammond never pried into their business asking questions, he guessed there was a problem, but it was nothing to do with him. Their business was their own, he was always friendly though. Anyway he also had his problems being parted from his wife and not wanting her to know where he was, as she would take every bit of money he had. The man wanted her off his back and when he could afford it, he would divorce her he'd told John. That's why he lived in a lonely spot, with only a farm nearby. He made his furniture and sold it to people in the district, after advertising in different shops using the name 'Flex Furniture' so his wife couldn't find him. She lived in the next town, which was quite a way away, she was always on his mind and he was afraid that he might bump into her at any time. Well he wasn't ready for that, not yet. He knew his wife would pester him for money and he didn't want her to get a penny of his. She was a nutty, vindictive person, who wanted all she could get. When he had enough money it was a divorce and then off to New Zealand to start a new life. Then if that happened John would have to look for something else, which he'd told him.

So John was lucky again, to meet this man who never asked any questions, as he had his own troubles. So making furniture for him suited John for the time being, of course he didn't intend to do it forever, and wouldn't stay longer than necessary. Still the other man seemed to want to talk to someone to tell his troubles too and John was it. Jess's car was handy at times for collecting and taking the furniture back, when it was made. He just managed to get two chairs in the car with the back down. But most of the time Clive would deliver and collect the bamboo furniture. Anyway that was John's life now. And Jess was such a decent person who deserved the best and that was what he was going to try and give her, the best, but it would be difficult.

Jess was stirring with a contented look on her face. She saw he was awake and she stared at him. "What would you like John? A girl? Or boy?"

"A girl just like you," he smiled.

"I'll see what I can do then," she laughed happily. Thinking now that John seemed to be getting used to the forthcoming event. When she suddenly told him, it will be like when I had Becky in this house. I never thought this would ever happen to me again."

John squeezed her hand "Don't worry Jess everything will be fine, I promise you nobody will ever touch our child. I'd kill them first!"

Jess sat up and looked at him, his face was so hard for the minute, this was a side she had never noticed before.

"JOHN! I wouldn't want you to do that. Still I promise you it won't happen again because I shall watch our baby all the time. Don't say things like that, it frightens me, with such talk."

He was hoping she hadn't seen the bad side of him at that moment. Too late she had! "Sorry Jess, my temper got the better of me again."

"John you looked like thunder then and hearing the anger in your voice frightened me for the first time." She'd never seen him so angry like this before, the lines in his face had become more prominent too.

"I didn't mean to frighten you, but knowing what you've been through and losing your daughter and all. That violent person made me see red, forgive me." He then took Jess's hand in his.

She turned to him. "It's sick to think of murderers, or paedophiles, are walking around on this earth who are so dangerous and violent. When caught they should be locked up and the key thrown away. Mind you this man that killed Becky had a disturbed mind," she told him. "John are you alright?"

"Yes Jess I'm alright. But I must go downstairs and let Stamper out in the garden he's barking," however he was now wondering what she would do, if she ever found out about him? She didn't deserve all this. How was he going to be able to hide his past from her for ever? If she did find out the truth his life would be over. He now had a good woman and a child coming into the world. Soon he would have everything he'd ever wanted. He would dearly have loved to marry Jess but he knew that couldn't be yet. If ever!

"I'm getting up too now," She leaned over towards him, before he made a move. "Would you like a cup of tea John Turner?"

"Yes I would thank you Jess Sinclair." They had one of those moments where they both roared with laughter.

"I'd better put a drop of brandy in your cup. It might make you feel better."

"I doubt it," he actually laughed at that comment. Every day he'd tried to put what he'd done behind him, but it was difficult. Everything seemed quiet where he was concerned, but he knew the police and other people would still be looking for him which did put him on edge. Jess's television had something wrong with it he knew. So one day he decided to see if he could get it going, when she was out. He had a feeling it might be a fuse, he found another one in the work box and put it in and bingo the television worked, but he wouldn't tell her not yet. When he felt it might be safe for him, he would put the fuse back in. The thought that they might mention an escaped prisoner on the television petrified him, he would lose everything in a minute. Especially if they put his picture on the screen that would be a nightmare for him. It was two months on now, the police must have made searches, but thankfully had never come up to the cottage and he hoped that they never would. Also they couldn't have put any photo's of him in the local paper, so that was good, because he was sure had they done, the phone would have been ringing with Stephanie on the line.

Life was marvellous here and working for Clive and earning money was great, because he paid him cash in hand. Again, he was so happy, like never before, and spent hours in Jess's shed, making these bamboo chairs which he loved doing and seeing the finished item. His boss seemed very pleased with his work. But John's favourite time of day was walking across the fells occasionally with Jess and Stamper, nobody ever seemed to be looking for the dog. At one point Jess thought they should take him to the dogs rescue home, as somebody might be looking for him, but they never did. As the two got so fond of him and he seemed quite happy with them. Jess loved the animal, but would never go walking over the moors in the direction where Becky was killed, it brought too many terrible memories back to her.

Chapter 21

Then one idyllic Sunday afternoon in late May, when all seemed right with the world and Jess was sitting on her lounger under the huge apple tree, in a large floppy hat and loose-fitting colourful dress. John was now staring at her from a distance, when he saw her eyes gently close, she looked so content and lovely, pregnancy suited her. He loved her so much it hurt, he couldn't have been happier and knew she was too. It was the perfect summer's day, but very hot. He had some spare time, so he was sorting their little allotment out. The lettuces, onions, tomatoes and most other things were coming through well.

When suddenly Jess opened her eyes to the sound of a car hitting the loose shingle on the drive. John also heard the noise as he looked up with panic in his eyes.

"Who's that?" he shouted across to her, feeling very tense now, as it was unusual to hear that this wasn't a walker. This time it was definitely a person in a car who had probably lost their way, he began thinking.

"I don't know, I'll go and see shall I?" She said, struggling to get up from her chair.

"No you stay there I'll go," he told her nervously.

"If it's anybody selling heather we don't want it. We have enough luck," she laughed.

"He wished! Okay I'll do that." Hurrying to the small back gate, he was now apprehensive, at what might confront him. It wasn't the police, however.

"Hello there!"

John jumped!

"Frightened you, did I?" She said peeping round the large bush.

Relieved, he said, "Oh it's you Stephanie!"

"Well don't look so surprised, I won't bite," she laughed. Wondering why John had looked so alarmed.

He began to relax a little now, she had probably come to see how Jess was. Having been surprised when she had heard about the pregnancy situation. But he had to admit he also thought it rather too soon to have this happen, still it had and that was that. Looking at the woman he began thinking he and Jess didn't need anyone to join them today, they were quite happy on their own, in their blissful surroundings. But for once he was glad it was her friend and not the police, still he had to be careful what he said to her.

Then it just happened, as he asked. "What are you doing here?" rather curtly without a smile which would have helped. Suddenly realising he'd said that wrongly.

She sighed (arrogant devil.) "I was in the area and decided to pay you a visit, because there's something I want to ask you both."

"Oh what?"

"I'll tell you in a minute. Where's Jess?"

"In the garden under the apple tree."

She pushed past him, holding the gate for John and the dog to come through, then turned her back and walked towards her friend.

"Thanks!" (Bitch!) This woman irritated him.

"Your welcome." (Cocky!) "Ah there she is. Hi Jess!"

"Hello Steph! What a surprise, come and sit down," she told her. Patting the deckchair beside her.

"Sunning yourselves are you on this lovely May afternoon?" Stephanie smiled.

"Well it is rather warm for me, but thankfully sitting here in the shade is perfect," Jess told her, "and I'd rather this than the rain and snow. I'm hoping there are many more sunny days to come. You know you made my John jump when you arrived."

"Did I? Sorry! Who did you think it was?"

He thought he'd better lighten up. "The bogie man," he smiled at her.

"You are funny John." Jess laughed.

"So what are you frightened of John?" asked Stephanie.

"Wouldn't you like to know?" He told her in no uncertain terms.

Jess couldn't make out why her friend irritated him so much. But what she said next, threw John completely.

"I didn't want to say anything Jess but, I feel you ought to know. A convict has escaped from the prison." She noticed

John wasn't smiling now. He definitely wasn't pleased to see her today she could tell that.

"Oh no." Jess stared at her friend, as she sat up more in her chair.

Johns hand went up to his dripping forehead, wiping the sweat from it. He didn't want to hear this. "What a sweltering hot day it is. That digging has made me so hot," he told them forcing a smile, as they both stared at him. His hands were soaking wet now and he was wondering who had managed to get away this time. "So when did this prisoner escape?" he asked Stephanie, sounding light hearted as he composed himself.

"Didn't you see it in your paper this morning?" The woman was saying to them.

"No!" Jess said quietly, "we don't have paper's do we John?"

"No if we want one Jess buys it in town, but we haven't been anywhere today to get one."

"Oh I could have brought one up for you if I'd known. It's in all the papers, in actual fact there's two now. Apparently, they haven't caught the other one yet, they must be getting a bit lax at that prison."

John didn't want to hear this.

"Well don't let's talk about convicts," Jess told the two, "it really frightens me!"

"Don't worry Jess you have John to protect you now," her friend told her as she looked straight at him. But then she suddenly felt uneasy, he seemed to have that effect on her. She just couldn't make out why Jess had fallen for this individual in the first place? But she had to admit he was very good to her friend and was very protective towards her. Also he was quite a looker and the two seemed really happy together, so that was the main thing, after all Jess had been through so much over the years, losing her little daughter to that maniac man. And on this lovely day she'd told her this piece of news, she shouldn't have done that and was cross with herself. Stephanie knew Jess was so looking forward to her forthcoming baby and she didn't want to put a downer on it because she looked so happy Anyway that was fine by her and she could suffer Johns innuendos. When she heard…

"Jess doesn't really want to hear this at the moment Stephanie, with what happened to her daughter."

"Of course not, sorry Jess I didn't mean to frighten you." She told her. "Just thought you ought to be on your guard after what happened in the past."

"Now what are you really doing here?" Jess asked, "it wasn't just to tell us about the convict was it? Anyway I thought you would be at work today?"

"Well I should have been, but I took the afternoon off, part of my holiday, because there was something that I wanted to ask you both? I've decided as the weather is so good I would have a barbecue this coming Saturday and I want you both to be there."

She had to get back in John's good books, "I thought you never go out and this would be a change for you both, please say you'll come?" I know it's short notice.

"You're not holding this barbecue just for us are you Steph?" Jess asked.

"No silly, I'm hoping there will be about ten of us altogether, that's if they can all make it." She stared at the man in front of her but he didn't seem that pleased with her invite.

This situation was not good, there might be people who might recognise him even though his entire look was different. They just might have seen his photo somewhere; blow, he was so enjoying his new life now. As he began to stare at Jess noticing her cheeks were glowing with excitement, she wanted to go to this barbecue, he could tell by her face.

"Can we go?" She asked him, it would make such a change for us. She noticed he didn't look to happy but suddenly he smiled.

"You want to go? Then we'll go." He had to, after all it wouldn't look right if he said no, we're not going!

"Stephanie had gone quiet, as she watched the two discuss the evening. When she suddenly burst out. Right then that's six I can cross off my list."

"Are these people going to your barbecue, locals?" John asked casually.

"Well my two friends Jan and Rick come from around my way. He's a doctor like Nathan, and at the hospital and she's a nurse like me," she hurriedly told him. "Except she's on casualty and I'm on maternity, suddenly saying. So how are you Jess? And how's that little one?" She pointed?

"Wonderful," Jess told her friend, as she reached out and grabbed Johns hand, squeezing it with tenderness.

"Yes, she's fine now," he answered, "but she had a lot of sickness at the beginning." He did wish he could get out of this barbecue situation, but, Jess looked so excited by the invite, he couldn't disappoint her by not going.

"Well I'm thrilled you can come, hopefully the weather will be kind to us on the day and that it doesn't rain. Nat has worked hard to get it nice for the barbecue. Hopefully little mother to be can sit and relax and enjoy the evening." She smiled, squeezing her friend's arm.

"I'm nearly three months pregnant not nine."

Well it was a good moment when all three laughed out loud, with that remark.

He knew about one couple now hoping they didn't know about him. So at the moment it seemed quite safe. "Who else is coming to this barbecue?" he asked. Stephanie.

"Oh Amanda and Howard are not from around here. Well they used to be, but when they got married they moved to Cornwall and have lived there for five years now, anyway they happened to be coming to see me for the weekend. She works as a nursery nurse and he is an estate agent. So I thought, what can I do to entertain them and that's when I decided on a barbecue. Then there's Andy and Jill they live in the village, we've been friends since we were at school together. He's an IT person and my friend works as a hairdresser. Oh then there's my partner Nathaniel he's a Doctor."

"What?" Asked John smiling.

"Don't you start?" She laughed. "He's always having his leg pulled, about his name. No, most people call him Nat. Me included."

"John you're horrible smiled Jess. Nathaniel is very nice. You know it's funny you haven't visited us since John arrived all those weeks ago Steph."

"No! No! I haven't," she had thought at the time that Nat wouldn't like John very much. So she made excuses for him. "Well I am sorry, but I've been so busy at the hospital. Nat is usually working on in the evening and it's been too late for us to pay you a visit, by the time we get ready. Also it's quite a way that we have to come to visit you. But I know you'll like him, when you meet him, at the barbecue John."

"He certainly will," Jess told her.

"So we look forward to seeing you both on Saturday and you now know whose coming. Ok? I must say you look really well Jess, John is definitely taking good care of you."

"He certainly is. I am so lucky that he came into my life on that snowy night. We were destined to meet, weren't we John?"

"We were," he answered quietly. "It pleases me that Jess is happy, because that's what she deserves and when our baby comes along I hope we live happily ever after. The three of us." He momentarily felt wicked to think he could tell all these lie's to Jess and Stephanie, he was getting in deeper and deeper. They would hate him, if they ever found out about his past.

"You do say such nice things," Jess told him. Now who's for a nice cup of tea? Here in the garden, it's such a beautiful day." She began to get up out of the chair.

"You sit still and have a chat with Stephanie while I go and make the tea," he told her. Wanting to get away from her friend.

"Can I help?" Stephanie asked hm.

"No its alright I can manage. Thank you!"

"There's some cream biscuits in the tin." Jess shouted to him.

He waved his hand in the air.

"He's settled well here hasn't he?" Stephanie remarked.

"Yes he has, it was the best thing that ever happened to me when I met John. Peculiar really, it was as though I was meant to meet him."

Her friend was in deep thought now as she looked over towards the kitchen door.

Dare she? "Jess you don't know anything about John do you?"

"Well I know he walked out on a very difficult situation where he lived. His sister-in-law sounds a dreadful person, who was always arguing with him it was a terrible life for him. He couldn't stand her snide remarks all the time, I think the last row was the last straw for him. Why are you querying everything Stephanie? I love him and that's all that matters. He's good to me and I'm having his child, which we're both so thrilled about." In the next breath she said, "you don't like him do you?"

"He's ok, but we seem to rub each other up the wrong way. I'm just worried about you Jess, that's all. You've had such a lot of knocks in your life, I just want you to be happy."

"I am! I am!" But she felt a little agitated now as she saw John heading towards them both with a tray. "He's coming, no more doubts Steph, I'm very happy, let's enjoy the day shall we?"

Stephanie nodded she wasn't going to get anywhere with Jess on this John subject!!

"Alright darling did you find everything?"

He smiled, "Even the cream biscuits," he told her. Putting the tray down on the small wicker table, before turning to sit on the grass.

"Good, thank you my lovely man," Jess grinned. The rest of the afternoon went off swimmingly. He, holding her hand as they laughed at funny things the three had done at times over the years. What about when you tripped John whilst painting the living room and nearly dropped the whole can of primrose paint all over the floor. (Not funny at the time.) He had a job to stop himself from sliding." She laughed.

He felt a little easier now because he wasn't so worried about meeting Stephanie's friends. But didn't think anyone would know who he really was after all.

Thinking about the birth of the baby. Stephanie told him: "Remember you have to keep calm and get Jess to hospital, as soon as she thinks she should go John. I do hope I'm on the ward that night." She said.

He hoped not!!

145

"Yes so do I," her friend answered.

"Well I really must go now. Would you believe Nat said he would try and get home early to take me out tonight, for a meal? His early is not mine, once I'm ready I want to go. I suppose that's unusual but being a nurse I am rather disciplined as you can't keep these babies waiting, but he also has to move fast at times when an operation is needed. It's funny but it's usually the man waiting for the lady. We haven't been out together in months in a way just like you two. John never takes you out, does he Jess?" Why did she say that? She knew at that moment she'd gone too far, the man in front of her wasn't looking very pleased, with her remarks.

Jess got in quick. "No you're right we don't go out much, but we're quite happy to stay at home as long as we're together. Still we both look forward to the barbecue, it will make such a change. Won't it John?"

"Yes! Yes! It will, I can't wait," blast why did he say that? Jess was now staring at him again. He'd got to cover that remark up as it sounded rather cynical. "No seriously, thank you for the invite." Saved!

"Yes thank you again Steph, look forward to it." Jess told her, but was looking at him now, wondering why he was always so curt with her dearest friend? "See you Saturday."

"Right shall we say 7 30." Stephanie wanted to get away before she put her foot in it again, as he also seemed to do as well. Rubbing her up the wrong way.

"You bet," Jess took Johns hand and squeezed it, "would you see Steph off for me please darling?" Noticing he was looking much happier now.

"Yes of course," he told her, the sooner the better, he did not like this woman around, even though she was so good to Jess. She was far too inquisitive for his liking. Well he'd have his chair back again.

After their goodbyes Stephanie hugged Jess before following John along the cobbled path, as he seemed to increase his step, but stopped at the gate, to let her through. Stamper was at his heel as always. Walking towards her car she turned to him. "See you John."

"Yes, see you," he replied politely, he was trying.

146

Jess was feeling so happy that Steph and John were talking she noticed from her deckchair. Then other thoughts came to her mind, when she could never understand why he always wanted to stay at home, but hoped one day he would come out of his shell. Anyway this party was a start. It would do them both good to go out and mix with new people, before the baby came on the scene.

Stephanie was now shouting out through her window. "Bye!" As she pulled away in her little Mini car. "See you Saturday." She was now wishing it would just be her friend coming! What was the matter with Jess? She seemed to be besotted with this man. But she had to admit they did look as though they were in love and as long as John was good to Jess that was all that mattered. He did treat her well. She'd enjoyed sitting in the garden with unfortunately the two on this beautiful sunny day. When she suddenly felt awful because he had made the tea and brought it out to them. So yes it had been quite relaxing afternoon, but would have been better if he hadn't been there though. Anyway time for a spot of music she thought turning her car radio on.

He waved and began to walk back into the garden with Stamper who hadn't left his side so he bent down and stroked him. Looking up towards Jess now he noticed she had her earphones on.

Chapter 22

"They're still talking about those escapes," she told him as he joined her. "It puts me on edge, when I hear things like that." She reached up to take the earphones off .

"You know I will not let anybody hurt you Jess."

"Oh thank you, I do feel so safe with you around. She put the radio onto another station as Frank Sinatra belted out. *I Did It My Way*. I love this one," she smiled, holding the ear piece out so that John could hear.

He strained to listen. "Me too," even though he hadn't heard much music in the last few years. John was now very worried that Stephanie and Jess would have a fit if they knew he was one of the prisoners. But who was the man that had escaped from prison? Also how did he get away? He began wondering, as he looked at the dog who had settled down on the grass again quite contented and wished he was without a care in the world like Stamper.

"Okay boy?" he said, as the animal licked his hand.

"You alright John?" She asked pulling her earphones from her ears, as she noticed he looked pensive.

"Yes. I was just thinking how your friend is so looking forward to her barbecue on Saturday."

"She is, it's probably because she hasn't done anything like this for ages."

He had to try and be nice, about her friend.

"I wish you could get on better with her John. She's really lovely when you get to know her."

"I'm trying! I'm trying! but she comes out with things that really irritate me. Anyway let's forget her for now and go indoors you've had enough heat for today and so have I," he smiled, as he helped Jess out of her deckchair before taking her arm and walking towards the house.

She did love him, she thought, with all his awkward ways. It was the day before the party, when she was pottering about in the kitchen she asked him. "Would you mind picking the cleaning up for me in town? As you know I took my dress in on

Wednesday and they told me it would be ready today. I'm hoping that it's cleaned well. After making all those alterations on my machine I don't know if I've done them right? If so, I can wear it tomorrow for the barbecue. I can't wait to see if it fits, because I'm sure you've noticed I've put a little bit of weight on?" She smiled. And was now wondering whether he would say. You go? But he knew she really wanted to stay home and do some baking.

What could he do, or say? He was taken aback for the minute. "Of course I will," he told her. However he didn't fancy going into town and would have to be on the alert because of the CCTV cameras. Not that he went to the shops much at all, but on one occasion, he was alert and aware when he'd been into the town on his own. It was when Jess needed some shampoo and hand cream, at the time. John would do anything for her, but he always imagined that somebody wherever would spot him, but they didn't. Still he had to take a chance and do this for Jess again. She needed that dress so he would be very careful, well the cleaners was on the outskirts of the town, so that was good. He really shouldn't drive the car though because he didn't have a valid licence yet. Jess was always telling him to get one, but he passed the question over. So he didn't drive if he could help it.

"Thank you darling and she kissed him on the cheek. I do hope I won't look like a bloated fish in it?"

"Of course you won't, you'll look lovely I'm sure."

"How sweet of you to say that, but I am nearly three months pregnant now."

"Yes that time has flown, but I think you will look beautiful. Anyway to look good doesn't matter really, it's what's inside the person that matters, and you have a good heart Jess. As I've said before," he reassured her.

"You are kind for saying that. I can't believe you at times as there's this wonderful caring person, then all of a sudden your character changes and you become rather bitter."

John looked into her face. "I'm sorry I'm like that, I suppose it stems from my childhood when my father used to be stern with me, but I'm harmless." He then felt terrible for saying that as the man had been the perfect father.

"I know you are, now here's the ticket she said, explaining where the dry cleaners was. So go on I've got things to do. My keys are on the sideboard there, see you later." When all of a sudden she thought and be careful because you shouldn't be driving my car and I could be in trouble for letting you do it."

"Alright I will and I promise you I'll sort that out sometime, so you're not to worry. Now don't you over do it," he told her walking out the door.

"Of course I won't silly." She blew him a kiss from the doorway.

He reciprocated. What a mess he was in and how much longer could this situation go on for? He couldn't keep fobbing Jess off about everything, he shook his head not knowing how far this was going to go, nearly all the words he uttered were lies. John really didn't like himself very much. Anyway he had to concentrate now because he didn't want to be caught by the police or whoever? He decided to get the dress quickly from the cleaners, and scarper out of town. Being confident that it would be difficult to recognise him now. Well that was thanks to Jess, without her realising what it was all about, seeing to his present look with his say so, of course, which was good. Firstly she hadn't wanted his beard to go, because she liked the mixture of black and grey peeping through, his hair was also the same colour now anyway she cut it slightly, which made it look neater and told him that he looked quite handsome in a rugged sort of way; with that they had both laughed. "Thank you," he'd said. Also now he was wearing smarter clothes, thanks to her.

She also bought him a nice pair of trousers. He always made an excuse though not to go out to the men's wear shop himself. But she didn't seem to mind doing his clothes shopping though that was until she said, 'you will do this yourself one day." Needless to say he did pay his way for most of the items from his wages now. So he felt as good as anybody else. Reaching his destination now he parked the car in Drakes Road car park. Trees surrounded the area, which led to a park with a very large pond, which he noticed through the trees. So he was quite happy where he was and pleased the cleaners was on the outside of the town, and thankfully there weren't many cars about, just mainly people in the park. How wonderful this was to not be in prison? But enjoying life with a lovely woman and looking forward to their baby being born.

It was a beautiful day and he began to appreciate all he had. Now as he opened the door to the cleaners the bell began to jingle, such a lovely sound he thought. Walking to the counter he handed the woman the ticket. A few minutes later he had the dress on his arm keeping his head down until he got to the door again. As different people pushed past him, he just wanted to get out of there and back to his car, where he felt safe, just in case he might be recognised. Looking down through the clear wrapping now he hoped the dress had cleaned well for Jess? But he knew she would look lovely in it, with the bright orange and brown flowers on it. It would complement her auburn hair. He was looking forward to seeing her wearing it. As he went towards his car, he noticed a little secluded seat tucked in amongst the trees, so on the spur of the moment he went over and sat down intending to stay only a few minutes, enjoying this fantastic day, he felt so happy. Of course he was able to walk round the pen at the prison, but it was nothing like this. Children were having such fun on the swings and slide that would probably be his son or daughter doing the same in the future. Would he ever get to that situation, where his child would be on a swing and he would be pushing it? As he then gazed across the pond, which was gleaming in the sunshine, Jake began to feel quite relaxed sitting there. That was until suddenly, he felt a hand being placed on his shoulder!

Chapter 23

"OH NO!! That was it, they'd got him!! Why had he not been more vigilant? He'd relaxed a little bit too much and had not seen anyone creeping up to the side of him. He must have been in a trance? What with all the different things that were happening in the park, happy people walking along, children chatting as they sailed their boats on the lake. An ice-cream man making up wonderful cornets. Stupid me! Jess it's over, he began thinking. It must be the constabulary. If only he'd not come to the district for the dress today.

Turning round slowly, he thought it must be the law who would confront him. This was it, he shouldn't have stopped here that's for sure, but it wasn't them, it was someone much worse LUKE STAMFORD!! He got caught, when Jake managed to get away from the prison, this man was unfortunately his partner in crime. The criminal who he thought was safely in prison. He stared at the person in front of him now, sweat breaking out onto his brow. That voice was a terrible sound from the past.

"What are you doing here? Where did you come from? He couldn't stop ... And how did you recognise me?"

"JAKE FARRENDON? I have to say you do look different but I would know you anywhere even with that beard and hair, but you look pretty good and quite fit from what I can see, also I like that tan you have. He was smiling that sinister smile he always had in prison (nothing changed there.) It's almost three months now since you've been on the run, so where have you been hiding I'd like to know?"

Jake looked round as an elderly couple past by with presumably their grandchild giving the two men a look.

"Keep your voice down," Jake told him. He had to get away from here he thought, staring at the man in front of him, they must look like the odd couple. The bearded man with a dress on his arm and the worried look and the scruffy looking individual next to him. "I can't believe this, he was saying. Let's go over there near those trees, where we won't be so noticeable," he told Luke, folding the dress again as he walked quickly to the secluded spot, where they would be able to speak more easily. How the hell did he get out of prison? He was wondering now. This unpleasant looking individual before him, came back like a nightmare. He noticed now that he had a very bad limp. Which he didn't have before. Jake would like to swipe his smug face which was smirking now. His black hair flattened to his head was thick with grease but the one thing that put him on edge and had before, was his scary eyes, which stared right through you, they seemed to look more prominent now. The scar on his forehead was slightly covered with that awful lank hair.

"I bet you didn't think I'd break out again from the prison did you? Well not after that last failed attempt?"

"As it happened I heard someone had, but didn't know it was you?" Jake informed him shaking.

"Don't forget we were both supposed to escape from prison on that unforgettable day, but all my planning went to pot for me, when I couldn't release my chains with the cutters, which had gone blunt. So I threw them over the road into some bushes which went down into a well and I heard the plop. But being big didn't help I twisted my leg that day and I've done some damage which hasn't repaired, so I have to live with it. Those heavy chains were a nightmare for me." He sneered, "but not for you. Anyway the doctor at the prison said I could have it operated on. I told them to stuff that idea. But you were the lucky one, cutting your chains off quickly. We made one big mistake, overlooking that the cutters would go blunt. That's because they were heavy chains and the cutters weren't that big to deal with that. Still I just managed to loosen one of mine pulling my leg out from the chain, but it was too late then. Those two sodding officers brought me down. And you had scarpered. Anyway did you wait for me in the wood as we planned?"

"Yes! Yes!" Jake lied! "But when you didn't come I got out from my hiding place and made a spurt for it."

"You're a liar Jake Farrendon," he said, getting closer to him. "Because two of the warders said when they came back, there was no sign of you."

153

"Well good job we had that snow, as far as I'm concerned."
The other man was now staring straight at me, I had to be
careful what I said. "Err …well I was hiding in the bushes."

"The warders said they saw your footsteps in the snow,
nearly up to the roadway and then because of the snow it
covered some of your tracks. You must have moved very
quickly and deviated into the wood? So tell the bloody truth
will ya?" He moved closer to Jake breathing heavily on him.

"Ok! Ok!" Jake said feeling a little nervous of this inmate. "I
couldn't hang around when I looked back, I saw you were
having difficulty with those chains. I had to move or else I
would have been caught too and all our planning of escaping
would have been for nothing. Rather one escape than none."

The big man had calmed down now. Noticing the cleaned
dress in the flimsy plastic. "Who's is that then?"

"None of your business," Jake told him.

"Got a woman have we? So where have you been hiding her
then?"

"That's my business," Not wanting Jess involved, if he
could help it. "Anyway how did you get away? Those officers
must be slacking in their job?"

"They must be, to let you go for a start." Luke said
smirking. "Well it was quite easy for me. They let me work in
the library after a lot of consulting with one another. They
thought it might improve my mind. That was a load of shit! I
don't think you could improve me. HA! HA! Well one day one
of the inmates had a fit in there, it was pandemonium for a time.
The warders were all busy with this new inmate Eddie Finch
who was also a diabetic. So whilst they were attending to him
and not looking my way, I quickly went into the office and
found the keys from one of their jackets hanging up, took them
and then literally walked out. The warder on the gate had just
gone for his break and the next one was due any minute. So I
unlocked the door and threw the keys onto the desk, because
the library was next to the outside gate. It was more difficult for
me being big though, as I don't move so quickly either,
especially with a gammy leg now."

He wiped his nose on his cuff before carrying on: "I wasn't
sure what I was going to do as it was difficult for me to hide

with my large frame, I do tend to stand out in a crowd. But my mind was made up for me, when a lorry came past with rubbish bins on board from the prison. It goes slowly through the grounds to the small lanes and so whilst the men were busy and weren't looking, I hid in the bushes and then jumped on the back. When they started up thankfully, there was only two stops as we went round the lanes. I was out!! (Plus the snow had gone, it had played its part, well for you anyway.) Funny the two men in front must have been chatting so much, because the man that was driving never saw me in his mirror hanging on for grim death. Then before the main road came up, I jumped off, and I've been walking ever since, and I ended up in this town. I've had to keep my head down though. I wouldn't have come here, but I was so hungry I had £3.00 I'd saved from the allowance they give you from the prison. So I bought a meat pie. Then I saw this wood and thought I would hide in here for a while and eat it, when I spotted you sitting there," he pointed. "Now come on Jake tell me where you're living? Out with it?"

Jake was now very worried by this situation. "It's not Jake now, it's John."

"Oh, oh ... John eh? Well I have to say you've been clever not having been caught yet. So how do you like being out?"

Staring at this horrible person in front of me, I began thinking. What had ever possessed me to get involved with him? But of course I knew, his idea had been good for getting out of that dreadful prison. So I just had to tolerate him. "It's great and I don't intend to get caught. So I'd be pleased if you would leave me and go somewhere else. After all we don't want to end up back in prison do we?"

He had to keep this man sweet, as he really didn't want to get involved with him again, knowing he could be dangerous. As he also began thinking it must be getting late and Jess would be wondering where he was. "I must go now," he said, turning.

"Hold on, you're not going anywhere, because I'm going to need some help."

"Why should I help you?" John asked in a nervous tone. He didn't need this everything had been so good these last few months. I'm sorry but you have to do your own thing, just like

I've had too. I really must go now goodbye" …And he began to walk away when Luke grabbed him.

"I think the prison authorities would like to know where you are."

"You wouldn't?"

"Try me? All it takes is one phone call to the police."

Jake was frightened now of what he might do. He really didn't want to have an altercation with him here in the park.

"I have a new life now and I like it, but of course I don't know how long it will last, still I'm going to see that it does. So leave me alone and get out of my way."

The burly man stood in front of his path, grabbing his coat for a second time. "You needn't think you are going to get away from me now?"

As Jake was pushed heavily to the ground the dress fell from his arm, into a heap at his feet, he struggled to get up. Luke was strong when provoked, as he knew from their time in prison. Thank goodness they couldn't be seen from the park, being on the edge of the wood. There weren't many people about, only the ones that were engrossed with their children, feeding the swans on the lake nearby. How was he to get away from this man?

Suddenly looking down on the ground he saw a thick stick. Jake bent down to pick it up. Luke pushed him again and that was it. Wham! He landed the man with a hard blow to his body, surprised Luke fell to the ground. With that Jake picked up the dress turned on his heel and walked briskly from the wood, before the man could lay a hand on him again. He didn't need all this, he thought, his legs beginning to give out on him, so he decided to slow down, not to give any heed. And walked across the car park to his car, feeling relieved that Stamford wasn't behind him. Well he couldn't see him if he was.

The sweat began to pour down his face, and he looked dishevelled he realised. As the public walked to their cars they began to stare at him, he was sure they could see the frightened look on his face, but Jake paid no attention to them. He was more intent on getting out of this car park. At that moment he reached into his pocket for his key to the car, hurriedly opening the door and throwing the cleaning onto the passenger seat, as he got in relieved. The dress looked ok thank goodness after accidentally dropping it on the ground, when he had the fight with Luke, he was pleased it was covered with the plastic protector. He was now hoping the car would start first time, only it did have a tendency to play up but this is one time he hoped it wouldn't happen. He had to get away from here quick.

Turning the key it choked into life. 'Thank you God,' he said under his breath, as he steered the car away from the car park. What had gone on in the last hour he could have done without. He tried to steady his hands as he thought of what had happened. How could he have hit this man with this heavy stick? It wasn't like him, but he'd had to defend himself. The other man would only have been dazed, he was tough. However he had to hurry. He couldn't see Luke anywhere around now. His life had been so good, over these last few months with Jess. He didn't need all this aggro.

If only Luke hadn't come into the town today and they hadn't bumped into each other? Why had he ever got involved with him? It was only that the escape seemed possible with his plan, but after all he'd concealed the cutters and got them out of the building, of course to his advantage, but he couldn't forget it had been Luke's idea. Tough! No way did he want him as a friend. He knew he could be dangerous, even though he didn't know what deed he'd committed, but had heard from one of the prisoners that they thought he'd killed somebody, Jake was only using him to get out of the prison that's all, he hated the very ground the man walked on and was never going to stay with him, once out of that awful place. Which he'd done up until now. Nobody argued with Luke, when he was over there side in prison, Ginger and Mack were sort of friendly with him because they got him drugs and cigarettes, he thought from a repair man that came in. Luke was dangerous! Jake didn't have these attributes he wasn't that sort of person. There really was nothing brutal in him, only when provoked, like he was just now in the wood.

It was just so weird that Luke took to Jake, the young fellow thought, not realising that the man had an ulterior motive as it came about later. What he was to do, with the (cutters.) And not being frisked properly before going out thanks to George Trent.

157

Most prisoners must have been pleased when Luke was caught and taken back to the prison after trying to escape. He had helped Jake with his breakout yes, never thinking he would be caught. Having planned everything. So now it was Jake's turn he supposed to help this awful person, this was all getting out of hand. Still perhaps he wouldn't see him ever again after this altercation. when all of a sudden he began to feel a little easier.

Reaching the lane all he could now think of was Jess, as the car carried on over rough ground and tight bends up to the cottage. What would this sweet woman whom he had deceived, think of all of this? She wouldn't want him he knew. She was too caring and straight herself. He had to keep all his terrible life from her. Why did this happen on such a beautiful sunny day? Drawing nearer to the cottage he saw Jess dead heading some roses. This was what he'd always wanted, contentment, but now in a short time his life had become so complicated. Pulling up in the car he sighed before steadily getting out, feeling shattered at that moment and probably looking a mess, he had brushed himself down though and combed his hair, he hoped he looked okay?

She turned round quickly when hearing the car and the gate opening and shutting. "Oh!" She yelled, as he made his way towards her.

"What's the matter?" He called out, going quickly across to where she was. The dress which had been through hell like him, was over his arm.

"Oh it's nothing I just pricked my finger on these darn roses she pointed." Staring at him!

"Let me see? He took her hand and put her finger in his mouth sucking the blood away. There! You'll live, he smiled, at her. Not noticing the look from her. Let's go indoors and put some Dettol on it, shall we?"

"Thank you for being so concerned about me," she kissed him. Suddenly noticing the state he was in. "Where's all that dirt come from on your cheek? Why are you bleeding? She went on, John you've also torn your shirt on the pocket and look at the dust on your trousers."

Dam! He hadn't checked himself as well as he thought, at the time he'd wanted to get away from the wood so quickly. "Oh this?" He pointed.

The smile disappeared off her face.

"Yes that!!" "John whatever's happened? You're as white as a ghost and that graze on your face looks sore."

He thought for a moment. It was just like a web of lies.

"Well I came out of the cleaners having picked up your dress. Didn't see this stupid dog lying on the ground and I fell straight over the top of him, dress and all. He tried to smile at her wondering would she believe him? Now I've got a terrible headache," he told her. "I think your dress is alright though Jess and that's the main thing."

"No the main thing is you," she said, putting her arms around him and kissing his grubby lips. "I bet you could have throttled him."

"Who?"

"The dog of course. Who did you think I meant?" she laughed.

"Oh sorry I was miles away then. It's that bang on the head that's done it," he said, his face breaking into a smile.

"Yes of course."

"Let's put that Dettol on your finger and a little on my grazed head." Because we're both in the wars now." Yes he could have throttled him, not the dog though!

After they walked indoors she unwrapped the dress "Look it's fine, so don't worry. I'll just hang it up. Now we must get you a couple of tablets for your headache. Then you can take that shirt off and I'll mend it for you, because it's torn under the arm, as well as on the pocket. So go and put a clean one on, I've just hung a couple in the airing cupboard. You sure you're alright? You're quite pale?"

"Oh I'm fine, don't you worry I'll be even better when I've had my dinner." She really was a kind considerate person, he thought, but if she'd only known what had really happened to him, he wouldn't be in this house anymore. Anyway, it was over now. "I'm glad your dress is okay?"

"Well I hope so after having it cleaned?" Next breath, she said, "I think it should be fine now at the front, after my bit of sewing. Anyway that's enough about my stupid dress, which has caused you all this trouble." She turned to him carrying on. "How does this brighten you up? We've got roast beef and Yorkshire pudding also your favourite strawberries and ice-cream."

"Oh great! You spoil me and I know you'll look lovely in your dress for the BBQ." He smiled. Trying now to forget the last hour.

"What nearly three months pregnant I don't think so, but thank you. Now are you sure you're alright?" She asked him again.

"STOP FUSSING JESS," he told her. Which he knew took her by surprise.

"I didn't mean to go on, I just love you so much, that I don't like to know you're in pain."

"Oh sweetheart, I'm so sorry I didn't mean to upset you," he kissed her lovingly.

What was the matter with him? One minute he was nice and the next minute nasty, but he couldn't help it. Luke was hovering at the back of his mind. He was wondering what the man would do next.

Jess was thinking where does that nasty temperament come from? Perhaps it was his family that were always on his mind? She knew that he loved her though, because he showed her in so many different ways. It could be his headache from the nasty fall getting him down. That was it. 'Fancy falling over a dog.' Anyway better not say anymore.

Later when John had had his shower, he changed and felt so much better, but Luke kept coming into his mind. It was like a dream in actual fact, or more to the point, a nightmare. He was hoping he was far away now.

"Dinner's almost ready," Jess told him later.

In the kitchen John put his arm around her. "Sorry I shouted at you."

"Oh that's okay, I know you don't mean it, you never do." They both sat down at the table, when they heard an almighty knock at the front door.

Jess turned round. THATS UNUSUAL "Just when we're about to have dinner too." "I wonder who that can be?"

160

"Don't answer it," he told her briskly, feeling very apprehensive now.

"I must, it might be something important."

Leaving him wondering who it was. Jess walked out into the newly decorated hall which John had worked so hard on in the house, doing it in between his furniture jobs and having repaired mostly everything that needed doing. Opening the door slightly now, she looked hard at the person in front of her, he was a very tall man. He must be over six feet she thought, what she could see through the crack in the door, she did notice that he was rather rough looking and was shaken by it. His hair which was dark and not much of was flat to his head. Well she would notice that having been a hairdresser herself years ago. She was now remembering John's hair when she first met him, it was such a mess, but now since she had been seeing to it herself, it always looked nice. Anyway she didn't like this man's deep-set eyes and sly face, who was he? "Yes, can I help you?" She asked him, leaving the double chain on the door, wishing John had answered this knock instead of her.

Chapter 24

His voice was gruff as he said. "I'm looking for a friend of mine his name is John. I was told he lived here?" He'd followed him from the town in the car he'd stolen. It was very nice of the woman to leave the keys in the ignition. Anyway when he arrived in the lane he decided to sit and wait until it was very dark. So this must be the cottage? Yes that's where good old John was. Now he was waiting for the right moment to surprise his partner in crime. He intended to spoil his perfect little life.

Jess's mind was muddled now, wondering where John had met such a low life as this man who was looking at her. Still she had to tell him. "John it's for you," she called out. She stood waiting for him, eager to get back into her kitchen.

When Jess had gone to the door, John had been listening, thinking it was Stephanie. It wasn't … It was Luke. How on earth had he recovered so quickly and followed him here? John decided he had to stay calm and was about to go out, as Jess called him again.

"John! John!" She saw the man was still smiling and looking her up and down. She didn't like the look of him at all.

"I'm coming." He wasted a couple more minutes wondering what to do. How had this man found him? He must have pinched a car from somewhere and followed him because that's the sort of man he was dealing with and knew that's what he would do. After the fight he thought that would be the end of it. Hoping he'd never see him again, how wrong he'd been. Pushing the kitchen door open now leading into the hall, he looked at Jess who seemed perplexed and white as a ghost. What was she thinking of him knowing somebody like this man?

Luke was dangerous and it seemed as though he wasn't going to let go. If he didn't get rid of him they would have very big problems and his life with Jess would be over. So he had to do something but what? It was a shock to think the bloke even followed him! The last thing Jake wanted was for him to spoil their contented life!

162

"This man, she pointed to the gap in the door, said you were a friend of his." She looked at John because she hadn't removed the chain on the door yet, being very dubious of the situation.

Waiting for his reaction as he stared at Luke outside in the rain, she could see he didn't look very happy at all.

John put his arm around Jess's shoulders seeing her distress, telling her gently. "Go and get dinner whilst I sort this out darling."

She was pregnant for goodness sake, she didn't need this predicament they were in. Also she was very delicate at the moment, carrying their baby. He kissed her on the cheek, before she turned and went through to the kitchen. John took the chain off the door and walked outside. Then with all his strength he grabbed the man's collar. "Go over there under that tree where we can't be seen," he pointed. "I don't want Jess to hear our conversation and I don't want to get wet."

"Me neither," Luke agreed.

"I'm really not worried if you get wet it's not my problem."

That's not very nice to say that J-a-k-i-e after all I've done for you. But I can see what you like about the woman, she's a bit of alright. You didn't tell me she'd got a bun in the oven though. Whose been a naughty boy?"

"Don't be filthy and don't ever talk about her like that." Jake told him. Yes she's going to have my child and I will take care of her, as long as I can. They were now facing each other. You've got a cheek following me here. What do you want? I thought we'd said all that was to be said, after our heated argument and the fight we had in the town? Anyway how did you get here, when I left you on the ground? I evidently didn't hit you hard enough with that piece of wood and where did you pinch that car from?" he pointed, "because that's what you did, pinched it didn't you?"

"Well when you hit me, it was nothing and didn't hurt me much at all. So I got up quickly and followed you to the car park, then I saw an elderly person go and get her parking ticket. I had this feeling, when I looked into her car, seeing she'd left the keys in the ignition, as I'd hoped. So I jumped in and followed you. Then I waited in the lane until it got dark hoping

163

nobody would come and see me there, but nobody did and here I am!!"

Jake felt ill at that moment. "The police will be looking for that car, and you've come here? Stupid!!"

"Don't call me stupid? Nobody will venture up here I'm sure. I wasn't going to let you get away that easily. You've got a short memory I think. We both come from the same place and we both escaped from there, and we're both no good. If your woman only knew who you were, Jake Farrendon. That would be the end of your relationship."

John stared at the man. "As you know I have a new identity. I'm a different person. Jess has made me what I am now. My life is here with her. I know what I did in the past was partly wrong, but what I did was a total accident, one which will be with me to the end of my days. Nobody has ever found out about me around here, I'm living a good life. Well I was until you came onto the scene. You made your escape from prison, now it's up to you what you do with your life. So clear off do you hear me."

Jess peered through the kitchen window and just caught sight of the two under the tree, they seemed to be arguing, but, about what?

"Sorry old buddy."

"I'm not your buddy." Jake told him.

Luke looked around before saying. "This is the perfect place for our hideout, you've done well, no wonder you've never been found by the prison authorities. Well you know what, living on the moors away from everything suits me fine, for the time being, because I have to lay low for a while like you?"

"Think again, because you're not staying here."

"We'll see about that, you cocky devil?"

At that moment John looked towards the cottage as he heard Jess calling out for him to come indoors John!!

"Won't be a minute Jess."

She thought he sounded very agitated. She'd never seen him like this before.

"I think you'd better ask me in JOHN!! don't you?" Luke told him.

164

"No I don't think so. I don't want you in our house, do you hear me?"

"Well I'll tell you, it's either that or I'm going to spill the beans about you, to your lady friend and that will be the end of your relationship. Okay!"

He felt ill with worry now. What could he do? He began to wipe the drips of rain off his face from the trees.

He could just see Jess who was standing in the porch now watching them. She didn't like this dreadful looking man, but what could she do? To get John indoors she shouted. "If your friend would like to have a bite with us, I'm sure I can stretch the meal,"

"No I don't think so, you've got to go haven't you?"

"NO! NO! I'm in no hurry. Thanks, I'm starving," Luke called out to her. Ignoring John and what he was saying, as he hurriedly walked towards the front door and the woman.

John followed quickly alongside him. He was so angry and suddenly afraid of the consequences, with this individual around. He knew what Luke was capable of having a violent temper was one, which he saw in the prison once with an inmate whom he'd nearly killed. Jess had gone indoors now, when John pulled the man's sleeve. "Listen? You eat your meal and clear off. Right?"

"Sorry mate I don't think so."

"And don't call me mate, because I'm not your mate."

"Okay, but you owe me and I think your little woman would like to hear about us two. Because you were glad of me when you wanted to get out of prison."

"Biggest mistake I ever made. Anyway watch what you say in front of Jess. You hear?" John told him.

"Yeah man!" He laughed with a sneer on his face. As he found his way into the kitchen. Slinging his worn donkey jacket onto a chair and plonking himself down on another, pulling it up to the table. Now he was staring at Jess as she dished him a few slices of meat on his plate, before putting a dish with all the veg in, on the table. And then got John's and hers from the oven, where she had put them when this man had knocked at the door. He was about to eat her and John's meal for the next day. Ah well. She had to be hospitable towards John's friend.

"Good old John hasn't told you my name has he?" He stared at the other who looked really worried, not knowing what he was about to say.

"John began thinking his relationship with Jess and his wonderful contented life was over, when he heard.

"It's Nichols ... Frank Nichols.

"Well Frank, she said forcing a smile, enjoy" She was feeling very uneasy now with this awful individual beside them. John slid onto another chair and she felt him touch her arm, but she noticed he had gone very quiet. Whilst Frank helped himself to more food.

"Good job I got a larger piece of beef," she was saying nervously, trying to get a better atmosphere into the room. As she watched the man pile his plate up with vegetables and Yorkshire puddings, too. Not bothering about anyone else and would they like any more as she watched him ramming huge amounts of food into his mouth.

Jess stared at John. "You're not eating!" She smiled.

"Sorry Jess I'm just not hungry." He was wondering where all this was going. His new life had been so good, being with her. He didn't need this situation. He began to think of giving himself up for Jess's sake. She was such a good woman and he didn't want her to get hurt. Looking across at Luke now with disgust. What was Jess thinking inviting him in for a meal? He wondered as he watched her gently putting her knife and fork down, she too had only eaten a little. He stared in disgust at Luke shovelling the potatoes into his mouth, as though there was no tomorrow. (There probably wasn't,) John thought.

Jess broke the silence again asking. "Where have you come from Mr Nichols?"

He looked up. "My names Frank Jess!"

How dare he call her by her name he'd better not say anything though. John felt as though the blood had drained from his body, as he waited with bated breath for the man's answer.

Luke stared at him. "I've been working on boat repairs, he lied, but they don't pay enough money so I left."

166

"Oh I see. What brought you here?" She asked him.

John got up and went to the sink as his body got hotter and hotter. He turned on the tap and drank a glass of water. What was Luke about to say? He wondered as the lies flew out of his mouth once more.

Luke looked at John noticing the beads of perspiration on his brow, as he carried on talking. "Well I wanted a change from working on boats and packed it up. And came to this town for a change. When I bumped into my old friend John! He turned and looked at him. Wasn't that a piece of luck us bumping into each other? I haven't seen you for how long? ...."

John could have been violently sick at that moment, his stomach was churning, but he had to keep control. "Five years," he made up quickly.

"Is it that long John? I would have said months."

Chapter 25

"You didn't tell me you had bumped into Frank?" She sighed.

When would this situation ever end? Lies, lies, and more lies as he made things up. He hated all this lying to Jess. Why had he ever got involved with this man? An evil individual who wasn't liked inside the prison and most of the men gave him a wide berth, because they knew he could be very dangerous when he was out of his cell and walking amongst them all. Thinking deeply now his life had been so good with Jess. He began to wonder, like he had done many times before what Luke had been in prison for? John didn't really want to ask him, as he knew he would regret it. What he didn't know was best left alone. He knew one thing though. He hated the man with every fibre in his body especially when he was on drugs, like a lot of them were inside, that's why he was so hateful at times.

Officers tried to find out where these were coming in from but the men were very devious. There were many illegal things going on which got past them, as they were so busy doing whatever they had to do, the drugs carried on coming in. But John wasn't into any of that sort of thing, he did realise that's why the mans mind was up in the air at times having taken these awful drugs. The inmates really hated him when he was let out to mingle with them, as the plumbers worked on his cell. And as far as they were concerned he could do one!! Now it had backfired on John because Luke was now sitting here in front of him, in Jess's house. Eating a meal at her table which she had prepared and her not knowing he had escaped from Slate Moors Prison and he felt terribly upset by all this. Where were those men who should have been watching this man? How could he have put her in this situation when this so called bloke could blow the gaff on him, if he was caught. The only good thing to come out of all this was meeting Jess. They loved one another and she was having his baby. All of a sudden he began to calm down a little, he had to play this game carefully now, as they were both staring at him. "Oh sorry

I totally forgot to mention it after having that fall, it went right out of my mind."

"Well I forgive you," she smiled. "But do you know Frank? John came home with his shirt torn and dirt all over his trousers, also he had a slight gash on his head. I thought he'd been in a fight." She told the other man but no, would you believe he fell over a dog having my cleaning in his arms, poor John. The only time he goes out and he falls. Anyway my John wouldn't get in a fight when I think about it, he's not that type of person. She managed a laugh.

"YOU DIDN'T SAY THAT TO ME JESS?" John said to her in a loud voice feeling very agitated again.

She gave a weak smile. "Oh sorry, well when you said you'd fallen and it was the dogs fault, which caused the problem, I didn't push the subject, as you know?"

"No you didn't," he answered sharply, seeing her flinch. "I can't believe you thought that."

"JOHN!" She wasn't used to being spoken to like this.

He'd gone too far. "I'm sorry Jess for talking to you like that. I'm just not feeling my bright self at the moment. I've still got that rotten headache," he told her, staring at the man in front of him. Then feeling so sorry for his outburst, he gave her a gentle hug.

"Ah!!" Frank was enjoying this, as he stared from one to the other. Must keep my gob shut, especially as he had managed to get into this house and have a scrummy meal. It was difficult to keep silent though.

"Would you like another tablet John?" Jess asked. "You've been in the sun a lot, perhaps you have a bit of sun stroke." She was saying, noticing his red face.

"YES HAVE A TABLET JOHN!" Frank told him loudly.

"No! no! I'll get over my problem. Let me help you wash up Jess?"

"It's ok you speak to your friend," she told him nervously.
He really didn't need that request, this man was no friend All he wanted was to get back to normal and for Luke to leave him and Jess. But he knew he had to talk to him again. He looked at the man who was just about to light up a cigarette, perfect!

"Let's go outside," John told him, "then you can have a smoke. Jess doesn't like anyone smoking in the house."

She turned from the sink, miming 'thank you.' As she saw him blow a kiss to her, realising probably that he knew he had to get back in her good books.

Frank smirked, but was quite impressed by the homely scene between these two people.

"Right," he said, "good idea." He was going to have to be pleasant to this woman, even though he wasn't bothered too. He had more plans up his sleeve and had to play his cards close to his chest, being careful what he said, because he wanted more out of this, it would take a little planning. "Great meal Jess, thank you." he said to her.

"Surprised by this, she answered. You're welcome," but didn't mean it. Wanting this awful looking man to go and leave her and John on their own again.

John certainly didn't like familiarity from this individual, calling his lady Jess, and didn't want her anywhere near him. Outside he and so-called Frank walked back over to where they'd been before. Thank goodness the rain had stopped. Suddenly he grabbed the man's arm. "You've had all you can get, now go, you hear me?"

"Tut! Tut! don't get nasty you know the prison warders and police are looking for us both. One word from me and your cosy little life will be over."

"John stared at him. "I've been safe here and have another life now, for however long that might be? Living at the cottage with the woman I love. Now you've turned up and put a damper on it. Why don't you go and leave us alone we're happy and also look forward to our forthcoming child being born?"

"Well you didn't waste much time did you? Ha! Ha! How very cosy. Frank scratched himself under his arm, before saying. You don't think I'm going to go away now do you? This is the perfect place for me too. I don't know how you came to be here. No doubt I'll eventually find out. This will suit me fine to stay here, perhaps for a while. Then when the time is right I might go."

"Look enough!!" "You must leave today Frank." He had to play this right, not knowing if it would work or not? "But thank you for your help in getting me out of that dreadful place, however that's as far as it goes."

"No way, you've got a good set up here and I'm sure you can fit me in. After all you don't want me to disclose to your woman that she has two convicts in her midst."

"You wouldn't?" Being nice to him hadn't worked.

"Wouldn't I?"

"I don't believe this. You really are a nasty piece of work." John said loudly.

"Now as I seem to remember, you're the one who killed his wife. Perhaps you'd like me to tell your lady friend, I think that would be the end of your little romance."

"You keep your mouth shut, you hear me? It was an accident perhaps unlike your situation which I don't know about, but it must be bad for you to be in a cell away from everyone and only being let out when it's absolutely necessary, like the work that's been going on in your cell. Nevertheless he guessed this man before him had done something dreadful. He felt it, but it was kept hush, hush, in the prison. Luke didn't like inmates talking about him, well I don't want to know about that either." He didn't intend to become his best friend. God forbid! He had only wanted to get out of that dreadful building which he did."

"Alright keep your hair on John. The other man was looking him up and down now. I have to say, you do look very different. But still I recognised you in that park, I would know you anywhere!! The perfect so-called prisoner. You can bet the police will too," he smiled.

"Shut up."

"Now I have a proposition if you put me up for a few days I won't disclose who you really are. YET!! How about it?"

"That's the very last thing I want," John told. him.

"Look I'm sure your woman wouldn't mind, she seems very obliging."

"Why don't you sod off." John was fuming, how dare he say that?

"Tut! Tut! That's not nice J-a-k-i-e

When all of a sudden the front door opened once more and Jess stood there. "WOULD YOU LIKE A CUP OF TEA?" She shouted to the two. Looking across now she began to think how the weather had changed, thank goodness it wasn't raining, as the two would have got soaked. But why didn't John and that awful man come indoors to talk now?

"YES, THANK YOU JESS! Frank called back. You know when your fed up with old John here I will be first in the queue." He shouted to her.

'In your dreams.' She had taken an instant dislike to him, but was trying to be polite, because it was Johns so called friend. How did he ever meet such a low life character? She began wondering again. Where did this man come from? Frank didn't need asking again as he began to make his way across the drive to her. John following close behind, but was very quiet. It's so weird; how he never explained a great deal about his past, only about the argument he had had with his family. She didn't really know anything about his mother either. This situation was going to have to be sorted out soon. Jess had always trusted John whatever he would say, but now she was wondering about everything. They were going to have to talk about this at some future date. Surely he would never lie to her, not her John. Then there was Stephanie she knew he wasn't keen on her, or she on him. Her friend saying at odd times he didn't ring true. These last few months had been so perfect though, now it seemed to be crumbling. She was going to have to tolerate this despicable man for Johns sake, well for now anyway. She waited at the door as the man pushed right past her. Jess raised her hand and brushed the strands away from her face, feeling very hot and bothered now.

"I'll go and pour the tea," she told John as he entered pale faced. His look told her everything and she was sure he didn't like this man Frank, but was committed in some way.

John whispered in Franks ear, whilst Jess had her back to the men. "Have your tea then go." He told him.

"SORRY OLD SON. NO CAN DO!" He told him behind his hands. I'm sure she will ask me to stay he whispered."

"I DOUBT IT!"

When Jess suddenly turned round hearing raised voices as she looked over at the two.

When Frank asked. "Jess do you think you could put me up for a couple days?"

John felt ill, this was getting totally out of order, he had to get rid of this dreadful person who was terrorising his life. Whatever made him think he would ever be able to lead a normal existence now? What was Jess going to say? She was looking at him for support. But what could he do? The man had a hold over him and he knew that and would shout this out if he could, from the roof tops. There would be no holding him back.

Jess couldn't believe what she heard and John had gone very quiet again, "Well I don't know, we haven't got an awful lot of room here, but I suppose two days wouldn't hurt. What do you say John?"

Frank was staring at him in such a way, he had no option. "Okay but that's all." He suddenly felt sick.

But she was now looking at him, "you know we're going to Stephanie's tomorrow for the barbecue?"

Without hesitation, "Are you indeed? Great I'll join you." Frank told them.

"You haven't been invited," John responded.

"John!" She stared at Frank who didn't look very presentable to go to a party, he looked down right scruffy in his tatty clothes and by the looks of it, he didn't seem to have much in his duffle bag, as it looked almost flat. She was worried about her friend Stephanie who wouldn't be too happy about this man in her house, that's if she let him come, but Jess felt she had to ask this for John's sake, there was really no alternative. Although he wasn't saying much. She felt that he didn't seem to be happy with his so-called friend.

'Were they really friends?' What hold did Frank have over John? Because that's what it seemed like. It was a puzzle she couldn't fit together. Looking at the two men, she told them. "I'll just ring Steph and see if it's okay for you to come. If so, perhaps, and she stared at Frank we could find something more appropriate, for you to wear."

Although that might be difficult, because you're very broad, but from what I can remember there's a large shirt up in the case in the loft. It was bought for my husband's birthday once and he didn't like to tell his relation it was too big. So it just went into the case with all the other clothes."

"Thank you Jess. Do I look that awful?"

"Well if you don't mind my saying your jeans look rather dirty and that jumper has seen better days. Sorry!" This was going from bad to worse. Stephanie would be horrified to see the man as he was looking now. So she had to try and make him look a little better.

He had to say something. "Jess is right your clothes aren't very clean, did you get like that from working on the boats?" John asked.

"Yes that's right and I never bought any new ones, lazy me."

Jess was in the hall now with the phone to her ear: "So would you mind Steph? She asked in a very low voice, not wanting Frank to hear her. It put us in such an awkward position, it's either bring him along, or we can't come."

"Oh bring him along," came the reply. "One more won't make much difference."

Jess had always wished her friend would like John more for her sake, but she always had her doubts about if they would ever like one another. "Well I must warn you I don't think you will like this one," she whispered into the phone.

"Let me be the judge of that. See you at 7.30pm tomorrow, okay?"

"Thank you, yes okay bye." Five minutes later she was back in the kitchen, where the atmosphere was still strained between the two men.

John wasn't happy, and was thinking with a bit of luck Stephanie might not want Frank to come. She was a fussy girl as he'd found out and he knew she didn't like him.

"It's okay you can come with us tomorrow evening," she told Frank. But she had heard in Stephanie's tone that she wasn't too keen, already finding it hard to tolerate John. Wait till she sees this one, because he had such a hard face. I'll just go and make the box room up for you Frank, It's only small but alright for a couple of nights."

"Great that won't matter I'm used to small places, aren't I John?"

"I suppose," he watched as Jess shut the door and made her way upstairs. The two men heard her walking backwards and forwards going about her job of making the bed up, as the floorboards creaked. John glared at the man opposite. "Just behave yourself tomorrow you hear? Then we want you out of mine and Jess's life as soon as possible, got it, you slime ball"?

Frank walked over to John and grabbed his collar, "I hear you, but I'll go when I'm good and ready because this is the perfect hiding place. Well you haven't been found yet. You've got a good little set up here with your lady friend, haven't you? It's perfect," then in a low voice he mumbled. "I've never forgotten!!!"

Picking that remark up John asked. "What! you knew this area? Have you been here before?"

Frank was on his guard. "No! Take no notice what I said I was just goading you."

"You have brought my past life back, which I'm not happy about," John told him sadly. The police have never found me, but now there're two of us. How long will it be before we're caught? Plus it will break Jess's heart and she's had so much unhappiness already. We were happy and I was contented here. Please go away," he begged. "I mean Jess might be in the town and meet someone, casually saying you're here. What then?"

"She'd better not! Or else."

"John was blazing now. Don't you go making threats to Jess or you'll have me to deal with. I know exactly what your like and how ruthless you can be. So don't ever try it on or say anything nasty about her, because I'm not frightened of you."

Thank goodness they got through the night, but John and Jess didn't sleep well with this man in the house. But thankfully there were no incidents they could here him snoring. Saturday came and it was a lovely sunny day. Frank ambled about with John following him. As the man whittled what looked like the shape of a knife, when sitting in the garden. She thought he was interested in her different nick knacks she had there, so she took no notice. But John knew he was up to something but what? Why did he want that

175

piece of wood what was it for? He had questioned him but Frank just smiled and said, "I like doing this whilst I'm waiting to go to that fantastic barbecue. I used to do things like this in prison. John was worried about that remark, so he would keep close to Jess.

Chapter 26

The three were quiet driving to Stephanie's to say the least, by what had happened earlier. Frank had been walking from room to room of the cottage, before they left and walked in on Jess just as she was putting her dress on. He had stared at her as she hurriedly covered herself with her dressing gown, shaking. But he had seen what he wanted to. "WOULD YOU GET OUT OF MY ROOM? JOHN? JOHN?" She had called.

John had been downstairs feeding the dog at the time. When he heard her frantic call. Jumping the stairs two at a time, he had this sinking feeling in the pit of his stomach. Where was Frank? Suddenly he was confronted by him, as he walked boldly out of their bedroom.

"What are you doing in our room?"

"Looking at the scenery," the man had whispered, in Johns ear.

"Out!" he said pushing Frank. Noticing Jess was transfixed to the spot. "Are you alright Jess?"

"Yes, yes, I'm okay," she said standing there holding her dressing gown in front of her. John had walked across the room and put his arm around the woman, telling her to get dressed as he kissed her and closed the door.

Frank was smiling a sinister smile, leaning against his bedroom door. John joined him grabbing the man by his collar and pushing him hard into his room. But he was so solid it wasn't easy. "If you ever go into our bedroom again I promise you you'll not see another day. Got it?"

"You think that frightens me? She's a good-looking bird, even though she's up the creek."

"Shut your mouth, you hear?"

Jess heard enough peeping through a crack in the door, as she hurriedly got dressed and quickly ran down the stairs. Feeling frightened now of what might happen between the two. She wanted this man to go, as a shiver ran up and down her body. It was weird but she felt she had seen this person before, but couldn't think where? The same thing had happened in the bedroom, as he stood in the doorway, perhaps not! So brushing the thought away, how would she know such a person.

"Enough you two," she yelled out from the kitchen.

John was feeling apprehensive about the evening. Two convicts going out to a barbecue, it just didn't ring true. Why hadn't he told Jess everything and then taken it from there, because he couldn't go on with his life like this. Frank was dangerous, but if he shopped him to the police he and Jess would be through and he would end up back in prison. He had to keep quiet at the moment and put up with the situation.

When John joined her she asked him. "Do I look alright in this dress John?"

"You look lovely as I thought you would, it's such a pretty dress and it suits your beautiful hair. I am sorry about Frank. I will get it sorted."

"Not with violence though John because I saw you together and you were about to hit him weren't you? Friends don't do this, even though I have to say you don't act like friends."

"No true, we aren't, but I owe him unfortunately I will tell you soon. Anyway going into our bedroom when you were changing. I won't have that, well not as long as I'm here, I will always protect you and our baby. Forgive me for this person entering our space. I will get rid of him soon."

She hurriedly kissed him: "Don't worry it will all work out in the end, one way or another."

Frank looked more presentable she thought, having the check shirt on now which she had given him. It was big as she had thought and had fitted the man well. So it had come in handy today, although she would rather have got rid of it, than let this man wear it. But he couldn't go to Stephanie's looking like he had. He'd had a wash and brush up in her bathroom which she wasn't too happy about as he'd left a mess. However he had sponged his jeans after Jake told him to. His hair had been combed which looked better and he had shaved off the thick stubble on his chin with the razor she gave him. So he was cleaner but was still wearing the old trainers much to John and hers disgust.

John as it was, hadn't wanted to lend him any clothes, he didn't deserve anything, that's the trouble Jess had such a soft

178

nature. She was right he couldn't have gone to this barbecue, looking like he had. Her friend would have had a fit, as she probably still will. She wasn't going to be to happy having this person in her house, anyway. John thought why had he put Jess through all this? She was such a lovely kind person, thoughtful and caring. He was determined to make it right in the end. Well he hoped he could! So now they were off to the barbecue and Jess was driving. The ride to Stephanie's was not the most pleasant trip. Franks snide remarks, at times, had put John on edge.

"Do you remember when we used to play snooker in that huge place, well it was just like a hanger, wasn't it Johnny?"

"Where was that?" Jess asked him. Wanting to know more about John who hadn't told her these things.

"That was a long time ago, darling. I don't think you would be very interested in our past life, that's gone, it's over. Is the house around here?" John asked her, trying to change the subject after noticing she'd slowed down.

"Yes it's that one over there number 44."

Stephanie saw the car draw up and ran down the path to greet them. She must be more civil to John after all her friend was happy with him and that was the main thing. She was looking forward to a good evening, having all the food ready to barbecue. chicken, lamb cutlets, turkey on skewers, with cut up peppers. Lines of small mackerel, bowls of beautiful bright green salads, and a beetroot salad also coleslaw and potato salad. Finished off with a mandarin gateau and strawberries and cream, all on a large picnic table. She was also pleased how the garden looked, with fairy lights strung here and there in between their large conifer trees and the coloured lights lit up the pond. Everywhere you looked in this very organised garden was lovely. Steph's partner had worked so hard to make it look outstanding. Thank goodness the rain had cleared up now, and it was a warm evening and dry. Stephanie was interested to see this person who had arrived with John and Jess. She was so pleased that her friend had decided to come this evening, but not so happy to have John. Still Jess loved him, so that was the main thing. She felt good in her black trouser suit with the gold chain. Nathan had said that she looked

179

fantastic, having put her long blonde hair up she felt great. Walking towards their car now she greeted them both. Deciding at that moment she must be nice to John for Jess's sake.

"Hello, you two thank you for coming," she smiled, planting a kiss on both as they got out the car.

"High Steph I say you look lovely," Jess told her brightly..

"So do you my friend, in that pretty colourful dress."

"Well I don't look that good, with my baby bump showing," she smiled.

"Ah well you do to me," John remarked, "actually you look beautiful."

Jess suddenly grabbed his arm. "That was a sweet thing to say John"

"Yes it was," Stephanie remarked. Anyway now she had this other man to contend with and didn't want to cause any upset, not this evening, because she'd been looking so forward to everything being perfect. But at that moment she caught sight of the man in the back as his large frame and long legs struggled out of Jess's car. Then he stood in front of the three hands on hips watching the scene from the pavement. Stephanie was to say the least gob smacked this was a nightmare. She felt sick at that minute. What an ugly looking individual. Oh my God! So this was Frank? Still she must not, show her feelings. "Hello," she said holding out her hand as she walked towards him. She had never expected this, he was awful in every way the hair, face, body and the man himself, she didn't like his look at all.

"Hi yourself I'm Frank Nichols," he said to her. "I was told there's a booze up, at this shin-dig, lead me to the poison."

"So your Frank? Well you don't waste much time do you?" She couldn't help saying, disliking him instantly and what would her friends think in the garden when they saw him? Well I'm Stephanie." She smiled.

"Hi yourself and you got the name right sweetheart. And no I certainly don't? Haven't got much time, have we John?"

He could easily have thumped this degenerate.

Jess was not feeling at all well now and was dreading the evening. What hold did he have on John? She didn't need all this stress, not tonight, not ever. But she knew she mustn't let her temper get the better of her. She had to take care of herself because of the baby. John would sort it out though she was sure, as she looked at him, but he was glaring at Frank now. As the man limped slovenly down the path away from them with one thing on his mind.

John took Jess's arm and said, "I'm so sorry about this situation, I haven't seen this man for years and I never realised at the time, how much I disliked him. But as I mentioned, he once did me a favour, so I'm repaying him, so to speak."

Stephanie listened to his excuse. "Well John I suppose we have to make the best of it this evening don't we?" She whispered, "I feel sorry for you two anyway come and have a drink, it might relax you and I will get a juice for the little mother to be," she smiled. "Ah there's my other half," she told them having spotted Nathaniel heading towards them.

He hadn't met John and she wondered what his reaction would be? Then meeting Frank was going to be an even bigger shock. He would not be very impressed with him, she was sure of that, as she noticed the man was outside in the garden gazing around and heading for the bar.

Nat smiled, joining the four in the hall.

"Darling, come and meet Jess's partner, this is John." Stephanie was saying.

"Hello John we meet at long last."

"Hello there Nathaniel."

"Please call me Nat, most people do, as my name is such a mouthful, thanks to my devoted parents, he laughed. It was a bit of luck I wasn't on call this evening at the hospital," He told them extending his hand to John before leaning across and kissing Jess on the cheek. Looking round he said I will meet your friend in a minute no doubt." "So now you two mingle," he smiled, as he and Stephanie walked ahead, hand in hand.

John and Jess were now worried as both were thinking Nat wouldn't like Frank they were sure of that when he met him.

"We will," Jess called out to her friends. What would the evening be like? She wondered as John put his arm round her, but she was now shaking as she felt him squeeze her to him and smiled, trying to reassure him everything would be okay.

He was so proud at that moment to have this woman on his arm. He knew what she was thinking. Let's get this barbecue over.

"Don't worry John it will be okay." Well she really hoped so.

Chapter 27

"What have I done to you?" He whispered in her ear. "You shouldn't be worrying at a time like this. I promise you I will get rid of him as soon as possible."

"Thank you John I hope so?" she sighed. Jess felt tired by everything that had happened in the last few hours, as they both strolled outside onto the patio, seeing Frank shaking hands with Nathan who didn't look too happy. When Jess suddenly spotted Rick and Jan whom she had met in the past, so they took a slow walk up to them.

"Hello Jess? Nice to see you again." Rick said as Jan raised a friendly hand to them smiling. Your John aren't you? Stephanie put us in the picture before you arrived."

"Yes I am, hello there," now wondering how much this woman had told them? After all the introductions the four seemed to be getting on really well. When John noticed out the corner of his eye Frank helping himself to a large drink, at the bar.

Jess's eyes were now on her partner as she saw Johns face change.

"Excuse me I won't be a minute," He nodded to the three, squeezing Jess's arm and then letting go of her as he swiftly walked over towards Frank. They'd only been there twenty minutes and in that time the man was helping himself to another rum and coke.

John grabbed his arm, "what are you doing?" He asked the inexcusable, devious, individual. as he worried that at that moment the people at the party might be watching. Apart from Rick and Jan with whom he and Jess had been talking most of the crowd had turned the other way and were obviously trying not to notice the situation and were in deep conversation.

"What do you mean what am I doing? I thought that was pretty obvious. pouring another one of these beauties."

"Well don't!" John told him, this is not your house so you wait to be asked whether you would like another drink." He saw the snide smile appear on Franks face which he always pulled.

"Yeah! Yeah! Well I a-i-n-'t waiting for them to ask me as I could be here all night, they are so slow with offering, so I'm helping myself. And I don't think you will stop me, as these people would be very surprised to know our big secret. I'd love to make your happy life a disaster." He smirked.

"You keep your big mouth shut," John told him. "I wish I'd never met you, because I hate and despise you. Why should these people have to put up with your obnoxious ways? Try and behave yourself here, remember these are Stephanie's friend's and she's been kind enough to let you come here tonight to this barbecue. Do you know what? If I wasn't in this position of being wanted by the police myself, I would be more than happy to turn you in." He whispered in the mans ear.

"Well it's a good thing we're both in the same boat then isn't it?"

"God forbid!! Anyway don't take any more drinks, unless you're asked. Behave yourself, you hear" John shouted over the music as it got louder, from the hi-fi.

"John!" Jess called beckoning to him.

"Oh Johnnie your wanted by your beautiful lady?"

"I'm coming," he waved. "So you behave, he whispered in Franks ear, prodding the man's chest. Or else we will both be back inside," then he turned to wave to Jess.

Everyone was dancing and enjoying themselves, as the music played full blast. But John was uncomfortable as people were now staring at Frank who was trying to chat Stephanie up. He was getting closer to her and she was edging away, when Nathan came up. "I think this is our dance darling." And took her hand pulling her away from the man.

"Yes you must dance with darling," Frank imitated.
Stephanie hadn't known this man long, but she was beginning to despise him with every breath she took. He was such a low life and she was now hoping he wouldn't spoil the party. As she'd been so looking forward to this evening, having put such a lot of time and effort into it as her partner had. She loved entertaining her friends probably more than Nat, he was a little

184

quieter, but it wasn't the sort of barbecue you could really enjoy, well not at the moment. If only this vile man would go?

Nat hadn't been pleased with Franks advances, towards her she knew that and could tell he didn't like Frank on first meeting, this person was something else. Rude and infuriating in every way whatever possessed Jess to befriend this individual. Still it sounded as though it was John's so-called friend. Well Frank had better not spoil everything tonight.

"I'm sorry for all this stress I've caused you Jess?" John was saying as they stood by the dancing platform, looking round at the crowd now. He could see people shying away from the infuriating man's advances. You shouldn't have all this worry carrying our baby. As I said I will get rid of him as soon as I can I promise you."

"Don't worry darling," she told him not wanting to say too much to him, simply because she didn't want to give him another burden as she was feeling so tired now, probably through worry? What had she let herself in for? Taking this man in and bringing him here this evening, when all he wanted to do was make trouble.

The food on the barbecue was sizzling away but John and Jess had lost their appetite, because of everything which was happening with this awful person. There was a lapse in the music now whilst all their friends ate their meal.

So Stephanie decided to have a slow walk up to the conifer trees at the top of the garden, which backed onto a cornfield. She needed to clear her head as her mind was all over the place, as she began to wonder why John and Jess had brought this man here? What hold did he have over them she wondered? What has happened to my friend to allow him into her home? But Jess had told her she didn't know what the situation was between John and Frank. However she had to take the man in she had no option. Even though John hadn't wanted him to stay with them but felt indebted to Frank for some reason. (Would you worry about that?) Stephanie shivered for some unknown reason, funny really as it was a lovely warm evening and she wasn't cold. But suddenly she sensed something, turning on an impulse she got the fright of her life, when who should be standing next to her but Frank, he reached out and made a grab for her arm.

"Come on babe lets walk up to those tall trees."

"She began to panic. "I really should get back Frank."

"Not yet, you're a nice-looking woman, do you know that?"

"Please let go of my arm," she told him, as he roughly pulled her along. Somebody must have seen them walk up here? She thought. But no everybody seemed to be enjoying themselves now, at long last. Probably because this man wasn't around, he'd tried it on with most of the women, here this evening, who'd thankfully shunned him. As their men stepped in, which nearly ended in a punch up at one point. Stephanie tried to turn round and walk back, but he wouldn't let her, pushing her forward with his big hand, all she wanted was to get back to her friends. Surely Nat had missed her? Somebody must have. She now cursed the small white love seat, which she and her partner had bought a few weeks ago. When he had carried it up to the quiet spot, so that they could sit there and look over the corn fields. How she wished the seat wasn't there now.

"Sit down Steph," Frank said, pushing her as he put his arm round her, holding her very tightly, he could feel her body stiffen and she began to struggle to get away. With that he pulled her head round, seeing the fear in the woman's eyes and he smiled planting a sloppy kiss on her cheek, when she screamed out but nobody seemed to hear her, as the music had started and it was loud. But after what seemed an eternity, things began to happen as John and Jess appeared from behind the huge ferns. They had been looking for Frank and had walked up the garden by chance when they couldn't see Stephanie which panicked them both. Then before Frank could do anything else John grabbed his coat and pulled him off the seat with great difficulty using every bit of strength he had. He was furious with this situation which had occurred as he pushed Frank away from Stephanie.

"Let her go?" he said as Frank then loosened his grip on the woman.

Jess hurried over to her friend and put her arm round her shoulder, she was shaking as they both began to walk back to the party, at John's request. Turning he lashed out at the man with every bit of strength he had. Hitting Frank was like hitting a brick wall and looking at him he saw the punch had barely touched him.

"Thank goodness you and John came up here Jess," Stephanie was saying. "I thought Nat would have missed me, but no, he never came looking for me at all. That Frank's not a very nice person, I was really worried when he followed me, I thought I was going to be raped, and all I could see was that dreadful scar on his ugly face as he pushed his hair back. Whatever possessed John to pall up with him?" I felt I had seen him somewhere before, on second thoughts perhaps not, who would want to make friends with him?

"Stephanie you must believe me John can't stand this man as you can tell? He just owed him this favour as I told you, it's a long story. Hopefully he'll go soon. He stayed with us last night, and I said he could stay tonight then he'll go we hope, which I'm so looking forward to. You see he came into my bedroom when I was getting ready for the barbecue. I shouted for John. Do you know I thought he was going to kill him when he saw he was in our room. This awful man is such a devious person. I don't know where he's come from? John didn't say. In fact he's not said an awful lot. I even had to find him something to wear this evening, because he was so untidy? It's because he's been working on boats at a dockyard so he told us and never bought any new clothes. Not that he'd look that good in anything.

"Is he married" Steph asked

"No I ask you, who would have him?" Anyway he'll soon be gone. I hope! Do you know I wish I hadn't sent John for my dress at the cleaners then he wouldn't have bumped into this person? Anyway are you okay now?"

"Yes I'm fine, thanks to John. But where was Nat? For goodness sake, these men are never around when you need them."

"He must be indoors perhaps sorting something out for the barbecue," Jess replied.

"Well Jess please don't tell him about this. I'll fill him in later." She looked at everyone enjoying themselves dancing now on the patio. Really it was a good thing the crowd hadn't heard her scream it would have frightened everyone.

"We were talking to Andy and Jill when John said to me, where's Frank? Then all of a sudden he saw you both turning the corner at the top of the garden. Well he ran, probably guessing what that awful man might do, I had a job to keep up, but I did my best, because I was so worried about you."

"Thank goodness he did. You know I hadn't taken to John very much, as you could tell we seem to rub each other up the wrong way? Well he was brilliant just now. I've changed my mind about him," she smiled. As the two walked down towards the crowd arm in arm.

"Good! I said you would like him in time. I'm so sorry about all of this. Look we'll be going soon. Are you *okay* now?" Jess asked

"Yes I'm fine, it should be me asking you. Are you alright? Running up the garden in your condition."

"I'm okay apart from being a nervous wreck with Frank's behaviour. Look here comes John. He looks okay, well he evidently coped with that degenerate, Jess told her friend and Frank is right behind him unable to walk straight, he's eaten and drank so much. Stephanie I'm so sorry we brought him this evening."

"It's not your fault Jess. So let's forget it now, as nothing happened but I really must thank John for his quick actions though."

Chapter 28

Jess smiled at her friend, well who would believe something good would come out of this evening? Because her friend was now thinking differently about her John. When she noticed he was almost with the two women.

Standing by Stephanie now he heard her say "Thank you both so much for your quick actions." "But mainly I thank you John for sorting your friend out, I wasn't sure what he was going to do, as he wasn't conducting himself very well. And then I became rather frightened of him at the time."

"You're very welcome Stephanie, I'm so sorry for his behaviour, but please don't call him my friend, because he isn't. And may I say he invited himself this evening not explaining anymore. I really want him out of mine and Jess's life forever."

"I feel sorry for you both," she told them. "Now I really must check on Nat. So don't worry Jess I'm going to do my best to keep this party going, in spite of Frank. You always seem to get one at a party don't you? But I have to say he is rather horrible, this one."

"Yes you're right there Stephanie we shouldn't have brought him along with us, but I really didn't have any option, neither did John. You know he's not lost for it, trying to dance with all the women here, no wonder their husbands stood there ground and said no!" Jess smiled.

"Good for them, anyway bye for now, enjoy yourselves if you can?" Stephanie called out to both as she hurried down the garden, to get away from Frank who was heading their way, Nat might be in their kitchen she hoped.

Amanda was pretty with long blonde hair and a slim figure and Howard her other half had red hair and glasses, who always had a very cheeky grin on his face. "How long have you two been together?" He asked later as Jess and John joined them.

"It's just coming up to three months, isn't it Jess?" John was saying a little more relaxed now, when he heard.

"Well joked Howard "you didn't waste much time to have a family did you?"

But Jess saw John's face change and quickly said. "It was love at first sight wasn't it darling?"

"Yes it was," happy now that Jess had called him darling, after everything. He moved closer to her putting his arm round her shoulders.

Howard changed the subject quickly: "What work do you do John?"

No hesitation. "Well I make garden furniture, which is all wicker work. He thought he'd better not lie, so he continued: "The man that gives me this interesting work lives near us."

"He's very good at his job and John is happy with him," Jess added.

Amanda was staring at Jess now. "Are you looking forward to your baby coming?" she asked in a quiet voice? Stephanie had told her about what had happened to Jess's first child, so she didn't want to bring that up. Better to ask about the new baby. She wasn't happy with what Howard had said to John though and she would have something to say about that to him later.

"Yes we both are," Jess smiled. "You know Amanda I haven't seen you and Howard for some years. I understand you live in Cornwall now? Do you have any children?"

"No we decided to get our home nicely furnished first. Before we settle down with a family. However we have been married nearly seven years, still plenty of time Howard says."

Jess noticed the look from the girl, that showed she would love a family. "Oh I see and do you like living in Cornwall?"

Her husband intervened: "Yes, it's great isn't it love?"

"Yes we're very happy there, it's such a pretty place. And we have a lovely little house with just the right size garden, which we can manage."

"Do you work?" Even though Stephanie had told her that both of them did, still she was trying to keep the conversation going.

"Yes I'm a nursery nurse which I love, looking after the children. And Howard is an estate agent and in actual fact that's how we got our house when it came up for sale, he was in the right place at the right time, and jumped in before anybody else got interested in the property."

"That was good then," Jess smiled.

John had heard enough he was now on edge. Where was Frank? He gently took Jess's arm before giving an excuse to get away from the two.

"Yes bye see you later," Howard said.

Jess had explained the worry of Frank to the two before and what was uppermost in their minds at this time. But she got the feeling Howard and Amanda could see how John was on edge because he seemed very uptight. Jess also was upset by everything, that had gone on, it was turning into the most dreadful evening. Frank was a nightmare. She had been so looking forward to this barbecue, it was to be her first trip out in months well for both of them. Why had they brought this individual here? Poor Stephanie must have regretted saying he could come.

"I am sorry about leaving those two Jess and breaking up the party." John explained. "But I was so worried about what Frank was getting up too. I did give him a talking to after that situation with Stephanie but, I still have to watch him. However he seems to have quietened down a little at the moment." He smiled at her but he could see how much she was on edge too.

As they walked a bit nearer towards the patio acknowledging people with a smile, or wave of the hand as they went. The two saw Frank eating spare ribs now, as the juices ran down his chin, dripping onto his check shirt. He began to lick his fingers, one, by one, before rubbing them down his trousers and butting in on people's conversation's.

"So how many operations do you do in a week Doc? Frank asked Nat. "I bet you lose more than you save?"

Nat was beginning to hate this man in front of him. "Well I don't happen to give out classified information he told him." This situation was getting unbearable now. Stephanie needed to tell him something, but she'd said. "Later!"

"That told me," Frank laughed. Wondering what he could do next?

John left Jess and walked up to Frank, digging him in the back. "Excuse me folks," he said. Frank's strong body rebelled against John's hand, as the other pushed him, with force, out of the way and into a quiet spot in the garden. People were now staring at the scene. "So you listen and listen good, use your manners, if you have any, towards these people. Or I will knock your block off when we get away from here. Because tonight has been a living disaster with you. I can see on everyone's face's you are not wanted here."

"Too bad, because I'm staying. Oh and what I could disclose about you would surprise all of them. I wonder what would happen if I said you and I were convicts. Be a different type of barbecue wouldn't it?"

"SHUT IT!" John said looking around.

"So be nice to me or I'll have no hesitation in shopping you and think what that would do to your lady friend, who is expecting your sprout? And let me say the police wouldn't get me. I'd be gone after I'd turned you in.

"If things were not as they are and we weren't expecting a baby. I would turn myself in and serve the rest of my term in prison, rather than put up with you. But I love Jess and I don't want to hurt her. Having deceived her this far. It just breaks me up with what she's been through."

"Well, if she knew what you'd done she wouldn't want anything to do with you would she?" Frank told him.

"I think that would be it, anyway that's my problem. Stephanie has given this barbecue and allowed you to come here, now behave yourself or we're going home. Then I want you out of our lives do you hear?"

"Huh, hark at you? I didn't know you had such posh manners J-a-k-e-y boy. So you want me to go away do you? Well I don't think so. I have always thought that cottage is a great hiding place, away from the world, well almost. So don't preach to me, or Jess will be told everything Okay?"

John was confused now. "Have you been there before," he asked.

"That's for me to know and you to find out," he smiled.

John was confused and worried. He would sort that out later, because the man had mentioned that twice now.

"If your lady knew about us, that would be the end of your romance."

John could easily have hit him, for the things he was saying. He saw Jess walking in the garden on her own, with her head bowed, so he hit Franks arm hard before going to join her.

She turned and stared at him, he looked very worried, by the expression on his face. "Is everything alright?" She asked.

"Yes, Yes, of course, don't you worry Jess I'm sorting it out. How I could put you and everyone else through this, I don't know?" He remarked, "he's put me in an awkward position arriving on our doorstep, that I couldn't say no to all his pleas. However he's shot his bolt today with his rudeness and I want him out of our lives."

The small crowd of people had been talking in groups. Having been watching everything that had been going on with this dreadful individual. Who did seem very unsteady now, having had lots of wine and spirits also he'd been eating for the country. He was an utter pig John thought and uncouth. This was what most of the inmates in prison were like, thankfully he didn't feel like he was one of them.

Frank stared after John watching as he talked to Jess. She was a good-looking woman he thought. The kid was another matter though. There might be an accident waiting to happen perhaps to her. That's why he intended to stay put. He would be getting rid of so-called John first, which shouldn't be too hard. He couldn't resist this food which had been barbecued by Nathan earlier on. Taking a plate he loaded it up with another lot of spare ribs, pulling them apart with his ugly teeth as the juices ran down his chin, once more.

Chapter 29

"Whatever possessed Jess to bring this awful man to our home? Nat was saying to Steph and where did she and John meet him? Look at our friends you can see the distasteful look on their faces. I'm sure they're thinking that our choice of friends has gone down. This will probably be the last party we'll ever have."

"I hope not. Don't say that? What could I do it wasn't Jess's fault, this man is supposed to be John's friend and she wanted to please him? When we were asked if he could come this evening we couldn't say no, could we? That would have hurt Jess. She did say that John owed him a favour whatever that was about? But I don't know why we have to suffer. I wanted this evening to be special. after all Jess hasn't been out for ages and I thought she'd enjoy a barbecue. Now its ruined by this dreadful man and her face looks so sad at times, I know she's not enjoying herself. Also I'm a little apprehensive about John too, even though I have to say he was wonderful when he rescued me from that awful man, like I told you a while ago. But it's a funny situation all round, him just appearing that awful snowy night and then leaving and I thought that was it, but he came back and they got together seriously, as you can see, hence a baby on the way. What next?"

"Glad you're alright after that situation you had. Oh well, let's grin and bear it," Nathan told Steph placing a plate in her hand and putting chicken and sausages onto it, she was now looking surprised by the little pile of food. "Well I cooked it, so we might as well eat it," he smiled affectionately. "Let's try and enjoy the rest of the evening shall we?"

She kissed him on the cheek. "Yes lets."

Time was getting on when John asked. "Are you alright Jess?"

"Well I am a little tired, I expect it's the situation."

John rested his hand on her stomach affectionately. But then he looked up; where had he gone? He began to wonder,

194

he'd lost the moment once more. Jess looked up at him. "What were you talking about to your friend just now?"

"He's not my friend, I really can't stand the sight of him and I gave him another warning to behave himself while he was here."

"Sorry I didn't mean that, slip of the tongue. What did he say?"

"No problem," he lied.

The music was going full pelt now and two couples were dancing. It was a lovely warm evening, no more rain. Under different circumstances it would have been great.

"Where did you ever meet such a horrible character as that dreadful man over there?" Jess pointed.

John had to think about this. "Let's not discuss it now, I'll tell you later, we must let the people here see we are enjoying ourselves."

She held on to his arm and squeezed it acknowledging his remark.

Stephanie was beginning to relax a little, as she watched her friends having fun, ignoring this huge bear like man, with the ugly looks.

John turned to Jess. "Dance?" Who would have thought he'd be at a barbecue after such a dreadful few years? And meet this wonderful woman, who meant everything to him and was now pregnant with his child.

"I didn't know you could."

"Oh yes, I have done it before you know?"

"With whom?"

"Ah! Well I did have girlfriends many moons ago. But they weren't like holding you in my arms."

She nestled her head on his chest. She did love him.

Stephanie watched her dear and closest friend dance with John, they did seem happy. But she could tell this big burly loathsome creature was making their life hell. It was upsetting Jess a great deal, she could tell by her face. She was usually so chatty but not so much this evening. She knew she had been looking forward to her evening out, but Steph now could see these two people were unhappy, but were trying to put a brave face on it. She would have to try and find out more? But was now wondering, why she ever got involved with John. I mean he had been a complete stranger, she had known nothing about him. Still it was not for her to comment on their relationship, after all Jess must have known what she was doing. Steph looked around at her friends that were dancing. She had enjoyed the food Nathan had given her, even if it did stick in her throat at times, because she had rushed it. A few of her friends were silently talking in groups. She could tell they didn't like that man by the worried look on their faces.

Nathan walked over to the bar where Frank was, "Excuse me I have to get some more drinks for my friends," and reached across for the rum.

"Let them get the drinks themselves, lazy buggers," Frank slurred.

"Excuse me I wish you wouldn't speak of our friends like that. Nathaniel told him. If you don't like it here you should go."

John and Jess were staring at the slight commotion, they stopped dancing and walked over to Nat.

"I'm sorry," he told them both, "but this man you have brought to our party is despicable and the sooner he goes the better." As he then looked at Frank drinking whiskey and eating as though there were no tomorrow. Shovelling it into his mouth again.

Stephanie joined Jess and John but was getting worried now by Nathaniel's attitude towards Frank when she heard what was being said. She didn't want him to get into a fight because this man could hurt him badly, being so big.

"I'm so sorry," John was saying to Nathaniel and Stephanie now. "We'll leave if you don't mind and I'm sure you don't?" He half smiled and pointed to Frank. "He's done enough damage for one evening." He looked across at Jess who looked so tired by the whole situation as he carried on talking to the two. "We've spoilt your barbecue, we wouldn't have done that for the world to you both."

"Yes we're terribly sorry everyone, this situation has been forced upon us hasn't it John?" She told the crowd bravely.

"It has, get your things Jess we're going." He noticed all the friends at the party had congregated together talking and pointing, this was awful.

Frank was so drunk he was getting clumsy too, knocking a drink off a table, as the crowd watched in horror. When he lunged his way forward towards Amanda who was standing nearby, pushing his huge body into hers. Whilst she stood there helpless and frightened by this big unpleasant person. At that moment she didn't know what to do, but the look on her face told it all, as he reached for her assets. He hadn't had a woman for many years, as he then remembered that tart Rhoda, different type of woman. This one felt so good in his arms as he noticed though her whole body was shaking. When her husband left the person he had been talking to and shot across the garden, pulling the man's arm free from his wife.

"What are you doing you big oaf? Leave my wife alone," Howard shouted, pulling him away, as others came forward to help too.

John was shaking now with worry, in case things came out about the prison. That would be it with Jess and everyone else. He had to get Frank away from this party. So he ran over apologising to Howard. "I am sorry" he told him, as the man cuddled his wife trying to console her.

"That's enough Frank we're going."

"Why's that J-a-k-e-e- John!"

With that John had had enough and gave him a back hander on the jaw. In fact he thought he'd broken his hand. The man was bleeding from his nose as pandemonium broke out, John realised he wasn't in his league because he was much tougher and could if he'd wanted to crush him.

"Oh no," yelled Jess.

"Do something," Stephanie shouted. Ring the police Nathaniel!!"

Both men stopped and looked at each other knowing they had a lot to lose.

John had stunned the man with the big frame, but he was only dazed. Looking now across to Steph he told her again. "It's okay we're going."

197

John pushed the big oaf towards the side gate, as he tried to raise his arm to the crowd struggling to keep the man standing up properly, he was so heavy. When he shouted out. "JESS!"

"Why couldn't you have left me alone a bit longer with that woman, I nearly scored," Frank told him slurring.

"I don't think so," John answered with a huge sigh. In one respect it was easier for him to push the man along as he was so drunk now and dazed. He would never have been able to cope with him, had he not been, because he would have retaliated and he, John, would have come off worst. That could have been very nasty indeed because this man was like a man mountain to fight, as he'd found out.

Well he'd eaten and drunk himself silly. As both struggled towards the car, he pushed Frank with difficulty onto the back seat, where he was now snoring. But John was looking for Jess wanting to get away, as soon as possible. He noticed that the party crowd had congregated at the gate and were staring at them and some were shaking their heads. As he looked again he saw Nat raise his thumb to him and John did it back. But where was Jess?

Nathan and Stephanie had been horrified by what had just happened and Jess wanted to sit down and gather her thoughts. What a terrible evening it had been, this man had to get out of their lives once and for all. She was going to phone the police if he didn't go, she knew that now. She would tell John once they arrived home, friend or no friend. How he ever got involved with such a man she just couldn't believe. Getting up now she swayed as Stephanie helped her walk towards the car. "I really don't know what to say. I bet you wish you'd never invited us this evening?" Jess told her friend.

"You're always welcome, it's just him, he's the pain," Stephanie admitted, pointing towards Frank who she could see was now sitting on the back seat of the car asleep.

The party had begun to break up and Amanda and Howard were clearing up the mess on the patio for Nat and Steph, wanting to help them after what had happened, telling them both not to worry about anything, things happen like this at times. People get drunk and impossible. Having said that they didn't like this horrible man. It was now 11.30 and the party was well and truly over, never to be forgotten.

Stephanie felt dazed by what had gone on, she said. "Do as I say Jess get rid of this man he's no good, he's dangerous."

"I don't want to go in that car," Jess told her friend. When she saw John standing by it waiting for her.

He walked towards them and took Jess's arm. "Don't worry darling he's quietened down now, come on let's go home."

Nathan had joined them too, if only to see this car load going home, but he did feel sorry for these two.

Stephanie noticed her friend looked really on edge now. "Jess you're not going home with that big ape are you? Why don't you stay with us tonight? Eh Nathan?" She saw that he looked surprised by that remark, but agreed. That would give John time to get rid of him.

John was staring at his Jess, before looking across at the small party of people on the front lawn, who were watching what was going on. He felt happier now that he'd managed to get so called Frank into the car, and the man was snoring loudly, not good.

"Don't worry you two, he said to Nat and Steph we'll be okay now, but thanks for that offer Jess will be fine, I will make sure of that. Come on darling!" He said gently.

She stared at him. "I don't want to go in that car with him, but I don't want to leave you."

"I know you don't but, you will be ok," he told her, "he's asleep now, and I will take great care of you Jess you know that, this man has to go, I'll see to that."

"If he doesn't I'm ringing the police John and I mean that. Okay I'm going home, she told her friends. So sorry to have ruined your barbecue you two."

"Please don't worry Jess we'll get over it, Steph told her, but, get rid of that man?" She pointed.

John didn't want to make too much of this situation. After all if Jess phoned the police that would be the end of it all. He had to sort this out if he wanted to carry on with his life at the cottage, with her and hopefully his baby? Everyone was wondering what he was going to do, or say? When he put his arm around the only woman he had ever really loved. That was apart from his mother of course, she had always stood by him. But of course it was a different love. In fact if he could get Frank out of his life, he would take Jess to meet her one day but sadly there would be a great deal of explaining. "Come on then darling," he said squeezing her arm affectionately. "I'm sorry, about this and you made us so welcome, he told the host and hostess. This man has to go, favour or not," he smiled at them trying to behave, as Jess would want him to. Actually he would like to have punched Frank's lights out, if he had the strength against this big man.

"Well please get rid of him?" Nathaniel told him, "he's a dangerous person, in fact. HE LOOKS LIKE A CONVICT TO ME. You don't think he is one of the escaped one's do you? They haven't caught them yet!"

Jake didn't want to hear that, it was too close for comfort. He felt Jess shake against him. "No I'm sure not, he hadn't been in prison when I first met him a year ago. He did me a favour and I wouldn't be here today but for him. That's why when he came to us on that day we tried to make him welcome, well Jess did. I was paying him back and that was it. So I do apologise for everything we should never have brought him to your house and I'm sorry about the fight, but he deserved it, what little I could do."

"Just get rid of him John for my friend's sake, he's a monster," Stephanie sighed.

John looked at Nathan now and could see the fury written all over his face. "I will. You know I feel really bad for ruining your evening."

He felt Jess's eyes on him, he had to get away from here. "Bye for now," he said, "and thank you." As Nat seemed to be weighing the situation up, because he didn't say anything back. Moving towards the car with Jess now snuggled into him he said. "I didn't realise what a pain in the arse, he was going to be."

He felt Jess's eyes on him. "Sorry about that word Jess but he is," he explained, "leave it to me I promise I will get rid of him."

"I do hope so John," she said nervously sitting down in the driving seat, when she turned to him. "You don't think he's one of those convicts do you?" She asked him in a very low voice. Not wanting to wake the man in the back.

"No of course not, now are you still alright to drive home, like we planned? As I have had a couple of pints too many. Anyway I want to keep an eye on him is that alright?" He saw her nod, knowing that he still shouldn't drive her car anyway. "Are you alright darling?"

"Yes I'm fine, I need to drive, it will take my mind off this evening," she said. Looking in her mirror at this horrible, horrible, man on the back seat with his head down, she shuddered as she started up the engine, where was all this going?

John turned round to see that this hateful man was now snoring, his mouth was open and shut by big puffs of air and dribble. Oh how he hated him now, what an evil individual he looked. He'd got to sort all this out, just supposing he couldn't get rid of him what would he do? First thing in the morning he was hoping he'd be gone, but he was feeling very doubtful about this and very worried about the whole thing, because he didn't want to go back to prison and what about Jess? She probably wouldn't want him anyway when she knew what had he got himself into? He should never have escaped from prison, especially with the help of Luke, how wrong it all was. In hindsight he should have done his time and come out clean, but then in his mind he would never have met up with Jess, their paths probably would never have crossed and he couldn't bear that thought. John and Jess waved to their friends who were standing outside by the porch. When they saw Stephanie mime something. Jess wound the window down, so they could hear what she was saying, as she saw her shout through cupped hands.

"Take care you two, I'll ring you in the morning okay?" As she watched them wave back, before she and Nat turned to go indoors. The little crowd had gone from the gate now and Amanda and Howard were almost finished clearing up the mess, with the help now of Andy and Jill. The four had been talking about the evening and the fight between Frank and John which had taken place on the patio when the barbecue chicken and other bits went all over the place.

"How awful that man has to stay with Jess and John tonight?" Stephanie was saying to Nat. They will be so on edge she thought and probably wouldn't sleep at all. If it was her she wouldn't sleep either, having him in the house. Still hopefully John will get rid of him first thing in the morning.

"Your right there, he agreed, I pity those two and shook his head. Taking her arm now as they walked through the hall, before going out into the garden to explain the things to the others. Seeing that Andy and Jill had joined them, after helping Howard and Amanda clear up.

Chapter 30

John was on Jess's mind now, she'd never seen him in such a temper, Frank had really pushed him to the limit this evening, so she couldn't blame him for losing his cool. He would get rid of Frank, that she was certain of, now she had to concentrate on the drive home. John and her were looking so forward to their forthcoming child, but with all this happening would they ever be happy like they were before? It was funny but she had a peculiar feeling that somewhere, sometime, she had met this individual perhaps not, what an awful evening it had been for one and all. However, John had gone quiet on the way home and was hardly talking at all, he looked as though he was wondering how he was going to get rid of this horrible man on the back seat. She took a sidelong glance to see his jaw was firmly set. Better not talk to him now as he must be so embarrassed by the other man's behaviour, thank goodness he was asleep, it was the only bit of peace they'd had all evening. The drink had knocked him out alright because he was snoring very loudly As Jess steered the car up the lane leading towards the cottage Frank suddenly began to stir with the bumps in the road.

"Where are we? he asked.

John turned round and stared at him. "We're at the cottage you drunken son of a bitch causing all that trouble tonight."

"Well it was you if you remember, that punch you gave me landed pretty hard on my chin, I didn't know you had it in you. J-a k-i-e or should I say John."

"WHAT?" Jess shouted out, looking in the mirror at Frank before taking a quick glance at John.

This was (Jakes) worst moment. "Take no notice Jess he thinks he's being funny, but he isn't."

As she pulled the car up to the side of the cottage, he said. "You go indoors and I'll be there in a minute. I just want a word with Frank okay?"

"Will you be alright John?" she asked, worried now at what he was about to say to this individual, also what he might do.

"Don't you worry I'll be fine darling," he knew she liked to here him say that. Look you go and get that kettle on and I'll be there in a minute. Now let's try and forget all that's happened shall we?" He said looking in his passenger mirror at the man on the back seat who had gone decidedly quiet for a change. All of a sudden John got out of the car and walked round towards the driver's side. Opening the door for Jess he gave her his hand and helped her out.

She kissed him on the lips, before walking away. Feeling very worried for him and wondering what was going to happen, because she didn't trust that man in the back of the car, whoever he was. "Be careful."

"Don't you worry he shouted, I'II be fine."

"She's a bit of alright that woman but, she needs a real man and that's exactly what she'll get. Me! Ha! Ha!"

"Get out you? Jake opened the back door and leaned in. Don't you say another word about Jess. Keep your mouth shut. First thing in the morning I want you gone, I want you out of mine and Jess's life forever, you hear? Do I have to repeat myself again? He went on. You are the most despicable person I've ever met. You're ruining our lives. GO AWAY. I wish I'd never got involved with you."

Frank suddenly pulled John towards him by the collar, he had great strength in his arms. "I'm not going anywhere, so let's get that straight, I intend to win your lovely girlfriend over and you won't be in the picture at all by then," he said, with a sinister smile on his face.

John began to shake, never in a million years should he have ever got teamed up with this man. It was the worst possible thing he could ever have done, he now realised. He was the vilest human being on the planet. A living nightmare, that's what he was and the man was out to ruin his life, how did he ever hit Frank the way he did when he's built like a tank? Well that lump of wood came in handy the first time when they were in the park. At the party he had used every bit of energy when he had hit him and just been lucky, probably because Frank had been off his guard at that particular moment, and not believing that John had it in him to do it. Still he knew he'd never win a fight when he was sober, the man was much bigger than him. What really

204

irritated him was he didn't like the advances he'd made on Jess. Thinking back he'd been so shocked at the time when she told him about the baby, but on the other hand he was thrilled to bits now and thought hopefully all would work out, but he wasn't too know? He hated Frank and was beginning to think, why the devil did he allow all this to happen? Why hadn't he told Jess everything and be done with it? Because it couldn't go on like this. "You'll never have Jess!"

"Just wait and see."

"Well I shall ring the police and tell them their escaped convict is here, then you will be put away again, where you should be. Behind bars!! And if it means me being caught too, so be it."

The man was laughing out loud now. "You wouldn't?"

"Push me too far and I would. If it means Jess not wanting me then as I've said before, so be it. You said at the party you were going to split on me, well the tables are turned now."

"What would happen to your lovely lady John if you tell? I don't think she would want you anymore. Especially when she knows you killed your wife and you know what? Your da-da days will be over."

John tried to pull Frank out of the car, but to no avail. The man sat there not moving just smiling at him and he saw he was losing this argument, when suddenly he yelled out in pain staring at Frank in total despair, not believing what really was happening. The man had stabbed him in the shoulder with the wooden knife he had made when he was in the garden, it was as sharp as a razor, which went straight through his shirt. He'd evidently planned to do this at some point, John realised that now as pain shot through his body and he fell out the car in a crumpled heap onto the ground.

Frank stepped over him laughing and running towards the cottage as fast as he could with his very large frame. Reaching the door, suddenly he turned and looked totally surprised at seeing John was right behind him. He'd got up fast from the ground and ran after the man as best he could, because he was worried about Jess now. Holding his shoulder he felt the sticky blood run down his arm, not seeing it properly though, because there wasn't much light, only from cottage inside, which Jess had put on. Frank was now making a hideous noise as he swayed back and forth, actually John realised he was singing if you could call it that? He wasn't going to let this evil man get the better of him but was worried for Jess's sake and after tussling with Frank for what seemed like an eternity, he noticed her standing there watching the two of them. her hand over her mouth, probably not believing what she was looking at. Stamper was by her side barking as she held tightly onto him.

"John, Frank stop it!" She shouted as tears run down her cheeks when she turned and ran indoors with the dog following and dialled 999 before rushing to the door again with him. When suddenly she saw Frank raise his arm with the dangerous weapon in his hand and charge towards John. Jess screamed!

It was at that moment John realised Frank had got the better of him, as the man moved towards him again to possibly kill him. He was swaying back and forth drunk, as he headed for John who thankfully jumped aside, as Frank fell heavily to the ground after tripping onto a large stone by the front door. He heard Jess scream the man wasn't moving and John was bleeding badly from his shoulder wound now, as the scene in front of him came to a climax. John stood over Frank's body on the ground, not believing what had just happened. Somebody up there loved him. He bent down and felt the man's pulse and realised at that moment that he was dead, the dreadful moment was over. When he had rushed towards him with the knife to hurt him again, he had fallen on it and it had pierced his heart. John began to think now how sadistic Luke had been to whittle that piece of wood with horrific intentions. He must have been planning this situation for some time. Thank God it never came off and the plan backfired on him, it was peculiar that he had fallen on a stone which Jess had painted a picture liken to her little girl who she had lost, fate certainly played a hand. The man got his just deserts big time.

Jess was by John's side now and in his arms. "Is he dead?"

"Yes Jess."

"But he was so strong,"

"Well it must have been on the cards, because through eating so much food and drinking himself silly at the barbecue he wasn't steady on his feet or else he might have polished me off.

It was his drinking which really killed him. As he ran towards me puffing, blowing and swaying, backwards and forwards, he tripped over your stone and onto the knife he'd made. So it had backfired on him and he caused the whole thing himself. It's over Jess he was a dangerous man. And now I have to tell you something!!"

"Me also, when I saw you in difficulty and bleeding from your shoulder, I rang the police they should be here any minute."

Swallowing hard he said, "OH! NO! Jess I have to tell you this before they come. He felt ill at that moment, the relationship was over he couldn't carry on like this. Going indoors he began to explain, sit down please. Frank was not who you thought he was. He wasn't my friend, he was one of the convicts who escaped from the prison, His real name is not Frank Nichols it's Luke Stamford."

"What? How do you know that?"

"Because I am the other one the police are looking for!!! My real name is not John Turner it's Jake Farrendon." He watched her reaction as her face dropped and she moved away from him. "Jess I must explain everything. I have been deceiving you over and over again, which I'm not proud of. My heart is breaking inside for what I've done to you."

"YOU CANT BE A PRISONER, YOU CANT BE? But my thoughts were right HE WAS THE ONE WHO KILLED MY BECKY. I've had it on my mind many times. I knew I had seen him somewhere before, but he looks so different from years ago. That was when I first saw him in court, he had a moustache and long side burns, also a pony tail and he was a lot thinner, and now he has that scar on his forehead and loose unruly hair, but it was those eyes. You see I kept putting it to the back of my mind thinking it couldn't be? Because he was your friend, but he's so bloated now and looks totally different. No it can't be him, I thought. Then in the next breath, how happy we've been. J a k e … how could you do this to me? We've had a lovely few months together, but there were times when I did wonder about that temper of yours."

"Sorry about that Jess. I can't believe Luke killed your little girl? That's horrendous please believe me, I had no idea. But he did say he liked it here which I couldn't make out. I said to him have you been here before, but he didn't say just smirked as usual."

She was becoming a little nervous of him again he could see the panic in her face.

"He fell over my daughters stone, so he got his just deserts." As tears began to fall and she stared at Jake but she wasn't frightened of him, because she really believed he loved her as he'd told her so many time's and she sensed he would never ever harm her. "That man took my daughter's life." She was now shaking uncontrollably, as she felt John's good arm go round her, that she couldn't take. 'Don't!" she shivered.

Jake was hurt by that remark, but didn't blame her. He was in such pain from his shoulder now. But all he could think of was everything he had to tell her and what he'd done? When he heard, "I must see to your wound." With all that had happened she was still concerned about him. "How did you ever get involved with that murderer I'll never know? And why were you in prison?"

When she'd bandaged his arm up he said: "Sit down, I have to tell you everything now."

She was shaking again and struggling with her words as she said: "I can't believe all this but it was brought to my attention at the party, I can't remember who said it now? ...Oh yes I do, it was Nathaniel, he said that so called Frank could be an escaped prisoner. Well that made me think that I'd seen him before, but where? Then it came to me on the way home in the car, that's why I was so frightened by the whole thing. Yes it was him, my child's murderer as I said. Stephanie and I hardly looked his way at the time in court because we just couldn't and I felt so sick and devastated by the whole incident. He killed my little girl, I felt as though I was going to collapse when my friend took me outside the courtroom. You see I didn't want to be in the same room as him. I can't believe that I hadn't recognised him straight away on that awful day, when he knocked at the door wanting you. And also coming back into my life again, which was the very last thing I wanted. Anyway all I thought was, he was your friend. So I did what you asked and let him enter my home, which I wish I'd never done now. He must have thought he was onto a good thing, getting into my house and me

208

giving him clothes to wear and then allowing him to come to my friends barbecue evening, I can't believe it. How stupid am I? That I made this dreadful mistake in trusting people."

"Poor Jess you are a lovely caring lady whom l love and you're not stupid your wonderful and trusting." He looked down at his shoulder the blood was seeping through the bandage onto his shirt again. So he gingerly got up and pressed a medicated pad onto it. "Don't worry I won't hurt you," he said struggling to dress the wound himself, when she suddenly leaned across from her chair and helped him. "But there's more I have to tell you before the police arrive, which won't be too long now." She looked so sad, when he tried to get close to her so she moved back. What had he done to this woman whom he loved?

Jess placed a hand on her stomach and began to cry. This anxiety wasn't good for her, or the baby at this time. It was difficult to look at Jake's face now to see him with a different identity. As she continued to sit she placed her hands in her lap, after hearing all this. As she thought of that evil man outside with a knife in him, which he'd thrust in Jake first. Now it was the reverse, his wooden knife had killed him in the end. This was all so unnerving. But there was only one thing she could think at that moment and that was he wouldn't hurt anyone else and that he was gone for good. And she had freedom for her daughter at last. What was going to happen to her life now though? As once more things hadn't worked out, and the man she had grown to love had deceived her in every way possible. Where would all this end? Jess was totally confused as she now listened to what Jake had to tell her.

Chapter 31

He turned to her, "I know what I'm about to tell you will be upsetting Jess and I realise you will probably never ever want to see me again after all this? But I have to tell you it all now and leave nothing out. I was married for five years, he saw the look of horror on her face which was as white as snow, (where this all began.) As he wondered what she'd say? Still he had to be honest now and tell everything, which he did, getting it all off his conscience and bringing this to a conclusion, never leaving anything out, because she had a right to know. He was loath to do this as he didn't want to hurt her. However, this was the day of truth, he'd had enough of all the lies. That was what you do when you love someone, you have to be honest in the end. She had over the last few months become his world, he lived for nothing else but to make her happy. But it was because of that, he just couldn't go on like this. Luke was dead outside the truth will out. He began thinking how surprised the police would be when they saw they had captured two prisoners in one day, but one was dead.

He also knew this would be the end of everything for him, he saw her face drop once more, when he told her he accidentally killed his wife. Her life had been awful and now it was again. He hated himself for what he'd done to her and said so. If he never loved again, she Jess, would stay in his heart forever. What had he done to her? She must hate him, he knew his relationship was over. He had no option now so it was back to prison, but it had all been worthwhile, he'd loved these last few months with this woman. Why was life so complicated? When suddenly he heard her say …

"Jake you killed your wife, how can I ever forget that? Then you broke out of prison."

"Jess I told you it was an accident, let me explain a bit more. I was so upset at the time to find out she had been having an affair with my best friend, at that, in our house. I thought she was happy with me. There was no indication anything was wrong, well not on my part, we were even saving for a new car.

Then the bombshell hit, their affair had been going on for some time apparently. Can you believe I was oblivious to it all?" He saw Jess shake her head. "Well I was in such a state about what she did to me. I only pushed her slightly but she accidentally fell onto the fender and hit her head on the hearth. It was such a terrible thing to happen, I didn't know she would fall. I've never ever been violent in my life, but the hurt came through. I was disgusted with them both. They even took all my money from my bank account. You know before all that happened I was a happy sort of bloke, but this situation changed me, especially when they sent me to prison for manslaughter. I got six years, and only had two more years to go, I know I was stupid to pal up with Luke but I was so unhappy in prison with all those maniac men, I was debating to do away with myself." He saw her breathe in deeply with concern for him, he was sure. "I was also fed up with being pushed around by the cons, so to break out was the opening I needed. Luke said it was fool proof, which I fell for. It worked for me, but not for him straight away and I was hoping it never would.

So you see that's how it all came about on that snowy day, when we first met and you gave me a lift. Which I thank you for from the bottom of my heart, because it's been a very happy few months for me being with you. Now you know things, it's such a load off my mind, but I hated lying to you. He watched as her head dropped in anguish. Luke told me of the plan to get out of prison, I never liked him and didn't know what crime he'd committed, so I was apprehensive, but my thought was it just might work and that's when you brought me to this lovely cottage. I am so sorry that I've had to lie to you in the past, you trusted me and we became so close and fell in love. You would never have given me a lift that night, or let me stay here if you had known. I needed a safe place and this was perfect. He watched as the tears fell down onto her cheeks. Then Luke found me that day in the park sitting on a seat enjoying life, thanks to you. But I wish I hadn't been there because look how that's ended up? He watch as she nodded back. But it's up to you what you say and do when the police arrive. But you're the woman I should have had at the very beginning not Kate, I thought a lot of her, but it wasn't the love that we have shared that's the truth, for once. Our lives would have been so good together, well as it has been these last few months.

"It has," she heard herself saying feeling sick inside.

"One more thing I must tell you is I don't have a brother or sister-in-law. You see I didn't know what to say when you asked me and I wasn't going to frighten you by everything that had happened, I certainly didn't want to tell you all those lies, but I was nervous that I'd lose you. But now I really hate myself and realise that I should never have escaped from prison, because when I go back, I will have to do more time there. You know what though, my mother is a lovely caring lady and I did see her when I told you I was going to, so that's no lie. Would you tell her though that I've been caught please?" "She will be so relieved I know because she was upset by my escape of course, but she would always stand by me though, and she made such a fuss of me for two days, but then there was a big problem. And he is called George Trent a friendly prison officer, who would you believe is going out with my mother now and that is also no lie either. The thing is he and I got on really well at the prison and he was one of the officers who was guarding me, the day I made my escape.

Now he doesn't know he's going out with my mother! You see she's also going under an assumed name as she has never told him about me." "Poor Mum she didn't want to lie either and has had her problems, what have I done to everyone I love? Then out of all the people in the world she dates my friendly prison warder. You know she would love to meet you, if that was ever possible? Jess this is something I'm really hoping will happen because she's a good person, so if you need somebody to look after you. Just go and see her, he added as he awkwardly wrote down the address with his other hand. She had been devastated by what I did. And I let George down too. He also will be so pleased to hear I've been caught, even though he's retired now, but I'm positive he will want me to serve my time and then get on with my life. He bent down and stroked Stamper who licked his hand. Woof!! Good boy take care of your mistress." He smiled.

212

Out of all the people in the world, my mother is courting she's got involved with George. But I couldn't choose anyone better for her. She's a widow, as I mentioned to you and she knows more than anybody what I'm like. As for me I will go back inside for a while, but I do intend to behave myself and be a model prisoner, to be released quicker." He saw her hand go up and cover her mouth. "Yes, I think that's the police I heard outside." As the noise filled the kitchen, one thing that made him really happy at that moment was that Luke was dead and would never harm anybody ever again. And when his baby was born whether it be a boy or girl, it would thrive with Jess's love and of course his. Even though he would be in prison. The two stared at each other. When all of a sudden hell broke loose as the police barged in through the door and the police officers walked towards him.

"Are you Jake Farrendon?" One of them asked.

"Yes!!" He wondered what Jess had told them now, on the phone.

"And we take it that is Luke Stamford lying on the ground outside?"

"Yes!!" Of course they'd seen their pictures over the months.

This was a nightmare, Jess felt devastated watching Jake get up and walk towards the two men in uniform, as they began to read him his rights.

She ran forward and grabbed his hand, "Jake I really can't believe you did this to me. I loved you and brought you into my home. We've been so happy together and all the time you were hiding this terrible secret, deceiving me with every single word you uttered. I never thought that you were an escaped convict, ever!!!"

The uniformed men were now handcuffing him and listening to the two's hurried conversation.

"Not every word Jess, not about what I think of you, that is definitely true, no lie. These last few months of my life have been the happiest I have ever had, never forget that." The police were pulling him towards the door. "Of course I shouldn't have done what I did and I've had to pay the price, but it was a total accident. You see I thought I owed Luke for what he did for me but, I was wrong. Anyway Jess would you please tell Mr Hammond how sorry I am to have deceived him and that I won't be going back."

She nodded.

All of a sudden Detective Inspector Pat Thornton entered and the look on his face was stern. "We've been looking for you Jake Farrendon for a few months. And Luke Stamford for a week, I saw your photo's down at the station. I have to say you look rather different now, with that beard and hair. Your partner in crime looks what he is a nasty piece of work."

"Let's get this straight I don't want him known as my partner because I hated the man, but all I wanted was to get out of that terrible place; Slate Moors Prison. But he was the only one that came up with the plan of escape which might work and it did. You know Inspector Thornton I love my life here with Jess and I didn't want to be caught. I'm not a bad man really." As he then began to explain what went on outside between him and Luke, saying how the other man had tripped on the stone, as he went forward to injure Jake, but it had gone completely wrong. He heard Jess say:

"That's exactly what happened because I was there at the time."

Jake looked away from the two policeman and began to stare at Jess, as he pleaded with her to forgive him, but she never spoke, so he said. "Please Jess if you never want to see me again, somehow let me know how our baby girl or boy is when it's born? I do hope you realise that I never wanted to get involved with that awful man out there. But I know that I have to serve my punishment now"

He watched as the Inspector frowned, probably he'd heard all this before from other prisoners, not knowing that this time everything was going to be true what Jake was saying.

"That's enough, save the rest Jake Farrendon until we get to the police station and then you have a great deal of explaining to do again, before you go back to prison." He said. Turning and walking towards Jess.

She looked so upset she couldn't talk, as she watched what happened next.

Placing their hands onto Jakes shoulder the Inspector's two men led him from the room after reading him his rights. Probably walking round the dead man lying on the ground outside as the ambulance had just arrived to pick up the body of Luke Stamford.

Jess was in tears as she saw Jake being guided away. Never in her wildest dreams did she think he had been an escaped convict. Ever since she met him she'd thought they were meant to be together. Everything had been wonderful, every day was a joy to them both. She got up from the kitchen chair and slumped down into the armchair, which she and Jake had shared, when she saw the Inspector staring at her. "We understand that Luke was the person who murdered your little girl four years ago Mrs Sinclair. We're so very sorry that all this is on your doorstep yet again."

Jess looked up from her chair at the Inspector. "So I was right, that horrible man Luke Stamford did kill my Becky?"

She saw him nod, as she began to explain everything that had happened with this awful man Luke and of course her life with Jake. "I did start to put things together, but this Luke has changed so much, I wasn't sure. So when this man came into my life the other evening and Jake, who I've known as John, for a few month's said he was a friend and he owed him, because he did something for Jake I felt compelled -to help him and I knew nothing about this horrid man. But somewhere there was a memory going round in my head, still I brushed it aside, thinking no this can't be. So I did what Jake- - wanted and invited him into my home, but I hated him, luckily it was only a short time but it became unbearable he was so uncouth and I couldn't wait for him to leave the house. Saying he was Jakes-- friend, I thought it was odd that John, as he was called, would get friendly with such a man. And what occurred now I've found out they were both prisoners." She began to sob uncontrollably. Then as she looked up he touched her, on the shoulder, shaking his head

"Will you be alright on your own Mrs Sinclair?"

Jess nodded and composed herself. "I'll be fine," she told him, "thank you. I rang my friend and she will be here in a while." With that he said his goodbyes and walked out of the door. She was thinking now about when she had rung Stephanie at work hearing her say.

'Oh no!! I will come straight over.'

Stephanie had been right about Jake. Now she couldn't stop crying. What was happening to her life? She looked through the kitchen window and saw the ambulance moving away with the body of Luke on board! And watched the van turn as it sped down the lane with Jake inside, until it faded out of sight. She felt exhausted now and began thinking of her muddled unhappy life. Whatever would have happened to them all if Luke hadn't collapsed and died? She and Jake might have been killed at some point, still they would never know now. Also could she ever forgive Jake. He had lied and lied. She knew what Stephanie would say: See I told you he wasn't to be trusted, also you knew I was never very keen on him. And how could you give a complete stranger a lift on that night? Still I have to say he's grown on me too now, when he saved me from that maniac man. And I feel there is a good side to him. I'm sure that would be her remark?

Well I gave him a lift because I liked him and trusted him, she'd have said, when I got used to him. Now as she thought of the wonderful moments they'd had together. Also when their baby was conceived, there was such happiness which had touched their lives at that time, when Jess had come back from the doctors with the wonderful news. There was going to be a baby, their baby. She had been very excited at the time and now realised why Jake hadn't been at first, because of where he'd come from at the time, prison. What was she going to do now? Never to see Jake again. She knew he had loved her as she had him, but could she ever forgive him?

Chapter 32

It was nearly Christmas. Since all those dreadful things had happened Jess had turned her life around. Jake was back in prison until his trial came up again. It would be another three years or more before he would be released, but with good behaviour who knows? He could be out before, the two hadn't been in contact since that dreadful day. She couldn't go and see him, she just couldn't, he had deceived her.

"Jess?"

"Yes what is it?" she shouted, as Jake's mother entered the kitchen.

"Do you want to keep these books?"

"No you can throw them away please they're old," she smiled. After Jake had gone back to prison, she went to see Jake's mother, like he asked her too. It took a lot of thought, but she went and never regretted it for one minute. The woman had taken her under her wing and treated her like a daughter. The two had become very close. Jess loved her. She was such a kind, sweet person, in fact she was going to give up her cottage and go and live with her next year, in her new flat, as the big house would be completed and ready to move into about the end of May. It had two bedrooms, so plenty of room. There would be four separate flats there eventually, not all taken. Amy would live with Jess whilst all the work was being done. So something to look forward too. The two had got very close over the weeks. She was like a mother to Jess. Well after all the upset with Jake her life had become a lot brighter since meeting this lovely lady. So today they were packing up with the help of George Trent, who had become Amy's partner and he had been delighted and surprised that they had caught Jake Farrendon, but was even more surprised when he found out it was Amy's son.

Well the whole story came out when Jake was incarcerated again. He had been shocked when he heard the story of Jake, Jess and his Amy. But how pleased he was that the young man was doing his time in prison and being a model prisoner,

217

behaving and doing everything he was told. Landing a job in the library where he began to write a book about his life and why he was where he was now, it was very therapeutic, he told George who still liked him and came to see him from time to time when he visited his old buddies the officers. And of course the governor was happy they had got Jake back in prison for George's sake.

Luke wasn't missed for all the terrible things he'd done. The prisoners seemed pleased that they didn't have to put up with him anymore.

Jake decided to wait and see what would happen when he came out of prison, to what Jess might think then about him, time would tell. He was hoping against hope that things would work out all round. If not, so be it. Jake had heard Jess was with his mum now, so that really pleased him. Except Stamper had to go to the dog's home as they couldn't take him to the flat. So George took him and what was unbelievable his owners were still looking for him, so all was well, he was back with them and seemed happy.

It was the 23rd of December. "Well we've almost finished," Amy told Jess, as she walked into the room smiling. This young woman had come into her life, making it so much brighter, she loved her. Jake had picked a good one here, it was a shame his life was so upside down. She stared at Jess, "you're tired, don't you do any more you hear? When she saw panic on the girls face at that moment. What?" Amy asked looking over to where Jess was pointing.

"Oh my God, your waters have broken," and she saw Jess nod. "Quick are you in much pain?" She asked her.

"Well let's just say the pains aren't too bad at the moment but getting closer, it's been happening for a while but I was busy sorting things out, so I brushed them aside, more fool me."

"GEORGE WHERE ARE YOU? We have to get to the hospital quickly my grandchild is on its way."

Two hours later Jess brought a beautiful baby boy into the world and it was delivered by Steph who had accepted the whole situation when told everything, but was terribly surprised by it all. Having awful thoughts of that Luke, especially who was no more thank goodness. She told Jess she was now very fond of Amy too. Now there was such excitement as Jess had so many kisses planted on her cheek. When Jake came into her mind. What would he say?

He heard the warder's steps as they got closer, putting his writing book and pen down onto his lap, he saw the bars sliding across his cell and a warder standing in front of him.

"Well Jake I have some good news for you. You have a baby son 7lb 11ozs he was born this morning, mother and baby are doing well. So what are you going to say about that then?"

He liked this fellow and felt sorry for him since he was brought back to prison, he noticed how certain men picked on him, but thankfully the chap took no notice now and always did as he was told never arguing, he was the perfect prisoner. Jake had learnt his lesson the hard way. The officer, Scott Mitchell, watched the young man, as a big smile crossed his face.

"I have a son?" He smiled, and hit the air. "Thank you Jess!! Thank you!!" he shouted out. As he stirred many inmates, hearing the nearest ones shouting out to him. "Congratulations."

Scott felt sad for him at that moment.

Jake was thrilled to hear this fantastic news, "Okay let's go."

"Where?" He asked the warder.

"Well you want to see your son don't you?" Scott Mitchell asked.

The excitement on Jake's face was a picture as he strolled into the decorated ward which looked colourful and glittery. Baby congratulation cards were everywhere as well as Christmas ones. He stared at his beautiful Jess as she sat up in a pristine bed holding their baby son, what a picture. Walking forward he kissed his mother, who looked so happy with her first grandchild. Shook hands with George and kissed Stephanie who was standing back, now at last friendly. Before he reached the bed he noticed Jess was full of smiles, she looked so happy, he thought, as he looked down at his baby son in her arms.

She began staring at him now. "Hello Jake. Well what do you think of your son?"

The warder smiled as he watched Jake's reaction; Jake couldn't stop smiling, as he thought his baby looked just like him, without the beard of course and the little bit of hair he possessed was the colour of his mother's, Auburn. He looked down at the tiny bundle, feeling so proud. "He's perfect, thank you Jess."

She couldn't take her eyes off him, not having seen him for six months, it had been June when he went back to prison. He looked thinner she thought. When all of a sudden lots of other people came into the room, it was a happy day, as they all began to sing. *'Silent Night'* Jess knew one thing, she still loved this man and she could tell he loved her, it was obvious, because he couldn't take his eyes off her, either. "What shall we call him Jake?"

"What about Nike?"

She laughed: "Very appropriate but I don't think that would be a good idea, do you? He doesn't want to think prison all his young life. she told him, looking down at her gorgeous son. But what do you say to Kane Edward Farrendon?"

"Oh Jess that's great because that was my father's middle name." He saw her nod and look at his mother, as she smiled at them both, happy at last, even though life wasn't perfect Yet! "Farrendon. Thank you."

Everyone in the room cheered shouting 'Happy Christmas' Even though he had to go back to prison. He had a son and life was looking up.

Jess began to think her daughter Becky would have loved *her* little brother, if she were still here.

It's anybody's guess how this story will end but, there's always hope. isn't there? Love will out.

THE END

Printed in Great Britain
by Amazon